Through
the
Rain

CAROL KNUTH

Dream Swept Publishing, LLC.

Dream Swept Publishing, LLC.
P.O. Box 18522
Erlanger, KY 41018

First paperback edition

ISBN: 0985924349

ISBN 13: 9780985924348

Printed in the United States of America

To my family and friends . . .

May you always find your way through the rain.

Through

the

Rain

Part I

1

Erin Grant, an assistant at the Weaver law firm, was bored out of her mind as she sat in a conference room overlooking the Ohio River. A Saturday morning, she thought, of all days to have a stinking training session and team building exercises. None of the employees at the Weaver law firm, Erin included, were happy about spending a beautiful spring day cooped up inside a windowless room at a work function, even if the room was inside a fancy hotel. It wasn't as if they were enjoying any of the amenities, such as the swimming pool or spa. No, over fifty employees were listening to a monotone man drone on about team work . . . *blah, blah, blah*. Yeah, I'll show him teamwork, Erin yawned.

Grateful for any excuse to leave the yawn-inspiring meeting, Erin walked out of the conference room located in the bowels of the hotel, and walked toward the ladies' restroom. She planned to stall as long as her bathroom break excuse would allow.

"Erin!" Dale, one of the junior partners at the firm, shouted from behind her. "Wait up!"

She rolled her eyes, then, pasting her most dazzling fake smile on her face, she turned toward the tall man. She could not stand him. He was a letch with a capital L, but he was one of the bosses at the firm, so she had to retract her claws. She knew he was one of Alan Weaver's, the owner of the firm, favorite attorneys, and one day he would be offered a partnership, so she had to play nice if she wanted to keep her job. Dale was the firm's womanizer, at least he thought he was. To Erin, he was a sexually harassing prick. As Erin looked at him, she noticed his perfectly groomed dishwater blonde hair with white strands popping free from the carefully hairsprayed mass. The white strands in his hair made it difficult to judge his age, but Erin suspected he was in his early thirties. He was wearing pressed blue jeans, a short-sleeved salmon colored dress shirt tucked smartly into his jeans, an expensive brown belt, and a pair of brown Armani loafers, the same shade of his belt.

Erin had dealt with Dale's type before. At twenty-six, she was the youngest of four kids, and the only girl. Three older brothers had taught her how to handle sleazy men, and she was annoyed that this sleazy man had disturbed her boredom break.

Wrinkling her nose at the strong cologne wafting in her direction, Erin asked, "What's up?"

"Let's go out for a smoke break," Dale insisted. Smiling, he grabbed her elbow and guided her toward the door.

"Dale, I don't smoke," she bristled.

Not relinquishing the firm hold he had on her elbow, he steered her toward the door.

"That's okay," he said. "You can hang out with me while *I* smoke."

Rationalizing the situation, Erin rolled her eyes, and thought, what harm could be done, even by Dale, on a Saturday morning standing in the entryway of a conference center . . . at a work event. Tugging her arm free from his grasp, she walked beside him through the lobby. Besides, he was the boss. There was always the possibility he wanted to discuss a work related issue, so she really didn't have an option but to follow him.

She followed Dale to a picnic table in a small garden area, screened from view by flowering bushes.

Dale lit up a cigarette, and watched as Erin sat down on the wooden bench. Blowing a plume of smoke in the air, he considered her. What was she he wondered, five foot eight, athletic build, but somehow she managed to come off feminine and sweet. He would love to run his fingers through

4

her shoulder length blonde hair, and her blue eyes, he could get lost in them. Dale wondered as he took in her casual Saturday work attire, blue jeans and crisp white blouse, if she realized she exuded sexy. He inhaled the scent of her perfume, just a hint, not overpowering like most of the women he knew. She knew what she was doing, he thought as his eyes locked on the top button of her blouse, too high to see even a peek of her cleavage. He would love to crack her uptight professional demeanor. Yeah, he considered, she was the type of woman who would be a hellcat in the sack, as he pictured her writhing beneath him, groaning in ecstasy as he gave her what he knew all women wanted . . . to be driven by a man. Oh, they might play the hard to get game, pretending they didn't want it, but that was just part of the game.

Women were all teases, flaunting their legs, tits and asses, and then when a man wanted it from them they'd try to leave him high and dry. Well, Dale didn't play that. If a woman teased she'd better be ready to give it up, or he was taking it. At times, some of his dates ended as a wrestling match, a woman pinned beneath him pretending she didn't want it. Fight just added spice to the sex chase. His eyes drooped a little as he remembered the woman he'd had the night before. She had played the hard to get game too, but she gave it up once he got her clothes off her.

Dale loved women, loved the smell, the feel, and the sounds of a woman, in the right situation that was. He preferred a little fight—a little challenge—in his women. Women who threw themselves at him bored him. What woman could turn him down, he thought with a smile as he continued to stare down at Erin. He knew she'd recently broken it off with her boyfriend and was just itching for a little bit of Dale right about now. A little fun—who didn't like a little fun? Live a little, was his motto.

Flicking his half-smoked cigarette into a bush nearby, he walked over and sat down next to her.

"So, what have you got going on tonight?" he asked easily, and draped his arm behind her on the picnic table.

Too close for comfort, Erin shifted on the bench, putting space between them so her legs were no longer pressed against his. "I have a date with my .

5

. . with Max tonight," she responded uneasily. He was just as sleazy outside the office as she had suspected he would be, Erin reflected in disgust.

"Max," he said with a frown. "I didn't know you were dating anyone. Didn't you break up with your boyfriend?"

"I did. Max is my dog," she explained, impatiently.

Relieved, Dale scooted closer, and swirled his thumb in a circle on her back.

"How 'bout you and me getting together tonight?" he asked, with a sly grin.

Annoyed, Erin shrugged her shoulder as if she were shrugging away a bug, and responded, "No. No thanks. It's just Max and me tonight."

"Awe, come on," he said. He leaned closer. "We could have a real good time. You broke up with your boyfriend, what, six months ago? I bet you're due for a little fun."

"Dale," I don't date men I work with," she said shortly.

"Who said anything about a date?" he asked. He stroked her upper arm. "We don't have to date to have a good time."

Erin turned, shoved his hand away, and said, "Dale, *no* thank you." She knew she was in shark-infested waters and had to tread very carefully with one of the owner's favorite attorneys. Nothing would make her feel better at that moment than to punch his smug face, but to do so would cost her a job, a job she needed, so instead she offered him a small smile, and said, "Thanks anyway."

Standing, Erin tugged the wrinkles from her blouse.

"Hey," she shrieked when she felt his hands tug at her waist and pull her down onto his lap.

"Come on," he said with a sleazy grin. "You can't tell me you don't want a piece of this." He grabbed her by her hips and began grinding her against him.

Erin felt the hardness of him against her, and struggled to get to her feet.

Dale wrapped an arm around her waist, pulling her tight against his chest, and using his free hand he grabbed her most private area.

"It's been awhile, hasn't it?" he said gruffly in her ear. He slid his fingers back and forth as she squirmed to be free, tears of anger and humiliation burning her eyes.

"Son of bitch!" she hissed, ripping away from him, not sure what to do next. Panting from the struggle, she looked down at him, into his grinning face as he reclined back against the table.

"Come on," he said. A smile tilted the corners of his lips in a Cheshire cat sort of way.

Dumbfounded, she stared at him. Panic bubbled deep inside her. He really didn't seem to get that there was a problem here, she realized as she shook her head back and forth. *Was this what he did—was this what he thought women wanted?*

"You know you want it," he said, looking up into her eyes.

"No, Dale," she said flatly. "*That* is not what I want or *wanted* from you. That's not what women want."

Dale stared up at the fiery blonde and considered, if she was this hot and he had just rubbed her a *little*, damn, the bitch would be on fire when he nailed her. Yeah, she wanted it, he thought.

Erin stepped back far enough to where he could not reach her without standing up. Not knowing what else to say, she turned toward the lobby of the conference area, and walked as quickly as could without breaking into a sprint.

Opening the door to the ladies' restroom, Erin rushed to a stall, and barely had time to close the door and lean over the white porcelain toilet before she started heaving—gagging—as her breakfast exploded from her mouth. Tears moistened her eyelashes as she leaned back against the wall of the stall, her body shaking. What just happened, she wondered as she closed her eyes.

Hearing the door to the ladies' room open, and the high-pitched voices of several of her female co-workers, Erin clumsily climbed to her feet, and kicked the handle on the toilet with the tip of her shoe. Ripping off a few squares of toilet paper, she wiped her eyes and then blew her nose, feeling as if she might throw up again. She couldn't let anyone see her this way. She shook herself internally, and chided herself, *you are not like those frilly simpleton women who cower when a man yells at them. How many times have you kicked your older brothers' asses? This is not a big deal. Pull it together! You can handle this.* Clearing her throat, Erin pasted a small smile on her face, and opened the door of the stall.

"Hello ladies," she said with false calm. "Are you enjoying the meeting?" Erin turned on the faucet, hoping her co-workers wouldn't notice that her hands were trembling.

"Boring!" Tanya, from accounting, pouted.

Erin glanced over at the red haired, short, chubby, forty-something accounting clerk, and smiled. Tanya had a way of making her smile, with her rather direct honest opinion about all things in life, including men. It was refreshing to work with such a strong female role model. Erin hadn't had many female role models, strong or otherwise. Her own mother had died in a car accident when Erin was just twelve years old.

It had been a cold and snowy December evening when Mellissa, Erin's mother, had begun the drive home from the mall after a day of Christmas shopping. Unknown to Mellissa, a forty-seven-year old man, after being fired from his job of twenty-two years, had spent the day drowning his sorrows in a bar. Then, drunk, he'd stumbled to his truck, and driven the wrong way down the highway slamming his truck into Mellissa's white Camry. She had died from injuries during the ambulance ride to the hospital.

Drying her hands, Erin responded, "I know. Not my idea of a fun Saturday either."

"You're looking a little peaked, sweetie. Are you feeling okay?" Tanya asked, concern lining her pudgy face.

Shaking her head, Erin said, "I'm *not* feeling very well. I think I might be coming down with the stomach virus that's been going around the office."

She wasn't feeling well Erin realized. Her stomach was still churning. Perhaps she would call it a day. Closing the blinds in her condo, and crawling into bed was an appealing thought. Suddenly, she felt exhausted. The situation with Dale had taken more out of her than she cared to admit.

"I think I'm going to find Katie from HR and let her know I'm leaving early," Erin said thoughtfully.

"You just do that," Tanya said, frowning. "You go on home and take care of yourself. You do look a little green."

Keeping her eyes averted, Erin walked quickly to the conference room and collected her purse, and then scanned the room for Katie, the HR Manager, the owner's assistant at the firm. Katie had been with the company several years longer than Erin had, and she was another one of the employees Erin was partial too. Where Tanya was strong and firm, Katie was soft and gentle, and all the employees trusted her.

Earlier in the day, Erin had seen Katie seated next to Alan at the front of the room, where all the important people had been seated, but as she looked now, her seat was empty and her purse was gone. Alan was standing near the table talking to one of the senior partners as Erin walked toward them. She stood and waited her turn to speak to the big man himself intending to inquire where his right hand—Katie—had gotten off to.

"Well hello, Erin," Alan said.

"Hi, Alan," Erin said, giving him the respect an owner of a law firm deserved. "Have you seen, Katie?"

Looking down at his cell phone, Alan began pressing away at the keypad.

"She had to leave early," he said. "Her niece came down with the flu." Looking up at Erin, he asked, "Can I help you with something?"

"I was going to see if it would be okay with her if I left early today," Erin stammered. "I'm not feeling well. I think it's that darn stomach bug that's been going around the office."

"Oh. Well that's too bad," Alan said, concern showing in his eyes. "Go on home and take care of yourself. Just let her know on Monday that you left early."

Feeling guilty for lying to the owner of the law firm, Erin offered him a small smile.

"Thank you," she said. "I'm sorry for leaving the meeting so early. I'm all for team building exercises, and hate that I'm bailing . . ."

"Don't you worry about it," Alan assured her. "There will be other team building meetings coming up. You go on home and get well."

"Thank you," Erin said, and with a slight wave of her hand she walked unsteadily toward the door of the conference room leading to the lobby. She felt like a fool leaving work because some man had groped her. Could you be any more girly, she chastised herself, and for some reason beyond her understanding, she wanted to cry. Keeping her head down, she walked as quickly as she could through the lobby and then the parking lot hoping she wouldn't run into Dale.

Tears streamed down her face as she clutched the steering wheel of her midnight blue truck. "Get a grip!" she told herself, sternly.

2

⌒♥

It was June, and Kate Sanders—everyone had called her Katie since she was a little girl—was thankful she was still sitting in her old office at the Weaver Law Firm in Covington, Kentucky. She wasn't ready to make the transition to George's cramped and unpleasant smelling office. It was the sour smell of rotting eggs, Katie had decided, wondering if George had dropped a boiled egg behind a cabinet, or perhaps it was just the stale smell of old backlogged case files that had the windowless space smelling so nauseatingly offensive.

George, a thin, nervous, balding man in his early forties, was a nice enough man, Katie mused, just incredibly disorganized. He'd been filling in as Alan's senior paralegal for the last year but was on his way out of the company, he just didn't know it yet. George had made one too many crucial errors on legal briefs, and had made a mess of a few depositions. Katie could still remember the day both parties, the defendant and the plaintiff in an upcoming case, had shown up for the same appointment due to an error George had made. It had been loud and messy, but Katie had managed to step in and take the more explosive of the parties to the conference room to cool down. It had all worked out in the end, but it had looked bad for Alan. Inefficiency in a law firm could not be tolerated.

Katie swiveled her black leather high-backed office chair, and stared out of her wall-to-wall window. Absently, she crossed her bare legs, swinging one of her low-heeled clad feet, lost in the exceptional view. From where she sat, she had a view of the Ohio side of the river—buildings set high on the hills. This stretch of the Ohio River was compared, in local travel guides, to the Rhine River in Germany because of the meandering river and hills that met the shoreline. Sighing, she thought, I am not looking forward to my new office with no window, closer to you know who . . . the boss. Nothing like being under Alan's thumb, not that he was a bad boss, Katie chided herself. Katie knew Alan had a tendency to become, as he liked to say, passionate about his cases, which often meant raised voices at the attorneys on staff, and it included a great deal of profane language.

Katie was seated with a yellow legal pad of paper, cell phone, and steaming hot cup of green tea on the desk beside her—on what would soon be her desk—waiting to review some of the case files she would be taking on. The desk was an organizational nightmare. She'd created a small space next to her by shoving mounds of file folders to the side and back, on what appeared to her to be a file folder avalanche waiting to happen. She watched as George flipped through manila file folders, searching for a key piece of data so he could explain a case to her. Alan wanted all the cases George was assisting with transferred over to Katie, last week!

She shoved at a file folder that slid onto her pad of paper, and continued to wait for George as he gathered his notes and his thoughts about the case. After a half an hour of watching George grumble and flip through the files, Katie, frustrated, realized they were going nowhere fast. She thought about the work she had on her own desk down the hall.

Snatching her cell phone off the desk, Katie slid the security bar to the right, and drug the text from her younger sister, Stacey, into view. She smiled as she re-read the text. Katie was forty three-years-old—three years older than Stacey—and looked like their biological mother, petite at five foot four, with long wavy light brown hair, made so each month by the color her hairdresser used to cover the sprinkling of white strands. She had beautiful classic features, carried herself elegantly, and was gentle and reserved.

Growing up in Illinois, Stacey had been the sister that had stolen the show. Stacey was tall at five foot nine, with hair a shade lighter than black, like their father's hair had been when they were little girls, and eyes the same color as Katie's, green, the same color as their mother's eyes had been. Stacey had always been a force, storming in and out of rooms, leaving her mark everywhere she went. That same force was what drew people to her, making everyone she met her friend. Katie, like her sister Stacey, was a native of Illinois, but unlike her sister, she had moved away her senior year of high school. She'd gone to live with her aunt in central Kentucky.

Katie loved her little sister, and was proud of all she had accomplished, especially how she had managed to keep it together after her husband, Sean—a police officer—had died the year before. Stacey had been serving in the Army reserves as a nurse in Afghanistan when she had gotten the news that Sean had been shot during what had at first seemed to be a routine traffic stop. The camera in Sean's squad car had captured the last moments of his life, as he approached the car that had moments before been weaving erratically through traffic, as he stood beside the car, and as he had fallen to the ground after the driver—high on drugs—shot him from point blank range. It had been a dizzying time of trying to make sense of what had happened to Sean, a good man, a son, father, and husband, taken too soon by a man that was not of a clear mind.

Stacey had been granted an emergency family leave, and had hopped the first military flight home. But until she arrived home, there had been Emily to consider, Stacey and Sean's only child, a beautiful little girl, only five-years-old at the time. Sean was an only child, a surprise blessing to older parents, and his parents, now in their seventies, had been in shock when they learned of their son's death. They had been little help with Emily or funeral arrangements. Katie had driven from the home she'd shared with Brad for the past ten years in Independence, Kentucky, to Chicago, to help Stacey with funeral arrangements, and to help care for Emily.

The day of the funeral had been an overwhelming experience, made as comforting as possible by the support of the police officer brotherhood. As a police officer that had fallen in the line of duty, thousands of fellow officers, judges, attorneys, firefighters and the many he had helped throughout the years, had shown their respect. It had been a long, and very emotional day.

Stacey had been granted only a three-week hardship leave for the funeral and to be with her family, but then she returned to her post in Afghanistan. Katie and her husband Brad stepped in to take care of Emily while Stacey finished her tour in the Afghanistan, bringing the child back to Kentucky to stay.

Brad and Katie both loved children, and had tried for five years to conceive before a specialist had announced the devastating news that Katie would never be able to have children of her own. Katie and Brad had been there when Stacey had needed them, but Emily had been a gift to *them*, filling an empty space in their lives.

Still smiling, Katie ended her text with, "I love you."

Katie and her sister had always been close, more so since their parents had died, their father from a heart attack when Katie was 18, and their mother when Katie was 21, from complications from a fall. Katie felt responsible for both her parents' deaths. The stress from what had happened the summer before her senior year of high school had been devastating for her parents. She knew the pain she had endured was a pain that had quite literally broken her father's heart, and her mother's accident years later was due to lack of sleep from nightmares that had haunted her. After the loss of her husband, Katie's mother had just given up on life. Her mother had fallen down the basement stairs, fallen into a coma, and within a few months was gone. Now, besides her aunt Nan, Stacey was the only adult living relative Katie had. The death of Stacey's husband the past year had been yet another reminder of how precarious and ever changing life was.

Putting the phone down, Katie looked up at George, taking in his disheveled appearance. He had run his hand through the wisp of hair on the side of his head, something he did when he was nervous. It was no wonder he was going bald, Katie thought. He was pulling his hair out when he was flustered.

"I am *so* sorry," George sighed. "I need to call our client. There's a key piece of information I can't find. I guess I must have misplaced it because I'm sure they gave it to me."

Katie responded perkily, "No problem. I will just go heat up my tea."

She walked out of his carpeted office, onto the tile floor of the hall, her heels echoing loudly. Carrying her cell phone in one hand and cup of tea in the other, she glanced into Alan's office. He was leaned back on his chair as if it were a recliner, with the earpiece of his office phone held against the side of his head. Quickly she walked past.

Katie walked into her sanctuary—her office—and sat down on her desk chair. She tucked her black knee-length pencil skirt under her legs, and knowing George would be tied up for a while, she began sifting through the manila files on her desk. After twenty minutes of sorting through various projects on her desk, Katie walked toward the break room. It was tea time.

A half an hour later, Katie walked down the hall to see if George was ready to resume client review. He was still sitting where she had left him, phone pressed against his ear with one hand and the other yanking through the tuft of hair on the side of his head. Katie sat down on the chair beside the desk and began making use of dead time; she made notations on the pad of paper she'd brought with her, of various things she needed to complete before the end of the day.

Several hours later, Katie was propped against Alan Weaver's desk, the owner of the law firm, as they discussed various cases they were working on. Finally he had moved on to the topic of George. It had been a miserably wasted afternoon, Katie thought. She had wasted hours as George struggled to gain control of his case files, and eventually she'd gone back to her office to play catch up—hours of work waiting for her.

"So, how's the training going?" Alan asked. He stared across his desk at her as he leaned back on his chair, hands clasped behind his head.

Crossing her arms across her chest, Katie looked across her boss's desk, considering him.

"Alan, it is so frustrating," she said. "George's office is a mess."

"Well," Alan said, "that's why you're in there, to clean it up. You," he said sharply, "need to be in that office. I expected those cases to be cleaned up by now. I want him *out* of that office. I mean it! You get your stuff in there and his out."

Katie stared at Alan as he quietly stared back.

"Any questions?" he asked.

"No. Well, actually—yes," Katie responded. "I know we talked about this before, but really, I think I should remain in my current office. George's office would be *great* as a storage room but it's just too cluttered to be an office. It has no windows, no air, no heat and the smell is atrocious," she rambled. "It's jamb-packed full of filing cabinets and boxes. Really, it would make more sense to just keep all the files locked in that room, *then*," she continued persuasively, "whenever I need to refer to a file I can easily access that room." She held her breath, hoping like a child at Christmas, he would say yes!

"No," Alan said, irritably. "I want you in George's office."

Staring at her boss in surprise, she thought, well that was quick. Katie considered Alan Weaver. He was ten years older than she was—fifty-three—had hair that at one time had been more brown than white, but now days was more white than brown. He was a little jiggly around the middle, she noticed. Too many nights spent at the bar with his friends, she suspected. He was tall, over six feet, which was a good thing because it gave him the appearance of being thinner than he was. His eyes were hazel in color, changing with his mood, some days a shade of brown with gold flecks and other days a shade of green. He wasn't unattractive—just ordinary— nothing about his features stood out, except for perhaps that he was always impeccably groomed, hair cut tidily the last Tuesday of each month and fingernails buffed and polished with a shiny clear coating. There was never a hair out of place, she mused.

She did not understand the relevance of moving her into George's office, and asked, "You have no plans to place a partner in my office do you, Alan? I mean, I know at some point you will wish to bring one on staff."

"Nope. I just want you closer to me," Alan said stubbornly.

"Fine," Katie said unhappily.

The meeting over, Katie stood up, walked to the door of Alan's office and pulled it open. Pausing in the hall, she turned, and asked, "Do you want me to shut the door?"

Now standing behind his desk, he looked up, and wrinkled his nose at her. "Nah," he said. "You can leave it open."

Alan stared after Katie as she walked out of his office, his eyes drawn to the way her hips moved in a grab my ass kind of way. He sniffed the air. It always smelled so good when Katie had been in his office. He knew she didn't know, but he always knew when she'd been in his office during the day when he was out, getting a case file or putting a note on his desk, or whatever it was she did while he was away. He could smell her unique scent, perfume so subtle it was barely detectable.

There was no real reason to insist Katie move into George's office, Alan reflected. It was simply a matter of comfort and candy. It had been a long time since he'd felt comfort from anyone, but that was how he felt when Katie was near. Few people in his life, whether it was at the firm, on one of the many boards he served on, or even in his personal life, seemed to notice anything but their own little worlds. Katie was different; she always seemed to notice the little things, seemed to know if anyone at the firm had a major or minor life event going on. She was the warmest woman he had ever known, and he liked that she brought that warmth to his law firm. That, he smiled, and what man didn't want a little eye candy to look at during the work day? Shaking his head, he turned toward his computer and clicked open an e-mail, trying to get his senior paralegal out of his head.

Disheartened, Katie walked to George's office, and resting her hands on her hips, scanned the mess. Alan had recently added acting human resource manager to her growing title. The manager of the firm's HR Department had resigned because her husband had taken a job with a company down south. Gretchen, the previous HR Manager, had given two months notice, plenty of time for Alan to find a replacement, but none of the applicants had measured up to his high standards, so he had the brilliant idea that

Katie should take on the role. Alan had great faith in Katie's abilities as she had always excelled at any challenge he had thrown at her, that and she had never said no to his project requests. She was still trying to figure out how she would possibly fit her new responsibilities into her day.

Hearing a soft knock on the open door of her office, Katie looked up, and smiled.

"I'm sorry to bother you," Erin said softly. "Do you have a minute?"

Erin had been thinking about this conversation all day, just how she was going to explain what Dale had done to her Saturday at the team building event. What if Katie didn't believe her, she worried? She hadn't told anyone else what happened, not even her dad, and typically, she told him everything. She had decided that this was something she needed to handle on her own.

"Hey, Erin," Katie said warmly. "Come on in." Erin was one of Katie's favorite co-workers, now employee, since she had taken on the HR duties. In the past three years, since Erin had been with the firm, she had never missed a day of work, had never been late or left early. She got along with all the other employees, overbearing attorneys included, and what she appreciated the most about Erin was her directness. She didn't beat around the bush. If she had something to say, she said it. Erin reminded Katie of her little sister, Stacey.

"Thanks," Erin said, and walked across Katie's office.

Katie detected the quiver in Erin's voice.

"Have a seat," Katie said. She swept her hand toward the two chairs placed in front of her oversized desk. It was obvious to Katie that Erin was upset by the way she slouched on her chair, pulled her long navy blue sweater tight around her in an unconscious hiding gesture, and wouldn't look her in the eye. Very un-Erin like.

Katie frowned. "Erin, are you okay?" she asked. "You don't seem like yourself. What's going on?"

Erin, dressed in navy slacks and long sleeved blouse, layered with a matching knee length sweater and a conservative one-inch black heeled shoe, felt cold. She leaned forward uncomfortably on her chair, crossed her ankles and forced a smile, feeling ridiculous. She was one of those women now—complaining about a man touching her. But she hadn't slept at all the night before, angry one moment and then a minute later crying in shame that any man could touch her as Dale had. He had just grabbed her, and then grinned about it. When she had gotten home Saturday, she'd stripped off her clothes, gotten into a hot shower, and scrubbed her skin raw, but she hadn't been able to get the filth off her. Now, as she sat in front of Katie, mortified, she couldn't stop the tears from spilling over her eyelashes and down her cheeks.

Stunned, Katie stared at the distraught young woman seated across her desk, almost huddled into a ball. She grabbed the box of tissues placed near the edge of her desk and rushed to sit beside her. Katie whisked several white tissues from the box and offered them to Erin who took them gratefully and began blotting her tear streaked face, wiping tears and make up away.

"I'm so sorry," Erin, sobbed. "Honestly, I don't know why I'm blubbering like a baby." She shook her head in embarrassment.

Katie was concerned, and as she looked at her friend, she could not imagine what had happened, speculating what possible tragedy had struck her family. This was so out of character for Erin, she thought, uneasily.

"It's okay," Katie said gently. "Take your time."

Erin grabbed several tissues from the blue flowered box, blew her nose, dabbed the tears beneath her eyes, and sighed heavily as she looked across the office out the window. She watched as a bright red cardinal flew past the window. She took a deep breath and turned toward Katie.

"Dale attacked me at the team building event Saturday," she blurted.

Katie stared at the tear stained face of the woman sitting next to her, close enough to touch.

"Attacked you?" Katie asked.

This was not the subject Katie thought she and Erin would ever be discussing. At least not in reference to Erin. For one, the very idea that any man could attack Erin without having his ass kicked, was shocking. That any man would even try, was potential suicide, Katie thought. She knew Erin was the youngest kid of four and the only girl in her family. Erin loved talking about her family, about her dad who had taken on the additional role of mother when his wife had died, and Erin's brothers who treated her just like one of the guys. For heaven sakes, Erin was a Karate nut! Katie knew she could quite literally kick a man's ass if she wanted to.

"Erin," Katie said as her friend continued to stare at her, "tell me exactly what happened. Where were you—inside the building or outside?"

"Outside," Erin whispered. She could still feel his hands on her . . .

"Erin—Erin, look at me," Katie snapped.

Erin blinked and shook her head, attempting to focus on Katie's voice. "Outside, it was outside," she said.

An hour later, Katie was sitting at her desk staring at the closed door of her office absorbing what Erin had shared with her about Dale, one of the junior attorneys. Sexual assault . . . at the firm. She needed to talk to Alan as soon as possible. Katie had known Alan for ten years. They had shared family stories over coffee and lunches, during work hours, and even if she hadn't been placed in the HR role recently, she would have shared what Erin had told her about Dale. Katie knew Dale's type. Most offices had one—the guy that thought he was every woman's dream. In reality, he was the office sleaze. She just hadn't realized how much of a sleaze he was. He was a liability to the firm. Alan had always come across as a loving husband and father, a champion of women, and Katie suspected as a man, he would be livid with Dale. Of course, as the owner and an attorney, Alan would have to follow procedure, even if he felt like kicking some sleaze ball's ass. Picking up the black receiver to her office phone, Katie dialed Alan's cell number. This matter could not wait until tomorrow.

After the fourth ring, Katie heard Alan's voice indicating that the caller should leave a message, or dial *her* number. "Thanks for that, Alan," she said aloud. As if she needed the extra calls during the day.

"Hey Alan," Katie said in response to her boss's voicemail greeting. She rolled her eyes. She hated leaving messages—hated the way her voice sounded to her ears—too girly. "It's Katie," she continued. "Could you find some time to meet with me tomorrow? An issue with one of the employees at the firm has been brought to my attention . . . a potential legal issue. Something you will have to address. Okay, well I will just talk to you in the morning. Night."

Katie clunked the hand piece of the telephone onto its cradle, and then began organizing files for the next day.

Katie stretched and then glanced at her wristwatch, surprised that it was later than she'd realized. Well, she thought, that's all I can stand for one day. She pushed back her chair, grabbed her peach colored spring jacket from the hanger on the back of her door and then walked toward the elevator that lead to the lobby and the parking lot. As she walked to her car, her cell phone vibrated, and looking down, she saw her husband's picture pop up.

She cradled the phone against her neck.

"Hey," she said cheerfully into the phone.

She pulled open the back door to the black highlander and placed her computer bag on the floor, soon to be at Emily's feet.

"Yes, I'm just now leaving. I'm going to pick up Emily at school."

She paused as her husband, Brad, responded.

"How was your day?" she asked with a smile. She climbed on to the driver's seat, and jiggled the key into the ignition. "Anything new going on in the world of 401K's and annuities?"

She paused, listening to her husband's voice.

"My day?" she asked. "Annoying. Once again I met with George. He tried to explain the cases he is handing over to me. Grrr! I still have no idea what's in all the files on his desk. I mean my desk. It's driving me *nuts*! Now Alan wants me to take on overseeing all the employees in an HR role. It's too much. This is insane!"

She listened to Brad's response of, "You said you were worried about taking on the added responsibility," and, "Don't give up just yet."

"I know," she said. She turned to look out the rear window, and applied pressure to the gas pedal, backing out of her parking space. "But we need the money. Since all this recession stuff began, Alan's gotten rid of a few of the attorneys on staff, and four paralegals. I could very well be the next one he gets rid of. I am well aware that my job is not critical to the day-to-day operation of his firm. I felt I had no choice. I *had* to say yes when he asked me to take on overseeing all the employees, even though I had and still have a very bad feeling about it, and so far I am being proven right."

As Katie drove down the road, she responded, "Okay. I'll see you when you get home. Love you too."

Twenty minutes later, Katie had a chatty six-year-old little girl in her car, and in her squeaky little girl voice, Emily shared exciting stories about recess, lunch, and craft time. Emily had gray-blue eyes and blonde hair, similar to what her daddy's coloring had been. Emily was tall for her age and slender, built like her mommy.

Looking in the rearview mirror, Katie marveled at the change in Emily's disposition. As Katie watched, Emily nestled her cheek against the cushioned backrest and gazed out of the window, a long strand of wheat colored hair falling across her eyes. The last six months had been a heart-breaking struggle for Emily. Even now, when Katie tucked the child into bed at night she asked about her daddy. When was he coming home, she would ask. Katie did her best to explain he was with Jesus now, but still, the questions of when would she see him next, brought burning tears to her eyes.

Crawling into bed several hours later, Katie giggled, "Hey, get off my side of the bed, missy! I'm going to squash you." She wiggled her giggly niece to the center of the queen-sized bed in the guest room, Emily's bed while Stacey finished her tour of duty overseas.

A giggle erupted from Emily as she scooted over, barely.

"Scootch your hiney over," Katie said laughing. "I'm going to fall off the bed!"

The freshly bathed six-year-old hugged her brown stuffed, fuzzy teddy bear dressed in matching pajamas, and giggled, to her aunt's delight.

Laughing, Katie said, "Okay, squirt. Just move it or I'll lay on you and squash you like a bug!"

"I'm not a bug!" Emily laughed.

"Sure you are," Katie said as she looked down at the little girl, and tickled her. A giggle escaped the little girl. "You are a b-e-a-u-t-i-f-u-l butterfly."

"What kind?" Emily asked.

"Well, you are purple with yellow dots on your wings and you flutter about like a fairy."

"Well," Emily said, "you are a magical fairy and we fly together."

"Yes, baby. We fly together," Katie said, smiling at her, continuing the game of imagination.

"Okay! Our show is on, so Shhh," Katie whispered.

"Can I snuggle you?" Emily asked, as she wiggled closer.

"Of course," Katie said.

She pulled Emily close so she could lay her head in the crook of her shoulder. A small leg flung across Katie's stomach, and soon the surprisingly loud snoring from such a small being began. Katie smoothed the hair that fell across Emily's eyes and looked at the beautiful child snuggled against her, remembering the painful end to her own childhood.

3

⌒

Tears burned her eyes as Katie stared at the screen of her computer. It had been one of those mornings already, beginning when she had pulled into the parking lot of the day care to drop off her niece before work. Slumping on her leather office chair, Katie thought about the sad crumpled expression on Emily's face when she had asked when her mommy and daddy were coming to get her. Katie had opened the backdoor, and with her hand on the car door, looked down at her niece.

With tiny little girl tears trickling down her cheeks, Emily had sadly, asked, "When are my mommy and daddy coming for me?"

Katie had managed to keep it together as she helped her niece out of her car seat and then climbed onto the backseat, not caring that her black business skirt was ripping in the back as she pulled the little girl onto her lap.

Katie had hugged Emily tight, and lied, "Oh baby girl, they will be here soon—any day now."

She didn't know what else to say. Some days it just seemed a lie was the most kind and sensitive route to take. This morning she just couldn't face the truth that Emily's daddy was *never* coming home.

Katie noticed the blur of a blue colored shirt and gray slacks as Alan walked briskly past her office as she continued to stare at her computer screen.

Alan whistled the tune from the song he had been listening to on his IPOD moments ago in his car, glanced at Katie sitting at her desk, and continued to breeze down the hall. Wrinkling his brow, he stopped in the middle of the hall. All was not well, he thought. It was rare to see Katie anything but happy, but the lady he saw had not been happy. Pivoting, he headed back to her office.

"Hey," Alan said. He walked into Katie's office with envelopes still held in his hand freshly retrieved from the mail center in the lobby.

Katie looked up in surprise.

"Hey," she said, offering him her best fake smile.

He walked across her office and leaned against the edge of her desk. Making himself comfortable, he hiked at the fabric at the front of his pants, crossed his ankles, and began ripping open one of the envelopes.

"Everything okay?" he asked casually. He noticed her red puffy eyes, and the twitch just to the right of her upper lip, one of the few signs Katie exhibited when she was upset. Even with the small smile, the twitch gave her away.

Alan had known Katie for years; knew that she had lost her parents at too early of an age, and that besides an aunt, Stacey and Emily were the only family, besides Brad, that she had. When Stacey's husband died in a tragic accident the year before, Stacey had leaned on Katie. Now Katie and Brad were taking care of her sister's little girl until Stacey completed her time in the military. Her life had been so very different from his life, Alan considered. He had never had to struggle at anything, a child from wealth rarely did. Alan had never met a woman as strong, soft, and sensitive as Katie. She intrigued him.

"*All* is well," she lied, offering him a small smile.

Alan knew she was lying. She wasn't one to bring her baggage to work. That was another thing that intrigued him. She was a woman who put on a happy front, no whining, even when she had legitimate troubles. "How's Brad's job going?"

Thankful for the distraction, Katie replied, "Good. His company is still strong regardless of the recession. We are *really* thankful for his job and mine right now with all the extra expenses, what with Emily, and helping out with expenses for the funeral and all that entailed for her daddy."

Alan watched as Katie leaned back on her chair, staring as her short-sleeved white blouse stretched across her breasts.

Katie stretched the kink out of her shoulders.

"God, Alan. I am so thankful for your generosity to my family and me during the past year with everything we have had to go through," she said. "I'm sure many employers wouldn't have been so giving during a tragedy. The flex time you allowed was huge in helping a little girl heal from her daddy's death." Tears sprung to her eyes as she thought about Emily and their morning in the car outside the daycare.

Alan looked at the tears sparkling like diamonds in Katie's green eyes.

"Thank you, Alan," she softly.

"You know," he said thoughtfully. He crossed his hands across his lap, the envelopes still held in his hand. "If you need anything, a hug, *anything*—I'm here."

"Thank you," she said. "I really appreciate the offer. Some days are just so hard." She sighed.

Alan tapped his opened mail on her desk, and looked intently into her eyes.

"I think it's great all you and Brad are doing. And the hug—I mean it, *really*," he said, pointing his mail at her. He paused for a moment and wondered how she would respond if he took her into his arms right then, but instead he stood up and walked toward the door of her office.

He paused in the doorway and turned toward her. "Just let me know—*anytime*."

Katie looked across the room into her boss's hazel eyes, today seeming a little more brown than green, and saw something she hadn't noticed before. His eyes glistened with weariness and something . . . unfamiliar.

Alan's eyes lingered on Katie's soft pink lips, and then slowly he turned away and continued on to his office.

Shaking her head to dispel the funk she was in, Katie said to the light gray walls of her office, "Good Lord! I forgot to talk to Alan about Erin. But then again," she said to the walls as she wrinkled her nose, "he didn't even ask about the voice message I left him last night."

Sighing, Katie decided to put the Erin talk off with Alan until after lunch. She thought it best not to approach Alan right now, especially after the slightly strange hug conversation they'd just had. Give him time to settle back into his work day, she mused. She did intend to tackle the Dale topic before the day was over, and she suspected Alan would be furious that one of his attorneys had assaulted one of the women on staff.

Alan leaned back on his chair and stared at his closed office door, the scent of Katie lingering in his nose, and thought about the meeting with the firm's accountant that morning. They had reviewed the numbers together, and as he feared, the firm was still barely keeping its head above water, even with the new cases and clients Alan had landed. Taking his glasses off his face, he rubbed his hand over his burning eyes, squeezing the bridge of his nose with his fingers. His thoughts turned to Katie and their brief talk moments ago.

Alan's cell phone belted out an obnoxious voice shouting, *Ring—Ring. Ring—Ring.* It was a new ring tone he was playing around with, and soon to be changed, he realized as he pulled his cell out of the case attached to his black leather belt. Glancing down at his cell phone, Alan saw his wife, Nancy's, face flashing at him.

"Hello," he growled into the phone.

Alan half listened as his wife rambled on, clicking open an e-mail as she chattered away about some event their daughter had that evening. When it seemed she might drone on, as she tended to do, he shouted into the phone, "God, Nancy! Can't you handle Reegan's teacher? I'm a little preoccupied here. Seriously, you are going to have to handle it! No," he shouted. "I cannot just *drop* everything and run to the school to pick Reegan up. I have a meeting in," he glanced down at his Rolex, "twenty minutes. I still need to review the client's file before they arrive." Pausing, he listened to his wife's explanation about being late to the school, but she would do the best she could.

"Nancy—*Nancy*," Alan interrupted. "We have a client dinner tonight. You did make the reservations for the restaurant downtown like I told you to last week, didn't you?" He paused for a minute listening to her response, fearing she hadn't made the reservations. As his wife, Nancy had limited involvement in the firm, however she was expected to help entertain clients and attorneys from the firm, and part of her responsibility was to make dinner and other event reservations. Over the past year, she had neglected to make arrangements for several dinner engagements, creating embarrassing situations when he had to find alternative arrangements in front of clients, an embarrassment he did not intend to relive. Since then, periodically, Alan had begun relying on various clerks at the firm to confirm reservations had actually been made.

Relieved, Alan said, "Be ready at seven! Bye."

Placing his cell phone on his desk, annoyed, Alan looked back up at the ceiling and ran a hand across his face. The woman was impossible, expecting him to drop everything to pick up their daughter at school. It was her job for Christ sake! Wives, he thought. Sometimes he wished Nancy would perform her duties as his wife more like an employee, and just do what she was told. It wasn't as if Nancy was swamped with anything important to do in her day. She was a housewife. How difficult could it be, he considered.

Katie reached across her desk and picked up the telephone on the third ring. "Hello," she said into the receiver.

She heard the deep growl of Alan's voice.

Sitting in his office down the hall, Alan asked, "Watcha workin' on?"

"The brief we discussed this morning—you know—for the Carson case," she answered. She moved her mouse, and clicked save on the document she had been working on.

"Hey," Alan said, "I'd like you to schedule some interviews for me."

"Oh. Sure," Katie said in surprise, wondering what position he was adding.

"I've decided to move forward with a search for another senior partner," Alan explained. "I have a list of names, all prominent attorneys in the region, and a few of the junior attorneys here at the firm. I'll e-mail the list to you. I want you to call each of the men on the list today and tomorrow, and schedule a first round of interviews for next week, for Wednesday and Thursday. There's a name on the top of the list, Jack Andrews. He's a strong possibility, so try to get him in as one of the first candidates to interview, for maybe Wednesday morning. The interviews will be the same format and process as any other interview—in the conference room with me and our senior partner."

Katie scribbled Alan's instructions on a pad of paper as Dale came to mind. She wondered if he was on the interview list. She needed to talk to Alan . . . today, about Dale.

"Okay. I've got it!" Katie assured him.

"Thanks," he said.

"No problem. Alan," she said in a rush. "I need to talk to you about something before I leave today. Could I have a few minutes of your time?"

Alan detected the worry in Katie's voice.

"Of course. How about at four, right before I leave. I have to be somewhere at 4:45 off site. Will that work for you?"

"Perfect," she sighed, not realizing she had been holding her breath.

Several hours later, Katie looked up when Alan popped his head into her office, and asked, "Is this a good time to talk?"

"Yes," she exhaled, with a smile. "Come on in, and could you shut the door behind you?" she asked.

"Sounds serious," he said, as he closed the door behind him and walked toward her desk, his bulging computer bag slung over one shoulder. Alan deposited his black bag on one of the chairs placed in front of Katie's desk. Then he pulled the other chair to the side of her desk, and sat down. Crossing one leg over the other, he hiked at the front of his pants, and dug at the front of his pants trying to shift himself into a better position.

"Okay," he said once he was situated. "What's up?"

Katie was amused and a little embarrassed as she witnessed Alan's obvious male discomfort issue and gave him a moment before delving into the Dale matter.

"Alan, I need to talk to you about Dale," Katie began.

Examining her face, Alan scowled, wondering what stupid thing Dale had done now. He was one of the younger attorneys at the firm and wasn't quite polished yet. Damned good attorney but he was a little rough around the edges, especially with women. Alan and the other older attorneys could appreciate Dale's enthusiasm for the ladies. Hell, what hot-blooded man with functioning parts didn't have a woman on his mind? But as attorneys, they had a role to play in the community, and they each had to look and act the part of concerned and conservative leaders.

"*Dale?*" Alan asked.

"Yes," she said, pausing for a moment. Continuing, she said grimly, "Erin filed an official complaint against Dale yesterday. She said he attacked her the morning of the team building meeting. He sexually assaulted her, Alan."

Katie watched Alan's face for a clue to what he was thinking, but his face was like a mask. No expression, if anything, all the lines seemed to have magically disappeared—as if he didn't want her to know what he was thinking.

"Can anyone corroborate Erin's claim?" Alan asked.

"No," Katie said. "Dale had Erin tucked away in a garden area hidden behind some bushes." Katie had asked Erin the same thing, knowing it would be helpful if someone had seen the incident. By chance or intent, Dale had selected an isolated area and it was Erin's word against whatever story Dale would present.

Relieved, Alan grinned.

"Maybe she misunderstood," he said. "You know how Dale can be, or any man for that matter. He's probably just attracted to her and wanted to ask her out."

Katie raised her eyebrows in surprise. Deep in thought, she considered what Alan had suggested. Could it be possible that Dale was attracted to Erin? Well, from what Erin had shared, it was certainly plausible. Still, she thought, as she shook her head, this wasn't a bar; it was a place of business, and although the team building meeting was off site, it had been a work related event.

Katie rolled her high-backed black leather chair closer to Alan.

"That may be the case," Katie said. "Maybe Dale *is* attracted to Erin, but I think I should tell you what she said, then you might have a different take on the incident."

Leaning back on his chair, Alan locked his hands behind his head, and looked at his assistant. "What did Erin say happened?"

Leaning forward, Katie took a deep breath, and said, "Erin told me that Dale asked her to join him outside while the other employees were still in the conference room. She had left the room to use the restroom, but before she could make it to the restroom, Dale came up behind her and insisted she join him outside. She didn't feel she could say no because it might have been business related and he was an attorney, a boss. She followed him outside to the side of the building to a garden area where they sat down at a picnic table while he smoked a cigarette, and then he began asking her about her personal life. Then he told her they should get together."

"So he *is* interested in her," he said with a smile."

"Not so fast," she admonished. "The story gets dicey from there. He *did* ask her out, in a manner of speaking . . . *true.* I'll give you that," Katie said, as Alan raised his eyebrows. "Erin told me that Dale said they should get together, and that she said no, that she didn't date men she worked with. He then said that he wasn't asking her out on a date-date. He was just looking to hook up, you know . . . have a good time, as in, sex."

Alan wrinkled his nose and grimaced. "Well that wasn't very smooth."

"It gets worse," she said. "Erin said when she got up from the picnic table, he grabbed her from behind, pulled her down on his lap, and with his hands on her hips began grinding her on him."

Katie paused for a moment to watch Alan's reaction. The smile had slipped from his face, and he was looking down at his hands, now hanging loose in front of him as he slouched forward.

"He touched her, Alan. He grabbed her . . . you know. There," Katie said.

"What do you mean—*there*?" Alan asked. "I don't know where *there* is. You're going to have to be more specific."

"Her *crotch*," she said, her face burning with embarrassment. She gestured her hand in a downward motion. "*There*. He grabbed her there, and said she wanted it."

Katie watched Alan as he took his rimless glasses off his face and squeezed the bridge of his nose. It was something he did when he was burdened down under the weight of immense pressure, when he thought no one was watching him. But Katie noticed.

Slumping back on his chair, Alan insisted, "Why don't you talk to Dale." Waving his hand in the air, he said, "Talk to him about being sensitive or something like that. I'm sure it was an isolated incident. We don't want to blow this out of proportion. It's probably just a case of misunderstanding. You know how it is," he said, grinning. "Remember those days . . . you know, the days of dating and new romance? It's probably just a young romance budding and pretty soon we'll hear through the grapevine that they're an item."

Wrinkling her forehead, Katie disagreed. "Somehow, Alan, I don't think this is going to bud into a romance. I think you need to talk to him. This is serious. Erin was crying in my office—Erin—*crying*. She, of all the women at the firm. She's not one of those women."

"Just talk to him," Alan insisted. "Just an informal talk. You're good at that sort of thing."

Well, yes, she *was* good at that sort of thing, if what he meant by *that sort of thing* was that she had a knack for communicating effectively. But she felt Alan was wrong. She couldn't believe he was sticking her with this. It was *his* employee, his very *large*, annoying, arrogant employee. He needed to man up and talk to Dale himself, Katie thought.

"Alan, I think the man needs more than a sensitivity lecture," she insisted.

"Katie, this sort of thing always blows over. Just talk to him, you know, tell him to be a little more sensitive. You're good with kids. You're good with Emily," he said, with a playful smile. "Just treat him like an overgrown kid, because he kind of is." He winked. "You'll be just fine. Don't make it more than it is."

Katie searched Alan's eyes. It must be her, she thought. She must have done a very bad job explaining the situation—what had transpired between Erin and Dale. It was the only way to explain Alan's lack of concern.

4

As Alan steered his car through rush hour traffic, he looked down at his vibrating cell phone and wiggled it out of the case nestled against his waist.

"Hello," he said. "Yes, Nancy. I'm on my way to pick the kids up right now, and then we're headed over to my parent's for a few minutes to pick something up."

Pausing, he listened to his wife's response.

"Yeah. My sister and her husband will be there with their kids." Feeling his blood pressure rise a little with Nancy's questions and accusations, he snarled, "What do mean, why didn't I tell you I was going over? I thought you needed the extra time to get ready for tonight. Why do you care? It's not as if you would want to go over to mom and dad's, anyway. Just last week you said you wouldn't go back over to their house. Remember? Someone said something that you didn't like, again."

Turning into the driveway of his children's school, Alan slowed to a stop by the sidewalk as Reegan and Tanner, weighed down by their backpacks, walked toward the car.

"Jesus, Nancy! I don't give a fuck! Come over then," he said in exasperation, and ended the call. As he reached to put the phone back in its case, it rang again. Looking down he noticed it was a friend from the executive business board he was on. Looking back at his children as they slammed the door closed, he acknowledged them, then turned back around in his seat, and pulled away from the curb.

"Hey, Al," he boomed. "Nah. You didn't catch me in the middle of anything. Just picking up the kids from school for Nancy. Tomorrow? Sure. I am *definitely* ready for a round of golf! Why don't you see if Phil and Gary want to join us? That'd be great. 3:00 o'clock at the club."

Alan threw his cell on the passenger seat and then gripped the steering wheel with both hands. His thoughts drifted to Nancy. Why couldn't wives be more like employees, he grimaced.

5

∽

"**E**rin," Dale crooned into the telephone. "Could you dig up the old Carver file? I'd like to review it."

Since the day Dale had attacked her in the garden at the hotel, as all the other employees from the firm sat inside the conference hall, Erin had found sleeping almost impossible. She had never been prone to sleepless nights, not even as a child when her mother had died, but for some reason this was different. When she turned the lights off at night and lie alone in her bed, thoughts of Dale rushed back, remembering how helpless she had felt . . . and his hands, everywhere.

Not one for medication, except for a daily vitamin, Erin had finally broken down and called her family doctor to ask for a prescription for sleeping pills. She had found herself sitting in his office during her lunch-hour tearfully explaining what had happened at work. The doctor had begged her to talk to her dad, and she had been frightened he would call him, considering he had been a golf buddy of his for years. He had stated the only reason he would not say anything was due to his duty as a physician. He couldn't tell, but he insisted that she talk to him, or call a crisis center . . . talk to someone. Something else new to her was stopping at the liquor store every few days to stock up on bottles of wine. She had never been much of a drinker, but a few drinks helped during the evenings until she could pop the little white pill that would allow her to sleep a nightmare-less sleep. Garbage day found her clinking her garbage to the curb . . . hoping her brothers and dad didn't discover her new drinking habit and press her as to why the binges.

Rolling her eyes, Erin responded, "You mean the case from last summer—the wrongful discharge case?"

Erin had walked into the firm a few days ago to the unpleasant news that she was filling in as Dale's secretary until a replacement was found. His most recent secretary, June, had quit unexpectedly, without notice. No surprise there, Erin thought. Funny, she pondered, he seemed to have a string of cheerleader-looking secretaries, and none stayed longer than a few months—couldn't tolerate his asshole attitude was more like it.

It wasn't as if she had nothing to do, Erin thought. Why the man couldn't walk down the hall to the file room, was beyond her. She huffed, her heels clicking on the marble floor as she walked to the large room used by the firm to house file cabinets for old cases.

"He's probably busy feeling up, Sonia," Erin muttered, as she pulled open a heavy green metal drawer and began riffling through the files in the cabinet. Sonia had worked as a clerk for the firm's marketing and PR department for five years, since her husband had left her and her three children for another woman. Erin had met Sonia's three little girls at a company picnic the previous summer—cute kids, she allowed. She couldn't understand why a woman that was raising three little girls would allow men, or a man—Dale—to treat her like a piece of meat.

Slamming the cabinet door shut, Erin scowled as she walked out of the room still thinking about how Sonia allowed Dale to grab her butt—in front of other employees. If they wanted to carry on, they should keep it behind closed doors, she thought grumpily.

And *there* was Sonia now, Erin mused, as she walked toward Dale's office and Sonia walked into the hall. Sonia was a tiny little thing, pretty, with long chocolate colored hair that hung below her shoulders. She looked much younger than her thirty-five years, with a petite figure and always looked stylish and professional in skirts, heels, and blouses maybe cut a little too low. Still, she could do so much better than Dale, Erin thought.

"Hi, Erin," Sonia said. She peered up at the tall blonde, and offered her a quick embarrassed glimmer of a smile. Sonia hated it when she had to meet with Dale in his office. She couldn't count the times she had walked away with his handprints on the back of her skirt. God, she thought, if only she didn't need the job. Sometimes she thought she might as well be half naked stripping on stage somewhere. She'd probably make more money and with a bouncer, she'd be groped a lot less.

"Hello," Erin responded stiffly.

Sighing, Sonia walked down the hall toward her cubicle. She knew what the other women, and even the men, in the office thought of her—that she was a slut—that she was screwing around with one of the attorneys. But she wasn't. It wasn't like that at all. She couldn't say what was really going on because she needed the job. So let them all think what they wanted, she thought with resignation. With three little girls to raise and an ex that had skipped town, she'd just have to put up with some ass groping. It wasn't as if it would be different anywhere else, she reasoned. Men were all alike . . . bastards!

Rapping her knuckles softly on the door, Erin called out, "Here's the file you wanted." She did not intend to have a repeat of the team building meeting, and planned to dump the file and make her exit quickly. As far as she knew, no one had spoken to Dale about her complaint, unless of course this was to be how she found out that he knew.

"Hey, Erin," Dale grinned. "Come on in!" His eyes lingered on her long toned legs. Leaning back on his leather chair, he clasped his hands behind his head and stared at her hips, the fabric pulling tight with each step.

Her face burning, Erin cleared her voice. She had watched his eyes as she walked across the room, and knew exactly what he was staring at. She slapped the file on his desk and pivoted on her toe, her spine tingling with revulsion knowing he was now watching her as she walked away.

"Hey—*hey!*" he stammered. "Shut the door for a second. I want to talk to you about this file," he lied.

Grimacing, she paused for a moment, trying to think of a plausible excuse to bolt out of his office, but finding none, nervously she closed the door, turned back around and faced him.

"So how's your day going?" he asked as he continued to stare at her. She was a tough one to crack open, he thought distractedly. "Have a seat," he said, as he motioned to the chair beside his desk.

With an audible sigh, she walked over and sat down on the chair beside his desk, crossed her legs and tucked her skirt tight, not realizing by doing so she was drawing even more attention to her legs. Dale's eyes lingered on the high point of her crossed legs, willing her skirt to shift up.

"It's fine, Dale," Erin said, annoyed. She had work to do, she thought, frustrated that the great Dale had the power to control her day!

"Now you ask me how my day is," he said with a sly grin.

Erin stared at him as if he was a lunatic. Flipping her hands in the air, just slightly off the armrests, she asked, "How is your day?"

"Well," he said, as he rolled his chair close to hers, pressing his knees into hers, "I'm much better now that you stopped by. It was nice of you to hurry in here."

She uncrossed her legs, crossed her ankles beneath her chair, and placed a hand in her lap.

"I hurried because you said you needed the file," she said, annoyed.

Dale cocked his head like a curious puppy. "You sure you didn't just want to see me?" he asked.

Placing her hands firmly on the arms of the chair, Erin prepared to stand, angry at the idiocy of the attorney wasting her time.

"Dale, I have work to do," she said.

She was in a half standing position when Dale lunged at her, wrapping both of his hands around her narrow waist. He jerked her toward him, causing her to lose her balance. She tried to catch, and right herself, her stomach muscles screaming with the effort as she fell across his lap. He wrapped an arm tight around her waist as his other hand rested on her backside, caressing her through her skirt as she tugged to be free.

Breathless from struggling, Erin could only squeak, "Stop!"

Dale held tight to Erin's waist, as she kicked and writhed on his lap. He groaned and shut his eyes as he felt her rubbing against him, feeling himself grow hard. Grabbing her hips, he moved her back and forth against him as she, breathing hard, grabbed the arms of his chair and lunged forward, pulling her body off his lap. Quickly he leaned forward and grabbed her hips and she lost her balance again, toppling back against his chest. She panicked, and tugged to be free as she heard him breathing heavily in her ear.

"Stop," she cried, hating the quiver in her voice.

As Erin struggled, she saw Dale stroke her skirt upward, and as she wiggled to be free, her skirt slid up even further. His hand slid along her thigh, almost to her panties, and she began to kick. Spreading her legs, she planted her feet on the ground. As she straddled him, leaning forward, she felt his hand grab between her legs, nothing between his hand and her but her satin bikini panties.

"Oh yeah," Dale growled as he thrust his hand between her legs. He groaned. "God, you're so hot."

Tugging forward with all her strength, Erin fell to her knees, and crawled, stumbling as her knee tangled in her skirt. Humiliated and shamed, she skittered away from Dale, and then got to her feet, backing quickly toward the door, watching to see if he would come after her. He continued to sit on his chair watching her. Not taking her eyes off him, she tried to catch her breath as she straightened her skirt and blouse, noticing the bulge and the stain on the front of his pants. Repulsion caused bile to burn the back of her throat.

"Stay away from me," she croaked. "Don't *ever* touch me again!"

He leaned back on his chair and considered her flushed cheeks, disheveled hair, clothes twisted from the struggle, and felt himself get harder, and tugged at the front of his pants.

Erin straightened her clothes as best as she could before pulling open the door. She didn't want anyone to see her like this, like—Sonia—as if she was one of his girls . . . one of *those* types of women.

She peeked into the hall to make sure no one would see her as she rushed to the ladies' room. As she walked down the hall, she thought hysterically, what did she care if someone saw her? She had just been attacked. So why did she feel such shame, she wondered, as tears sprang to her eyes and she walked faster across the marble lobby to the ladies' room.

Once inside the restroom, Erin walked toward the vanity. She leaned against it feeling the coolness beneath the palms of her hands. Bracing her hands on the sides of the white porcelain sink, she looked up into the oval mirror. Her eyes were bloodshot—puffy—with black mascara smudged beneath. She could see where her tears had created a trail down her cheeks through the pink blush she had applied that morning. She looked a mess. Shakily, she grabbed several paper towels from the dispenser, ran them under cold water, and tried to fix her makeup. Sighing, she stepped away from the vanity and walked to the mirror hanging on the wall to make sure her skirt and blouse were smooth and in place. Opening the ladies' room door, Erin straightened her shoulders and turned toward Katie's office, and with heels clicking on the marble floor, walked briskly to see the law firm's acting HR representative.

6

An hour later, Katie knocked on the door to Alan's office.

"Hey," she said, as he turned away from his computer screen and smiled at her. "I need to talk to you. Do you have a minute?" A serious expression pinched her face. She was still upset by the conversation she had just had with Erin about Dale.

Alan examined Katie's face, and noticed she looked strained. He wondered what had upset her—something at home or work.

"You bet," he said with an air of concern. "Come on in and shut the door behind you."

She paused in the center of the room. If it were an impromptu conversation, Alan half listened to her while he continued pecking away at his computer keyboard, as she leaned against the far side of his desk. When he called official meetings, the process was more formal, and they sat at the table in the corner of his office. Katie was uncomfortable with the situation she now found herself. It was all so new to her. So much responsibility was being dumped on her and she was wading into some murky water here.

"Alan," she said firmly, "could we sit at the table and talk?"

Alan leaned forward on his chair and grabbed a yellow legal pad from off the corner of his desk realizing something serious was up. He hoped he wasn't about to lose one of his most trusted and valued employees.

Sitting next to her at the table, Alan reached out and touched her hand. He hated to see her so distraught, and covering her hand with his much larger one seemed so natural to him. When she didn't jerk her hand away, he remained as he was, hands almost clasped.

"Katie, are you okay? Did something happen to Emily?" It was rare that Katie cracked her cool exterior. He knew she wasn't truly cool and aloof; it was fear, a wall of fear of letting anyone get too close. He'd love to break through that wall, he mused.

Absently, Katie moved her hand away and clasped it in her left hand on the desk. She inhaled deeply, and launched into her discussion about Dale.

"Erin talked to me again today, about Dale," she said.

Alan gave her a quizzical look.

"Alan," she said as she looked into his eyes, "it happened again. Dale attacked her again, but this time it was in his office—*here*—*today.*" She noticed his blank expression.

He slumped back on his chair and pushed his shirtsleeves above his elbows. What the hell, he wondered. That boy needed to be more careful—feel a woman out to see if she was into it. Jesus! Men had their moments—at work—it was to be expected, but *damn,* pick the right woman, he thought as he carefully ran his hand through his neatly groomed hair.

"What happened?" he asked sternly, not wanting his day ruined by a boy that couldn't find the right fuck around girl.

"Erin said she was in Dale's office when he grabbed her. He pulled her onto his lap, and started," using her hands Katie simulated what Erin had told her, "grabbed her by her hips and starting grinding her on him."

Alan stared at Katie, shocked that the word, *grinding* used in a sexual context, had just tumbled out of her mouth, again. In all the years he had known Katie, she had never used dirty or inappropriate language in *any* context. As he glanced at her moist lips, he felt something stir and shifted on his chair. Blinking, and taking a deep breath, he tried to think of something other than his assistant's lips.

He couldn't believe Dale would be so stupid to pick a girl that didn't want it. For Christ sake, it was a law firm! But he still wasn't convinced there was a problem. He couldn't count how many times this type of thing had happened at companies in the area. Sex on the job—it happened!

Alan noticed the twitch above Katie's right eye. His hot, librarian looking assistant, he thought, then blinked his eyes to clear the thought from his mind.

"How do you know this isn't some lover's spat? Are you sure they weren't screwing around and she just got pissed off at him about something? I've seen this before," Alan assured her. "Two people work together . . . become attracted to one another. As hard as we try, we are not going to keep emotions out of the workplace. It's just not possible, but when a lover's quarrel happens, typically the woman marches to HR to complain. I don't think I have ever heard of a man airing his relationship baggage in an HR department."

She couldn't believe what had just come out of his mouth—Mr. Family man—Father of the year—one of Kentucky's finest husbands, her mind ranted. Staring at him, she wondered, *just who was this man*? Horrified, she wondered if he really believed the crap he was saying.

"Oh my God, Alan," she said. "Are you serious? That is your response to me about this situation? You think they are in a relationship and she is pissed off at him so she is crying foul?" She looked down at the table wondering how to get through to him the seriousness of what had happened between two of his employees.

Katie wasn't like Alan. She hadn't developed the fine art of hiding behind a cool composed mask. She was passionate, and it showed in the intensity in her eyes, and the flush of her skin, as she flamboyantly gestured her arms, pinching her fingers together as if she were about to meditate.

"They are not in a *relationship*," she said exasperated. Shaking her head, she continued. "How on God's green earth, could you misconstrue this situation?" She clasped her hands together making a clapping noise. "How? How is it possible?" She pinched the fingers on her right hand together and lifted her arm in the air dramatically. "How?"

Alan flung his hands on the table and looked at his very angry assistant. "You mean to tell me, you have never heard of a workplace relationship gone bad?" he asked in disbelief.

"No!" Katie insisted hotly.

Alan had never seen Katie so fired up before, but even so, he was not convinced there was anything more than an innocent squabble between lovebirds.

"Alan, you need to talk to Dale. You *cannot* let this go on," she scowled. What the hell, she wondered. The man was an attorney. How was he missing the legal component of the situation?

Leaning back on his chair, he clasped his hands behind his head. "Katie," he reasoned, "has it occurred to you that maybe Erin is a little sensitive. Maybe she's blowing this thing out of proportion. Dale is a friendly guy, and the other women at the firm love the attention he gives them." Throwing his right hand in the air, he said, "What's that girl's name . . . Sonia. She doesn't seem to mind Dale's friendly nature." Opening his eyes wide and staring at her, he said, "I think she likes it!"

Katie laughed but not because she thought what Alan had said was funny. She was close to tears from frustration. Leaning back on her chair, she looked up at the white ceiling.

"Alan, you're not listening to me," she said. "You need to talk to your boy—tell him to back off Erin, and," looking him in the eye she said, "I'm telling you. Erin is really upset. You need to take this serious or you could have a lawsuit on your hands."

He didn't look overly concerned, Katie realized as she examined his face and body language. The same old Alan . . . but she was beginning to wonder if she really knew him. The same white button up dress shirt he had worn countless times, tucked neatly into his gray slacks, black socks peaked beneath his slacks, and the same expensive dress shoes were stuck on his feet. His shirt was conservatively buttoned, just one button undone to give him an air of casual, but not too casual . . . not a chest hair showed . . . perfectly groomed hair, soft hazel eyes . . . *impenetrable hazel eyes*. What was really going on in that seemingly gentle head of his, she wondered?

He flopped forward on his chair so quickly it startled her.

"Talk to him then," Alan said with a forced calm. "It's your job now."

She shook her head, and raised a hand off the table.

"Fine," she said, defeated.

"Anything else?" Alan asked.

"No," Katie said, with an insincere smile.

As her boss, Katie had to abide by what he said even if she did think he was wrong, in a dangerously legal way, wrong. What was his problem, Katie pondered? Could he be right? Could Erin and Dale be involved in a secret relationship, and he had pissed her off and now she was getting even by trying to get him fired? She sighed as she remembered Erin's tears when she had sat in her office and told her Dale had attacked her at the team building meeting. Her cheeks had been flushed and her hair was a mess. What Alan said just did not add up—but he was the boss, so what could she do? Nothing, she realized. It was his company to do with as he pleased. As she pushed back her chair, she thought, I sure hope his attitude doesn't come back to bite him on the ass.

Katie walked across Alan's office, brushing her hand over the back of her skirt as she did so, feeling for the seam, making sure it was straight.

Alan watched Katie's hips sway as she walked to the door. He squinted, trying to see how far up the slit of her skirt he could see. He grunted as he shifted in his chair. It was the first time he had seen Katie feisty.

As Katie opened the door, she turned, and asked, "Would you like the door shut?"

"Nah," he said. "You can leave it open."

"Oh!" Katie gasped. She'd walked out of Alan's office so quickly, and distracted, that she had literally collided with Kevin, the firm's accountant. She steadied herself by grasping his shirt-sleeved covered forearm as he placed his hand beneath her elbow. She stared up into piercing blue eyes.

"Excuse me," Kevin said with an uncomfortable smile. "Are you okay?"

Katie continued to stare up into Kevin's face, at a loss for words, her thoughts still in Alan's office. Kevin was one of the employees she didn't know very well, and as she considered him, she realized no one did. He was rather standoffish, keeping to himself during most of the workday, sharing few details about his personal life, and never seemed to have an opinion or idea to offer when the other employees took an occasional screwing off break. He was an odd one, she thought—not mean, or rude . . . just . . . kept to himself.

"I'm sorry," Katie said as she smiled up at him, and drew her hand back. "I should really watch where I'm going, that and slow down!"

"You were coming out of Alan's office pretty fast," he said with a knowing smile.

Kevin could guess why Katie was so frazzled—what had been the topic of conversation with their boss. Several hours before, Erin had been so distraught she hadn't noticed when he rounded the corner of the hall as she stormed out of Dale's office, her clothes askew, her hair a mess and tears in her eyes. As a married man with two little girls, he recognized her tears were not happy tears. Most of the men at the office knew the kind of man Dale was—womanizing, abusive—a sick asshole.

Kevin had continued down the hall to his destination to speak with one of the attorneys about client billable hours. After the meeting, Kevin had stewed over what he had seen, for about half an hour, and then called his wife to talk to her about it. Men like Dale really pissed him off.

He thought about his little girls, and what he'd do if a boy or man ever tried to treat them as Dale treated women. His first instinct was to slam open Dale's office door, grab him by his expensive name brand shirt, and beat the shit out of him. Kevin knew he could do it. Men like Dale weren't real men. They ran when they were confronted by other men bigger than they were. He'd had to dress down a few of his sister's boyfriends, but Erin wasn't his sister and this was his job.

He had a family to feed, which was exactly what Megan, his wife, had told him when he had called her to talk to her about it. "Leave it alone," she had insisted. "This kind of thing happens all the time. You can't change anything. But you can get yourself fired if you get involved." Scowling in anger, he had slammed his fist on his desk. Megan was right. He couldn't get involved, instead he had to cower, and let a man assault a woman. His dad had taught him as little boy that he was always to stand up for his sisters, or anyone smaller than him if they were being hurt, and in shame he wondered what his dad, an ex-marine, would think of his coward son if he knew he had just walked away from protecting a woman.

Katie's face burned, as she lied, "Just in a hurry to get a report done for Alan that he needs for a client. Sorry, Kevin," she said as she skirted around him and headed toward her office.

A few hours later, Katie had a very sleek junior partner sitting across her desk in her office. The corners of his lips were tilted up in a smirk as he considered Katie and the information she had just shared with him.

So, Erin was crying sexual harassment, Dale considered. Like so many women that complained of a little on the job attention, she'd regret it. No one wanted to deal with hypersensitive women in the business world. If you wanted to play in a man's world, you needed to suit up, and she had just shown she wasn't up to the game. Sad, he considered . . . they could have had a real good time.

As Katie watched, Dale leaned back on his chair, extended his long legs, and crossed his ankles. Propping his elbows on the arms of the chair, he splayed his hands, and lightly pressed the tips of his fingers together.

"Katie, do you really think I need to assault women?" Dale asked smoothly. "I mean, come on. I assure you, I am not the type of man that is so hard up for a woman that I have to force myself on one. What Erin says just doesn't make *any* sense."

Katie watched every move, even the slightest twitch for a sign of what made him tick, any sign of remorse, arrogance, or truth. She watched as he hunched forward on his chair, his legs spread wide, arms resting on his thighs, and looked at her as if they were conspirators in some plot against Erin.

"I wonder," Dale said as he wrinkled his brow with an air of artificial concern so thick it hung heavy in the room, "do you think she is having some kind of problem, you know, some kind of female problem? I've heard that sometimes women can get a little confused during that time of the month."

Dale examined Katie, her face, the slight lines around her eyes, and he could tell, although a soft and nice enough shade of light brown, he could tell it was color covering all that long hair of hers. She had a body that women of any age would die for, he thought, so it made it difficult to judge her age, thirty to forty years old. He didn't care how old a woman was; as long as they had a hot body, he was willing to help them out. Katie's wedding ring caught his eye, and he thought, he never let a little thing like a piece of jewelry deter him from a little fun.

Katie could feel and see Dale's eyes on her and wished she had thought to grab her sweater, which was hung on a hanger on the back of her office door. The lavender colored silk button up blouse felt suddenly too sheer. She wished she'd opted for slacks instead of the knee length gray skirt that seemed much too short, as she sat with her ankles crossed. Squirming, she tugged on her blouse and skirt, making sure both were covering as much of her skin as possible.

"Dale," she said, "a woman's menstrual cycle, if that is what you were referring too, has no bearing on this topic." Katie would have felt uncomfortable discussing sexual assault with any one of the employees, but especially so with a man who was openly leering at her across her desk, made even more complex by the fact that he was her superior. Alan may say she was now a boss, but attorney, even junior, trumped senior paralegal and even acting HR Manager. Alan should know that, so why the hell had he placed her in this position? *This was obviously a conversation he should be having with Dale, not her*!

"Dale, Erin presented the situation to me as *assault*," Katie said sternly. "I need your assurance that this behavior will not happen again with any of the firm's employees, on company grounds or elsewhere. Look, Dale, you're an attorney. You know the ramifications of sexual harassment, for the accused, the accuser, and the financial liability to a company. You know how messy these cases can be. I know you do, because you've represented companies in the community. This is no different except this time, we as a firm could be liable. We just cannot have this type of behavior here."

"I'm telling you, Katie!" Dale boomed. He pounded his right fist into the palm of his left hand. His face was flushed with anger. Fun was fun, he thought, but he was not going to let some cunt fuck up his career. She needed to learn to play or she'd regret it. "I did *not* assault her. We were getting a little friendly. I swear! She was into it! Prove to me she didn't want it!"

Oh my Lord, Katie thought. *I cannot believe I am having an argument, at work, with a man about a woman wanting it!*

Keeping her temper in check, she said stiffly, "Dale, it is your word against Erin's word. I can tell you this, that type of behavior, sexual behavior, regardless of who wanted what, has no place at the office. There will be no harassing, intimidating or even consensual fooling around on the job. While you are on company time, whether you are at the office, or a team building activity, or any other off-site business related activity, you will *not* engage in sexual activities with other employees. You are in a superior position to many of the employees. You're an *attorney* for Christ's sake! What are you *thinking*? Are you just asking someone to sue the firm? It is behavior unbecoming of a man that has hopes of becoming a senior partner. You need to think about that!"

Indicating the meeting was over, Katie pushed her chair back, walked across her office, and pulled open the door. She had every intention of discussing Dale's attitude with Alan. He needed to handle the situation from here.

Scowling, Dale looked down at her, and said between clenched teeth, "I have never forced myself on any woman," and then walked across the threshold into the hall.

She closed the door quietly after the very angry attorney, and let out the breath she had been holding, and hissed, "Asshole." Bending over, Katie placed her hands on her knees and closed her eyes for a minute, attempting to steady her breathing. Walking toward her desk, she whispered to the walls of her office, "What an asshole."

Leaning back on her chair, Katie ran the fingers of her left hand across her brow. It had been one shitty day and she was ready for it to be over. Alan had left over an hour ago. She would have liked to have gotten the Dale talk over with, but it would have to wait. She sighed.

After typing a few notes about the meeting with Dale, Katie grabbed her briefcase from under her side desk, grabbed her sweater, and walked slowly to the door, the click of her high heeled shoes muffled by the carpeted floor. Flipping off the light, she closed the door behind her, ready for a quiet evening at home. It would be the perfect movie night, she thought. She could really go for the movie *Toy Story* again, or maybe, Finding *NEMO*, Emily's pick—anything to forget the office crap for a few hours.

Thirty minutes from Katie's house, Erin sat hunched over the white ceramic toilet in the bathroom attached to her bedroom, bleary eyed, throwing up the partial bottle of vodka she had downed over an hour ago. Spent, she slid to the cool tile floor where she passed out. Max, watching from the doorway of the bathroom, cocked his head, and then lumbered across the floor toward his owner, and lay down beside her.

7

Katie knocked on the door to Alan's office to get his attention. As usual, he was staring intently at his computer screen. He was probably checking one of his social media sites . . . his Facebook account, Katie speculated. Typically he had all sorts of websites open during the day, and Facebook was left open all day at the upper right of his screen.

"Come in," he said slowly.

"I can come back if you're busy," Katie said hesitantly.

"No," he said, still staring at the large monitor of his computer as he pecked away at his keyboard.

She walked over and leaned against the edge of Alan's desk, knowing this was going to be one of those half-attentive conversations. Katie watched as Alan placed his index finger on the screen of his computer monitor, squinting at whatever it was he was reading. Perhaps, Katie considered, he should move the screen closer to his body so he could see better, but she said nothing.

"How's your day going?" she asked.

"Oh," he sighed as he squinted at the monitor, and leaned back in his chair, "busy. How's your day going? How's Emily?"

"Crazy busy day," she replied. "Emily—about the same."

"Don't forget," Alan said. "If you need anything, I'm here. I give great hugs," he said, still squinting at his computer screen.

Offering a distracted smile, she said, "Thank you."

The room was quiet for a moment as Alan leaned back on his chair, and clasping his hands behind his head, he examined her. Katie was wearing a pastel peach dress with white flowers sprinkled on it and a white elbow length sweater—so feminine, and her soft perfume filled the room in a nice way.

Leaning toward the screen of his computer, but looking at Katie, Alan asked, "So, what's going on with Dale?"

"I met with Dale yesterday afternoon," Katie said. She looked down at Alan's desk, and picked up a miniature brass clock and examined it.

"Well, how'd that go?" he asked, not taking his eyes off her face. She tucked a stray strand of hair behind her ear, not realizing how young and sweet the gesture was.

Resting against the edge of his desk, Katie crossed her arms over her chest, looked up with a small smile, and sighed. Her eyes locked on his.

"Not so well, actually," she said.

"And," he coaxed.

Shaking her head, she said, "The man argued with me that Erin," she raised her hands in the air and made a quote sign with her fingers, "wanted it. His claim is that they got a little friendly and that she was into it."

He leaned back on his chair, clasped his hands behind his head and stared at his assistant. "Well," he said, "maybe she was."

Wrinkling her forehead in surprise, Katie looked into his eyes and exclaimed, "What!? You have got to be kidding me."

They stared across his desk at each other, Alan with his blue dress shirt with white cuffs rolled to the middle of his forearms, one button opened near his collar giving him the look of a man that worked hard, and Katie a contrast in her flowing, feminine dress. The peach color of the dress seemed to make the green in Katie's eyes a deeper, darker shade.

Trying to focus on the conversation, Alan looked down at her hand, at the fingers of her left hand wrapped around the clock, and the diamond wedding band wrapped around her finger.

Scratching his forehead, he sighed, and said, "Katie, you weren't there. For that matter, neither was I. All we have is what Erin told you and now

Dale. Who are we supposed to believe? I'd say you believe Erin." He shifted his eyebrows.

Dammit! She thought. He was right. She did believe Erin. Dale was a womanizing ass. Everyone at the firm knew that. Alan knew it too. Katie knew Erin to be a levelheaded woman. She was not some loose woman that jumped into bed or relationships with any man that came along—not the desperate type. Dale on the other hand was a male slut! But she could not argue with Alan because he was right; there had been no witnesses.

"I do believe Erin," she said firmly. "I think this is exactly the type of thing Dale would do. He leers at women here in the office; stares at their breasts, down their blouses if he has the chance, and I have seen him slyly rub against women. Oh, I know he blows it off with the excuse that it was an accident. He couldn't reach a file so he just had to reach across an intern, or some young secretary." She looked up at the ceiling and laughed. "The man cannot keep any woman on staff for more than three months! Why do you think that is?"

"Did you see him touch Erin?" he asked patiently.

"No," Katie snapped as she looked at her boss. "So what are we supposed to do?"

"You just did it," he said, thumping his arms on his desk. He shrugged his shoulders and said, "That's it. You have done your job."

Wrinkling her forehead, she said, "*It*—that's it? Somehow I just do *not* think Erin is going to be overly pleased that, if she were sexually assaulted," Katie allowed, raising her hand to ward off Alan's interruption, "if she was sexually assaulted, and all we do is talk to Dale and tell him to keep his hands off her. I don't think she's going to be satisfied."

"Katie, it's all we can do at this point," Alan insisted. "There are no witnesses. It is her word against his."

"Okay," she said, placing her hands on her hips.

Trying to avert his eyes from the peach fabric stretched taught over Katie's breasts, Alan asked, "Anything else?"

"No. That was it." Offering him a small smile, she said, "I'm sorry Alan. I didn't mean to come off rude or disrespectful." This wasn't a personal issue; it was professional, and she knew she'd allowed her anger to show. "I'm sorry."

Wrinkling his nose, Alan grinned, and said, "That was you being rude? Wow, I'd love to see you angry. Don't worry about it, Katie. It's fine."

As she walked to her office, she thought, I have to get a grip. I cannot get angry with my boss. Exhaling, she closed her office door behind her, and with her hands on her hips, she considered her conversation with Erin. Alan was right. No one had seen anything. She'd just have to smooth it over as best as she could. But she felt for Erin. What a shitty position to be in.

8

Alan rolled over and reached toward the alarm clock beeping at him on the bedside table. He squinted at the clock and read, 4:00 a.m., and clicked the alarm off. Stretching, he sat up, swung his legs over the side of the king-sized bed, and planted his feet on the floor. He yawned as he walked toward the adjoining bathroom to turn on the shower. Once the spray from the shower hit his face he'd wake up, he thought with another yawn. He had always been an early riser, something he had learned when he was a kid from his dad. Several years ago, Alan had found the disturbances of his wife, crawling into bed hours after he'd slid between the sheets, bother-some, and had opted for his own bedroom. Their hours were different, she taking care of the kids, going to bed hours after him, and rising hours after him. Separate bedrooms worked for them. The weekly sex routine required of her was on a scheduled night so she knew the expectation, to be in her room early that one night of the week. It was little to ask of her.

"Hey, Lucky," Alan said as he leaned over to rub the fur of the black and white, four-year-old mutt that had followed him to the bathroom. "Man's loyal friend," he said to the dog. The dog whined as if he knew what his master was talking about, and curled up in the corner of the bathroom.

After showering, Alan walked downstairs to the kitchen to pour a cup of coffee from a freshly brewed pot. Walking into the kitchen, he smelled the fresh robust coffee and came fully awake. After pouring a cup, he headed to his laptop in the home office of his six thousand square foot Tudor-style house to check his e-mails. In Alan's world, appearances were everything, the house one owned, and even the grade school, university and church one attended.

After sending off a few e-mails to a couple of business associates inviting them to a golf outing that afternoon, Alan grabbed his laptop, slid it into its black bag, and headed to the office for a few hours before heading to church. He liked to catch the early service so it didn't eat into his day. Part of being a leader in the community meant putting in an appearance each week at the church he had selected years ago. Early in his legal career, a mentor had shared that to be successful in business, you had to endear yourself to the community, and one way to do that was to appear to be a God fearing family man. So Alan had picked one of the larger, more affluent churches in the area in order to be seen by the right folks. He had missed few Sunday services since. He realized that being a successful business man was part luck, being in the right place at the right time, and exceptional acting abilities—show the public what they wanted, that and it didn't hurt that his granddad had been rich.

"So, Alan, who are you doing these days?" Art asked with a laugh.

Alan was lining up his putt on the green, and thought, yeah, Art, you would pick now to start yappin' at me.

Alan turned toward a bear of a man with a flock of fiery red hair on his head and almost as thick covering his arms, the lead womanizer of the foursome. Alan had known Art for over twenty years, and he had changed little during that time. Even now, in his early fifties, he had his mind on the next sex score. None of the guys could keep up with Art, even with the annual bet.

Each spring, the group of men in their elite circle participated in a wager to see who could fuck their secretary, or assistant, or some newly hired woman at their company. The rule was that the woman chosen had to be someone they saw on a regular basis, not some random bar slut, and some form of sexual contact had to be made, either an all-out fuck, grind, blowjob or hand job. The most critical factor in choosing a victim was that she had to be married, and for good reason. Just in case the dim-wit should actually develop feelings for one of them, well, she was married and so was he. They could play on her sympathy for *their* wife, and if they had to, her husband. The other, probably even more important reason they selected only married women was that if they made an error and the woman they hit on was not in to it, they would use the old, we will tell your husband you were having an affair trick.

It never failed, even if the woman was not in to it and slapped them for grabbing her ass. The women never told. Funny how so many women feared their husbands would believe some man's version over the truth. Men knew other men. Plant the seed that some guy's wife was fucking around and the marriage was never the same, even if it was a lie. Most women wouldn't take that chance. It was a form of insurance, just in case they picked the wrong woman.

The reward for the winner varied over the years, from Cuban cigars, premium scotch, and one year the losers had to cough up ten grand if they couldn't manipulate a woman to play ball. Alan had his losing years but also his share of wins. Most of their wives were understanding of their husband's indiscretions. Sure, the wives probably weren't thrilled their husbands were sliding their hands over other women's bodies, their fingers penetrating their most secret places. When wives found out about one of the little stress relieving indiscretions, there could be months of sex dry spells on the home front, and they'd have to dish out expensive gifts of vacations, jewelry, plastic surgery and even the dreaded gifts to mother-in laws. But the wives knew if they didn't put out pretty damn quick, their husband would be sticking it to even more women, so they got over it pretty quick. They understood that powerful men had powerful stressors and needed powerful stress relief. Besides, their wives knew what they were signing on for, being married to power and money—knew their husbands would never be completely theirs. Alan had his flaws like his friends, and fortunately, as far as he knew, Nancy had been none the wiser. But occasionally he wondered if she knew about the other women.

The golf course was where the guys talked about their latest conquests, that and sometimes they had special holes arranged to make the game more interesting—blow job action from one of the pricey call girls in town. They knew in advance which holes had the special prize, and balls would be hit all over the course, finding them amongst the trees where a pretty little thing would be waiting.

"Art, I told you, I'm not doin' anyone on the side this year. Nancy and I are taking time for us," Alan insisted. "You know, trying to save my marriage, that and save half the money I've worked like hell to make. If she leaves, she takes half of what she did nothing to earn, other than spread her legs and pop out a few kids. I'm not just letting her walk away with my hard-earned life!"

The three men laughed.

"Yeah, taking some time," Art said as he slapped Alan on the back. "You're married man, and you're rich! You don't have anything to prove to her. She's got what she wants . . . a mini-mansion, everything money can buy, rubbin' elbows with other rich women and politician's wives. Without you, she's nothin', just the nobody she was when she married you. She ain't goin' nowhere. Hell, she done won the marital lottery. She don't give a fuck what, or who you do! Am I right boys?"

The group of men laughing on the green were impeccably groomed, hair in place, and nails buffed. They were what the community wanted in leaders, the appearance of wealth and affluence, a choir boy look. Now they were middle-aged, respected men, who had private lives—snorting cocaine for the rush and feeling of invincibility it provided, fucking prostitutes in their offices to take the edge off their day, and short-term affairs with employees who were fired when they tired of them—that could lose them everything.

"Yours is still my favorite, Alan, old man," Art laughed. "The line you gave your secretary . . . you know, that sweet little thing with blonde hair . . . and she bought it . . . left your firm without so much as a whisper. Tell us again what you told 'er to get 'er to leave without suing you."

Absently, Alan grinned. "It was supposed to be some sweet thing that couldn't be," he said thoughtfully.

The group of golf and business buddies laughed heartily remembering the single mom that Alan had come on to. He had managed to manipulate her into leaving the company without suing him after he realized, due to the slap on his face after one intense rejected come on, she wasn't willing to play his game of sex the secretary. She had left the firm with a few months of pay, thinking that Alan had a thing for her, and that it was best if she left because she was so desirable, she being all he could think about. He had gushed that he had just wanted something sweet with her, longing for more, but it couldn't be. Women were like puppies, Alan thought, wanting to believe that everything in the world, including men, were good.

Alan grinned as he listened to the men that he had called his friends for over twenty years talk about their latest conquests as he considered, was there anyone at his office worth entering the bet, and should he risk it with the fragile state of his marriage.

9

❦

"**M**ax, come on!" Erin shouted at the black lab as he dashed after a squirrel across the park lawn. It was a cloudless Saturday morning with just a hint of a breeze, and warming up quickly; she'd already tied her jacket around her waist. Her short-sleeved yellow t-shirt, blue jean shorts, and tennis shoes were a welcome change to her typical five day a week business wear.

Erin had been surprised when her brother, Tom, had called the night before and asked if she had a few hours free to spend with him this morning. He had no idea just how free she was, she thought. She'd been keeping to herself lately, no dinners or coffee dates with friends, no dates with any significant guy. Pulling away from her condo had become a chore. Typically, she loved being with friends—old and new—but what happed at work with Dale had really shaken her up and she needed time alone . . . needed quiet, to feel safe.

Tom was as casual as she was on Saturday mornings, dressed in navy blue running shorts, tennis shoes, and a white and navy colored t-shirt. As she glanced up at him, she noticed he'd yet to shave his morning stubble from his face. Of all her brothers, Tom was the closest in age to her, two years older—twenty-eight years of age. He was six-foot-four, and looked more like a linebacker than a fifth grade teacher. Anyone that glanced their way could discern they were related, he sharing the same shade of blonde hair, cut conservatively, and the same sparkling, friendly blue eyes.

Tom had noticed his kid sister had become a recluse over the past few weeks, very unlike her, even when she had a new man in her life. Something was up, and his gut told him his sister's reclusive behavior was not due to a mystery romance, but instead to something sinister.

"How's it been going, Erin?" Tom asked.

Looking across the park at Max, she replied, "Oh, it's been going okay."

Erin still hadn't talked to her family, not her brothers or her dad, about what had happened with Dale, and wasn't sure why. Her brothers and dad had always been privy to details about her life. This, however, was different, and looking down at the red and white dog leash in her hand, she wasn't sure why. Being the youngest kid, and the only girl, had meant she had three big brothers more than willing to fight her bullies for her, but she had stubbornly insisted, even when she was a little girl, that she could fight her own battles. And she had. But she didn't feel as if she was fighting this one very well, and it embarrassed her. She didn't want her brothers to find out just what a sissy-girl she was. That, and she couldn't bring herself to speak the shame of what had happened, that a man had touched her like that . . . had violated her. Surprised by the tears that pricked her eyes, she turned her face away from Tom, trying to hide her watery eyes.

There wasn't much Erin could hide from her brothers. They all kidded her about her independence, respecting her need to feel like one of the guys, but she wasn't. She was a girl. She was his little sister, and as Tom saw the tears she was trying hard to hide from him trickle down her cheek, he flung his arm around her shoulder, and pulled her close. She clung to him, releasing the pain she had been holding in for weeks. Finally, she pulled away, her face red and puffy, and wiped her eyes and nose with the back of her hand.

"You wanna sit down and talk about it?" Tom asked, gesturing toward an old wooden picnic table.

"No, at least not at a picnic table," she said bitterly. As they walked across the park, over the lush green grass, and under the brilliant blue summer sky, she shared what had happened at the team building event and then again in Dale's office.

"His hands, Tom, he wouldn't stop touching me and tugging at me. And I panicked," Erin said, shaking her head. With a grimace she said, "Remember when we were kids in high school, I actually insulted those simpleton girls that whined about things." Looking up at her brother as she shielded her eyes from the sun, she said, "Do you remember that girl in my grade, Tammy—Tammy what's her name," snapping her fingers. "God, she drove me nuts always tattling on the boys about how they pulled her hair or touched her! Well, I've become her!"

Tom felt his blood begin to boil, but he tried to appear calm, knowing exploding would not help his sister now. During his college days, a friend of his had been raped. He had seen firsthand the aftermath, watched as she had fallen apart, broken. She had never been the same since. There had been nothing he could do to help his friend, but Erin . . . his sister, Tom's instinct was to hunt down this Dale slime and beat him bloody. He knew his type. Dales' of the world were the arrogant assholes at high schools that used girls like toilet paper—used them to do their business—and then threw them in the trash. They were the guys at frat parties who preyed on girls that'd had too much to drink. Then, once the Dales' graduated from high school, or college, the low life scum-bags invaded and infected the work world, a new pool of women to assault.

Tom had learned a great deal about sexual assault from his college friend, enough to know victims never forgot. They had a future of being frightened easily by quick movements, suffered nightmares as they relived the attack, and unmercifully blamed themselves.

Gently, Tom placed his hand on his sister's forearm. "Erin, it wasn't your fault," he said softly. "You did nothing wrong, and you're not some whiny little girl. You were attacked."

She looked up at him with tears escaping from where they had been clinging to her long black lashes.

As Erin began to sob, Tom carefully pulled her into his arms as tears of his own coursed down his cheeks. They stood in the park clinging to one another. Tom held his sister in a bear hug, trying to shelter her from the evils of the world, as Erin clutched the back of his shirt.

When they parted, trying to keep the anger he was feeling from his tone, Tom asked, "Are you going to talk to dad about what happened at work?"

"Oh, God no, Tom," she said, shocked that he would ask such a thing. "I don't want dad worrying about me." Pulling her shoulders back, she said, "I'm a big girl. I can handle this."

There wasn't a man on the planet that Erin loved and admired more than her father. He had managed to raise four children on his own after his wife had died, and had made it look easy, organizing soccer games, football, Karate classes, swim classes, attending Girl Scout activities and leading a Boy Scout troop. But Erin knew it had not been easy. He had sacrificed a great deal for his children—dating, and even a VP position at the company he still worked at so he could play an active role in his children's lives. She couldn't let him down, couldn't let him think he had raised a sissy-girl for a daughter.

Absently, Erin tucked her hand in her big brother's hand, as she had done hundreds of times when she was a little girl, and they began walking toward Max.

"I know you are," Tom said, worried. "But I'm here if you need me."

Squinting up at her brother, Erin said, "I know."

"Have you thought about going to the police, you know, reporting Dale?" Tom asked.

Erin stopped, the shock of what her brother had asked registering on her face, and sputtered, "You can't be serious. Tom, this is my job. You don't just report something like *this*, unless of course you never want to work again. It's just not done."

"I think you're wrong," Tom said. "It's a crime. You were almost raped, at work! You can't let him get away with that. Who knows how many other women there have been, and how many more there will be!"

"Well, let one of them sacrifice *their* life for the good of all other women. I'm not going to be blackballed by every company in the tri-state area because of this," Erin said. "I can't press charges, and even complaining to Katie could seriously screw up my life at the firm. I don't know." She flung a hand in the air. "Maybe I made a mistake by telling her. Oh My God," she said as she squinted up at the blue sky. "What have I done?"

Grabbing his sister by the shoulders, Tom gave her a little shake.

"Done—*done*?" Tom said. "You haven't *done* anything. That asshole has, and someone needs to beat the shit out of him, and maybe that someone should be me!"

Startled, Erin said, "No, Tom. You can't tell anyone about this." She looked at the anger in her brother's face and worried that perhaps she shouldn't have told him. "Promise me," she pleaded. "Promise me you won't say or do anything."

"I won't say anything," he promised, shaking his head in frustration.

10

After selecting a song from her IPOD, Katie pulled out of the parking lot of Emily's school. It was one of her favorite times of the day, having a six-year-old tug on her hand to show her something in her classroom. This morning, hair bouncing in pigtails, Emily had excitedly grasped Katie's hand and skipped her across the classroom to the aquarium by the window. There on a table sat an aquarium with the class pet—a lizard. Tapping on the glass, Emily had tried to coax the white and tan colored creature out of its hiding place under a rock.

So this is what it would feel like to be a mother, Katie thought with a wistful smile as she pulled into the flow of traffic, and headed to work. It had been a crushing blow when she'd discovered she'd never be able to have a child of her own. Brad hadn't seemed to be overly concerned. He'd said it didn't change anything between them, that as a matter of fact, he liked having her all to himself, but the finality of never having a child of her own had torn a piece of her away.

A few days later, Katie was sitting at her desk at the firm when her cell phone rang. Before she could say hello into the receiver, she heard the voice of her younger sister, Stacey, her voice husky as if she had been crying.

"Hey, Stacey," Katie said anxiously. "Is everything okay?"

She hated having her sister so far away, in a foreign country. If Stacey needed her, it wasn't as if she could hop into her car and drive right over.

"Oh my God," Stacey sobbed. "I saw someone get shot. I know this is what I signed on for, and of course this is all part of the job—the military—you know."

Katie heard her sister sniff, and closing her eyes, she bent her head and leaned against her balled up hand.

"Katie, I've seen blood and gore as a nurse, but this was different. It wasn't some—some—controlled hospital setting. I don't know what happened. We were walking as a group during our off hours in town, somewhere that was supposed to be safe, and a shot came out of a small crowd. It hit Ed, the guy standing next to me. I had his blood splattered on me . . . on my face . . . it was still warm!" she cried. "He has a wife and two little kids in Texas . . . *two little kids*," she rambled hysterically.

Silently, Katie cried as she listened to her sister's tortured voice, needing to reach into the phone and pull her to safety, into her arms. She heard a fumbling noise and then the sound of Stacey blowing her nose, sniffing, clearing her throat, and then Stacey's voice again. "I'm sorry, Katie, for laying this on you so early in the day, laying it on you at all. I don't mean to worry you."

Katie sniffed as tears ran down her cheeks. In a thick voice, she said, "Stacey, stop trying to be so strong all the time." Her strong little sister trying to save the world, she thought, as she shook her head. Always trying to be the tough girl. When, she wondered, would Stacey realize it was okay to be soft?

"I wish I was there with you, Stacey, so I could give you a hug, so you could give *me* a hug," Katie said huskily.

"Me too," Stacey sniffed.

Katie knew her little sister wouldn't want to hear it, but she said it anyway, "I wish you could just come home, Stacey."

"Katie, I can't desert my team. They need me here. You know that. I'm just feeling raw right now. I didn't want anyone to see this—my break down.

It wouldn't do anyone any good. But," Stacey said with a watery smile, "you are my net . . . catching me when I fall every time."

Badly, Katie wanted to disagree with Stacey, wanted to insist that she hop the next military flight home, but knew her sister was right. Stacey had signed on for some scary stuff. She wasn't on the front line actually fighting the war, but that didn't matter anymore. As a nurse, she should be safe, but even if she were a supply clerk—an office type job—it still wouldn't be a guarantee of safety. Even so, Katie knew if every person in the military hopped on a plane and headed for home whenever they got scared, there would be no one keeping everyone at home safe. But, Katie worried, did it have to be her sister keeping everyone else safe? She couldn't lose her.

Trying to be cheerful for her sister, Katie said, a little too brightly, "I will catch you every time . . . just like you catch me, and together joined we make a mighty strong net for Emily too."

"How's my baby?" Stacey asked. "There are days I'm afraid she's going to forget me, forget who her real mommy is." Sighing, she said, "I miss my baby so much, Katie. My heart is not whole without her. I don't know how people make a career out of the military. Four years is all I can handle. Does she still remember me?" Stacey asked. She began to cry again.

Katie felt as if her heart were ripping out of her chest as she sat helplessly behind her desk. Pressing her hand against her heart, tears slipped silently down her cheeks, as she looked around her safe office with silly knick-knacks on bookshelves—her little world where nothing bad could get her. Closing her eyes, Katie pictured her sister's world, thousands of miles away in a war torn desert, far from all she loved, away from warmth, from home, and her safety net.

"She remembers you, Stacey," Katie cried, her shoulders shaking with silent sobs. "She remembers you," she whispered. "I won't let her forget you. We talk about you every day."

After Katie hung up the phone a few minutes later, with her chin resting on her clasped hands, she stared across her quiet office and thought about her sister and her niece.

Katie hid behind an artificial smile for the rest of the day, but her thoughts were far away, with her sister in the sweltering heat of the desert where the enemy lurked everywhere. Leaning back in her chair, Katie did a deep stretch, extending her arms above her head and arched her back. "Ouch," she said to the walls of her office. She was going to need to stretch the pain out of her back later with some yoga, but for now, she needed to drop a brief off to Alan's office, then on to her evening. She'd been grateful for the distraction of her busy day, but now, as she walked away from Alan's office, her thoughts turned to Stacey.

11

"How's business going?" Sam asked as he waited with Alan for their turn to putt.

"Slow," Alan responded with a sour expression.

"Yeah, mine too. The recession is killing me. I'm to the point I hate going into the office to deal with all my employees, wondering who I'm going to fire next, and I hate going home because all Maggie and I do anymore is argue. I can't remember the last time I had a good lay, at home that is," Sam said with a smile.

Chuckling, Alan said, "You and me both."

"The only thing getting me through this shit is the little thing I've got going on the side," Sam said, as he pumped his hips as if he was screwing a phantom woman. Grinning down at Alan he said, "You have to find the good in everything. Know what I mean?" He slapped his old friend on the back. "What you got goin' on? I know you aren't going without any. That's not the Alan I know."

Watching a man on the green line up his putt, Alan answered, "No. Nothing going on with me."

"The hell you say! You're so full of shit!" the taller man laughed.

"Nah. I'm too busy trying to keep my firm afloat." Looking up with a grin, Alan said, "And besides, man, there's no ass worth touching at my office right now. You know me. If there was, I'd be grabbing me some!"

The two men leaning on their clubs watched the short man on the green lean over, and then stroke the ball in to the hole. As Alan watched, his thoughts turned to Katie. Yeah, there was no one in the office he wanted to touch . . . except for her, but he wasn't willing to add her to the betting pool just yet.

12

Later that evening, lying next to a softly snoring six-year old, Katie continued to think about Alan. What did it all mean? Why was he constantly asking to touch her . . . if she needed a hug? Maybe it was the Erin and Dale issue . . . it was getting to her, that and Stacey. It's nothing, Katie, she chided. Alan is the same Alan he has always been. He probably senses you're stressed out and is just being nice. *Get a grip, Katie! You're becoming one of those paranoid women . . .*

The next afternoon, Katie leaned against Alan's desk and prepared for whatever task he was about to add to her list. He leaned back on his chair and clasped his hands behind his head.

"I want you to help me plan a company retreat, kind of like a team building event for the attorneys and paralegals," he said.

"Oh!" Katie responded. "A team building event. Like the one we had a few months ago at the hotel in Covington?" The event where Dale attacked Erin, she thought.

Leaning forward, he said, "Nah. Something bigger, for a few days at my cabin down in southern Kentucky . . . Lake Cumberland area. Years ago, several times a year, my dad used to get the attorneys together. It was a great way to really get to know one another, to develop loyalty for the firm. That and to reward everyone for their hard work."

Katie raised her eyebrows skeptically.

"A retreat, for a few days. Sure, I can help coordinate it for you." Hesitantly, she asked, "I won't be expected to attend, will I? I mean, I'm not an attorney . . ."

"Of course. You have to go!" Alan insisted. "As the head of the paralegal staff, and one of the leaders of this firm, your attendance is mandatory."

Inwardly, Katie groaned. Overnight, she thought. Perhaps there was some surgery, or something she had been putting off that would need to happen that weekend. Sighing, she knew she wouldn't be able to get out of it.

"Send out a memo to the attorneys, just for this office" Alan instructed. "That they'll be expected to attend the team building event." Leaning forward, he handed her an eight and half by eleven sized piece of white paper. "This is the list of employees I want at this event. CC me on the e-mail you send out."

Katie took the piece of paper from his hand, noticing her name was at the top of the list, and wondered if Brad would be okay to watch Emily for her while she was at the event.

"Two weekends from now," Alan said. "That's when the event will be. An extended weekend."

Alan rose from his chair, walked around his desk, and leaned against its edge and stared intently at Katie, a small smile hovering around his lips. He reached his hand toward her, wanting her to take it in his.

Cautiously, trying not to anger him, Katie walked toward the door, and turning, she looked back at him, still leaning against the edge of his desk. She offered him a small, uncertain, smile, and then eased out the door.

"Do you want me to shut the door?" she asked.

"No," he said, still smiling as he looked at her over his glasses.

Slowly Katie walked down the hall to the corridor that led to the firm's elaborate break room, furnished with several black leather couches and coffee tables. Relieved to find the room empty, she poured a cup of steaming black coffee into a cup and then walked over to one of the leather couches and sat down, relaxing into the overstuffed, worn leather. She shivered as a chill came over her.

"Good morning, Ms. Katie!" Tanya from accounting said brightly, as she breezed into the break room.

"Good morning, Tanya." Katie smiled at the large, bubbly woman. Tanya was one of the most cheerful women Katie had ever met, the unofficial comedian of the firm. Everyone loved her, except perhaps for a few of the good old boy attorneys at the firm. Right now, Katie could use a little comic relief in her day.

"How's it going, Tanya," Katie asked, welcoming a well-deserved girl chat break.

"Oh, I can't complain," Tanya said with a grin. She walked across the small room, and holding her coffee cup carefully, sat down at the opposite end of the couch. "How're you doin' girl? How's the boss man treating you these days?"

Watching Katie closely, Tanya took a careful sip of her steaming coffee. Not much got by Tanya and lately she had detected a definite note of tension around Katie, and she had her suspicions what was causing Katie's tension, not the specifics, just the cause. Tanya had been around the corporate world block long enough to know how messy it could be for women in the work world and the Weaver law firm had a reputation for use 'em up and discard 'em mentality toward their female employees. It happened all the time, at all types of companies, and there was really nothing women or their husbands could do about it. It was a, suffer in groping silence, and then when the owners or those at the helm of the companies grew bored with the chase, whether they ever actually caught the woman or not, she was let go. Tanya knew Alan and Katie had a great working relationship, but Katie, even at her age, was just a fresh faced naïve kid. If Alan put the moves on her, as he had so many other women at the office, she'd have no idea how to handle it. Alan had a special kind of respect for Katie, Tanya considered, and had hoped he'd give her a free pass, and leave her alone. Katie was a good lady, and had endured so much recently with her brother-in-laws death and taking on her niece. Tanya prayed Alan Weaver would surprise her and dig into the little decency she didn't think he possessed and leave her alone.

"Oh!" Katie said in surprise. She hadn't been prepared for such a direct question about her boss. "He's . . . he's fine . . . I guess," she stammered.

"Uh-huh," Tanya grunted. "What's that man up to?" she asked, and then took another sip of her coffee, hoping Katie would open up.

Waving her hand in the air, Katie tried to recover the conversation by saying, "It's great . . . I mean he's great . . . the . . . the . . . he's fine."

Considering the red head, Katie considered, Tanya might be the perfect opportunity to pry about Alan, considering she seemed to know everyone at the firm. Perhaps she'd have some much-needed insight into the head of the firm.

"Tanya, you've been with the firm a long time and seem to be the eyes and ears of the place. What do you know about the owners of the firm . . . Alan . . . his wife . . . and his parents?"

Tanya intended to grab the opportunity to convey just who the big man was, so if something was up, if Alan was hurting Katie, maybe the sweet kid could find a way to save herself before things got too bad.

Leaning toward Katie in a conspirator kind of way, Tanya exclaimed, "Oh my, Lord, girl! That man is a freak!"

It was not the response Katie had been anticipating, and in surprise, she sat back quickly. Raising her eyebrows, Katie said, "A freak."

"Yes! A freak!" Tanya said with a stern look on her face.

"Hey, ladies."

Startled, Katie recognized the annoying voice as her other problem at the firm—Dale. She looked down into her coffee cup to cover that he had startled her.

"Hello, Dale," Katie said uncomfortably. Taking a deep breath, she looked up at the office playboy, and asked, "How are you today?"

Tanya struggled to her feet, sloshing a little of her coffee on the couch and said, with a roll of her eyes, "I'm outta here." When she had wiggled to her feet, she looked down at Katie, wanting to say more, but needing even more to be free of the break room and Dale, the office sleaze. "I'll see you later, Katie," Tanya said, hoping they would have a chance to continue their conversation later.

Rising to her feet, Katie smiled at the other woman, and said, "See you later." She watched Tanya walk out of the break room wondering what she had meant by her freak comment.

Shaking her head, Katie walked toward the coffee pot with the intention of topping off her coffee, thinking, what Tanya had said didn't make sense, at least not for the people Nancy and Alan had presented to her. But then, she thought, Alan's most recent behavior was of the freak variety, the hug queries, and obvious disregard for Erin. Not what she would have expected from the man he presented to her and the community.

Dale leaned against the counter, as if he were leaning against a bar on a Saturday night. He smiled at Katie.

"I'm having a great day," he crooned. He examined Katie's face, surprised he hadn't noticed her classic features before. For a woman of her age, for that matter, any age, she was beautiful. Not in a cheerleader kind of way, but a soft, feminine kind of beauty.

"How's your day going?" he asked. His eyes traveled to the button that held her blouse together, hiding her feminine treasures from him.

"Oh, just busy. You know how it is around here. There's always something to be done," Katie said, trying not to clench her teeth together as she clutched her coffee cup in her hands.

Grinning playfully, Dale asked, "What crazy project has Alan got you working on now?" He knew Alan was a demanding boss, especially with Katie. But he also knew it was her own fault for taking it.

"A big case coming up," she responded shortly, with a fake smile pasted on her face.

"You should make him treat you to a nice lunch for all the extra hours you put in, and not at some cheap sandwich place. Hell, it won't cost him anything. It's a tax write off!" he laughed. It was common knowledge that instead of raises, Alan treated employees to lunches, some lunches much nicer than others depending on the job they had done for him, or just what he was hoping to get out of the lunch.

"Dale," she smiled, "I don't have time for fancy lunches with our boss, and as a matter of fact, I need to get back to work."

"Suit yourself," he said, leaning in a little closer, close enough to smell her soft scent.

Creepy, she thought as she walked out the break room. Get a grip Katie, she chided herself, the statement that seemed to be her mantra lately. *The man didn't touch you. You're just on edge lately with all the office bullshit going on.*

13

Saturday morning the black highlander was packed with Katie's favorite pillow, blanket, over-sized suitcase, toiletry bag, and a few inspirational books to read in the down time she hoped to have during the mornings and evenings of the firm's weekend retreat. Katie had been on the road for three hours. She'd gotten an early start to avoid the traffic, that and to arrive, per Alan's request, at his cabin a few hours before the rest of the team. Alan had scheduled a strategy meeting and pre-tour for Katie in preparation for the weekend. As his assistant, Katie was expected to know the flow of the weekend and serve as his right hand for all team events.

He had given her a garage door opener for the cabin and instructed her to do a walk-through of the cabin before he arrived for their meeting. A housekeeper was on staff to clean the cabin, however Alan wanted Katie to confirm his second home was in tip-top shape for the team; beds made, kitchens cleaned, living areas tidy, and weekend itineraries placed in all of the bedrooms. Add housekeeper to her growing job list, Katie thought sarcastically.

Leaning into the backrest, Katie sighed, happy for a few hours alone. She hummed softly to the soothing music that crooned from the speakers, reflecting over the events of the past week. The last week had been crazy busy preparing for the retreat, digging through a stack of client files, and a surprise drive to Illinois. One afternoon, while still at work, Katie had received a call from

Stacey, and could barely contain the tears of joy when her sister announced she would be home soon. She shared that she'd been granted an early release from the military, and was scheduled to arrive state-side in less than a month. Stacey had already shared the wonderful news with her in-laws and they had requested a visit with Emily, and since school was out for the summer it was decided now was the perfect time. Katie had packed a bag for the excited little girl, and she and Brad had driven Emily to northern Illinois to her grandparents. They had even extended their trip so they could enjoy a nice dinner and night in a hotel in Chicago, something they hadn't done in over a year.

"And now, here I am driving in the middle of nowhere," Katie said aloud. She leaned forward, squinting as she attempted to read the road sign she hoped would lead to Alan's cabin.

Fifteen minutes later, Katie slowed the car and turned onto the driveway that accessed Alan's three-story cabin. She knew it was his property because of the pictures he'd shown her, that and the over-sized black sign attached to the front of the building commemorating that he was the owner of the ridiculously large house—Weaver Cabin. It certainly didn't look like any cabin she had ever imagined, Katie reflected. Alan referred to it as his lake cabin retreat, and as she pulled up the long, narrow, twisting drive, the sparkling water of the lake caught her eye. Driving toward the back of the cabin, Katie clicked the garage door opener Alan had provided, and one of the doors to the five-car garage sprung into life. After pulling her car into the allotted space, she switched off the ignition and continued to sit for a moment, encased in the ridiculously large garage. It was quiet. Invisible fingers glanced off her spine and she shivered.

"Here we are," she said to the windshield.

Katie stared at the view in the rearview mirror, at the thick clump of trees beyond the garage. She clicked the garage door remote, closing the door, and shutting out the outside world and whatever might be lurking just beyond the cabin walls. Shivering again, she climbed out of the highlander, intent to tour the three floors of the cabin prior to Alan's arrival.

Her pillow and blanket tucked under her arm, Katie opened the door to gain access to the house, and then rolled her suitcase behind her on the slate floor. She raised her eyebrows as she walked toward a room lit by the bright sunlight of the day, windows stretched from floor to ceiling.

"My Lord!" she exclaimed as she stepped onto the buffed wooden floor and walked toward the window in the great room. She stood for a moment and looked out the window seeing thick treetops and hills—by Illinois standards, mountains—in the distance. Turning back toward the room, she looked at the giant stone fireplace in the corner of the room, and the leather furniture strategically placed nearby so those choosing to lounge against the cool fabric would have a view of a roaring fire on a cold afternoon, with a view of the wilderness beyond the walls of the cabin. She stepped onto a soft cream-colored rug, a touch no doubt, she mused, to add warmth to the room.

Her shoes echoed as she walked across the large room to explore the rest of the cabin. Katie wandered through each room of the cabin, all three floors, through nine bedrooms, two kitchens, three living areas, a game room, a formal dining room, and an area on the first floor she assumed would be used as the team meeting area. The large room was like all the other rooms. It had wooden flooring, and wood covered walls; one vantage point providing a ceiling to floor view from the windows overlooking the forest of trees, and on another side of the room, a peek of the lake. Five round wooden tables and chairs were sprinkled about the large room, giving the feel of a lodge dining area.

Each level of the cabin had decks. Two of the levels had hot tubs. There was even a theatre room with a giant movie screen that stretched the length of one wall, with eight couches for viewing. Two of the nine bedrooms contained two sets of bunk beds, two of the rooms had two double beds, two had two queen beds and the other three bedrooms each had king-sized beds. Alan had assigned Katie a bedroom with a king-sized bed on the third floor. Alan was staying in his bedroom which contained a king-sized bed on the same floor as Katie, and the only other woman attending the retreat was also issued one of the more luxurious and private rooms, on the second floor. After unpacking her suitcase in her assigned bedroom, Katie wandered to the second floor living area and made herself comfortable on the plush leather couch in front of the fireplace, and waited for Alan to arrive.

Turning to examine the expansive great room, Katie shook her head and said, "Wow . . . does anyone *really* need such a large house, cabin . . . or . . . whatever? There are people starving and homeless." With a sigh, she continued, "Surely there are better ways for Alan, or anyone for that matter, to spend his money."

Glancing at the watch strapped to her wrist, Katie sighed. What was keeping Alan, she wondered. She sprang to her feet and walked to the glass door leading to the second floor deck. The wind caught at her hair when she tugged the door open and walked toward the rail. She left the sliding glass door open so she would hear Alan when he arrived.

The deck ran the length of the cabin, and was deep enough for the white rocking chairs sprinkled about—waiting for occupants to while away an afternoon—and for people to mix and mingle. Leaning against the rail, she peered over the edge at the ground below. She closed her eyes, capturing the sound of the wind and feeling the warmth of the sun on her face. Opening her eyes, she sighed. The craziness at work is pushing me awfully close to the edge . . . to my breaking point, she thought, irritably. She looked down over the railing to the ground, hidden away beneath the green leaves on the surrounding trees, but at least, she thought, she wasn't like the hundreds of thousands of unemployed people due to the recession. She reassured herself, it will all settle down, soon. She just had to stick it out. Brad was right, it would all blow over, the issues with Dale and Erin, and Alan's odd attitude about it all, that and his recent compulsive behavior asking to hug her. Life at times became off balance; she knew that better than most, but eventually life had a way of righting itself.

"Hey!" Alan said as he walked out onto the deck, startling Katie out of her deep thoughts.

"Oh!" she exclaimed. "You startled me. I didn't hear you come in."

"I just arrived," he said with a grin. "So . . . what do you think?" He swept his arm grandly in an arc.

"I . . . I think it's beautiful," she admired. "Perhaps a little large for your small family, but then I suppose when you bring the family to your cabin they have a pick of bedrooms."

With a sheepish grin, Alan said, "I suppose it does seem a bit grandiose . . . like I'm putting on airs, doesn't it?"

"No," she stated. "The size of one's home is relative to their income, and when you think of it that way . . . this giant cabin makes perfect sense and . . . no, not so grandiose. Now for me . . . um . . . yes, a bit airish." She grinned to take the sting out of her words.

"You wanna go inside and have a drink?" he asked as he walked into the cabin without waiting for a response.

"I . . . sure," she murmured, and followed him inside.

He cocked his body toward her, grinned, and said, "My dad had this place built years ago and it just kind of became mine. It's a great place for a getaway. I've had friends and business associates down here and other times, just family weekends with the kids and Nancy. There was a time when Nancy and I would come down, just the two of us." Looking intently into Katie's eyes, Alan shared, "It's a great place for a romantic weekend . . . no one around for miles. Just trees, clean air, and the lake. I love water. Love just sitting and staring at it. Soothing. Then, during the evening, curling up in front of the fireplace . . . getting lost in one another."

"I could imagine one level of this house being nice for a weekend getaway with the one you love. Brad would love this place," she agreed.

Opening the door of the refrigerator, Alan said, "I have a housekeeper that cleans and a handyman that takes care of the place when I'm away. He stocked the bar so we have a nice variety for the weekend. I have wine already chilled and wine that's not been chilled. Red . . . white. You look like a wine kind of lady. Red or white?"

"Um—red, please. But just a little," she insisted. "It's just now after noon, a little early for alcohol, and I'm not really much of a drinker. Never have been. And the team will be here in about an hour. We still need to go over the events for the weekend before they arrive. Lots to do . . ."

"Just one drink," Alan assured her. "It was a long drive down, and I'd like to unwind just a bit before we kick off the weekend."

Glass in hand, Katie curled into one end of the couch in front of the stone fireplace while Alan sat nearby, at the center of the couch.

Placing his glass of wine on the rustic wooden table placed in front of the couch, Alan studied Katie's face, trying to judge where they stood. He wondered what was going on in her pretty head. Struggling to think of something to say, he fell back on his standard, how is your family question. He knew it was a sure way of putting Katie at ease.

"So, how's Brad doing, and did you get Emily settled in at her grandparents in Illinois. Chicago . . . did you say they live in Chicago?" Alan asked casually.

"Brad's doing great," Katie said, smiling. "He loves his job, and we had a wonderful time spending the night together in Chicago. Since Emily moved in, we haven't had a great deal of alone time. It was really nice to have a little alone time with my husband."

Katie wasn't much of a drinker; the occasional glass for her was more of an occasional sip with Brad finishing most of the glass for her. She had never acquired the art of casual drinking, maybe, she reflected, it was her need to be in control . . . completely aware of a situation. The few sips of the Pinot Noir that Alan had poured made her chattier than usual, and warmth spread through her, making her arms and legs feel heavy.

"Emily's grandparents live about ten minutes from Chicago, not *in* Chicago," Katie said, grinning. "Emily was so excited to see her grandparents." She took a sip of her wine and became teary eyed. "I'm just so happy her mommy will be home soon. It's been . . ." she placed a finger to her lips for a moment. Allowing her hand to drop to her lap, sitting up a little straighter and staring into the fireplace, Katie continued, "It's been such a difficult year with Emily's daddy passing away, and Stacey gone in Afghanistan." She sniffed, wiped an unexpected tear, and sighed. "God, I'm sorry, Alan. That was terribly depressing. It must be the wine." She leaned forward and placed her glass of wine on the coffee table. "I'm afraid I'm not much of a drinker, and with . . . just . . . the emotional roller coaster of last week . . ." Katie looked at Alan, smiled, and chuckled. "I suppose my past week and a few sips of wine just aren't a good combination."

"You know it's okay to have a human moment, Katie. You're entitled," Alan said softly as he scooted closer to her. "No one's perfect . . ."

She tucked one leg beneath her, and asked, "How's your family? How's Nancy and the kids?"

"Oh, they're fine," Alan said dismissively. He turned the conversation back to Katie. "I think it's admiral, what you did for Emily." Uncrossing his legs, Alan spread his legs apart and rested his forearms on his thighs and looked up into Katie's face. "Not everyone would do what you did—help a little girl," he said softly.

"I disagree," she said. "I believe everyone on this planet would do exactly what Brad and I did. You don't throw away children, and especially when they are family, *especially* when the mother—my sister—is fighting to protect our country."

Katie was unique, Alan considered as he looked at her, taking in the way her hair hung softly about her face, her soft lips, eyes so green, so deep he could get lost in them, but she was wrong. Not many people would take on what she had—a kid that didn't belong to them. It was tough enough being married, then add kids to the mix, and someone else's kids . . . no, she was wrong. Not many people would take on someone else's kid—he knew he wouldn't.

"How's Stacey doing?" he asked, for want of something to say.

Exhaling, Katie looked down and examined the tassels on Alan's brown leather shoes. "Okay. Stacey and I haven't talked about the shooting since that day at work."

Alan placed his hand firmly on Katie's arm, and peering up into her face asked, "What?! What shooting, Katie? You never mentioned a shooting."

Katie looked up at her boss, surprised by his reaction, and realized that she hadn't shared the phone call she'd received from Stacey, the devastating afternoon fearing for her sister's life.

"I . . . I thought I told you that one of Stacey's friends had been shot, not long ago. He had been standing next to her when it happened . . . close enough for Stacey to feel his blood, still warm, on her face." Katie stared blankly at Alan, her thoughts with her sister in another time and place . . . in her office that devastating day.

"No, Katie. You didn't tell me," Alan said with real concern cracking his voice. "My God . . ." He wanted to pull her onto his lap, feel the curves of her body tight against his, his arms pulling her close.

Shyly, Katie looked at her boss, feeling the warmth of his hand on her arm.

"I . . . I just . . . you weren't in the office. I guess that's why I didn't say anything, and besides you can't be bothered with personal issues," Katie said sleepily.

Alan rubbed his face with the palm of his hand and looked at Katie. It was not just that she was beautiful and wreaked sexy from something as simple as one leg gliding across the other as she crossed them. Or even the casual way she leaned against his desk when in his office. Or the way she turned and smiled at him as she brushed her long hair off her shoulder, and smiled at him as she walked out of his office, or now . . . as she looked shyly at the fireplace. She had such a sweet way about her.

"Hug?" he asked, with a small gentle smile.

"No, thank you," she said with a tired smile. "I'm okay . . . and Stacey and Emily are okay, now."

He cocked his head, stretched his hand toward her, and asked "You sure?"

Looking at him doubtfully, and confused, wanting to run from the room in panic, she hesitated.

"Come on," he said coaxingly.

Sighing, she stood up, tugged on her blouse, and looked down at the floor. She looked down at him, into his face, her eyes lingering on his smiling lips, peering into the depths of his eyes.

"It's not a good idea, Alan," Katie said carefully.

With a shift of his eyebrows, he dismissed their conversation. He smiled and stood up, towering above her.

"How about if we do that walk-through of the cabin together? We can talk about the weekend with the team."

With a relieved sigh, Katie smiled. "Now that, Mr. Weaver, sounds like a great idea," she said.

14

An hour later, Katie led eleven attorneys to their assigned bedrooms on the second and third floors of the cabin. Alan's team of attorneys seemed much more lively than usual, Katie noticed, which could have had something to do with the cocktails Alan had waiting for them upon their arrival and quickly consumed. Team building, she considered, so that's what he called the long weekend party. Oh well, she sighed, it's his business and his tax write off. Who am I to say how a company or law firm should be run, she grumbled.

The first evening of the team building getaway was spent settling into bedrooms, then eating a scrumptious meal served in the dining hall. Katie had begun referring to the conference area with the rustic round tables as the dining hall because that's what it looked like to her; a room that could have been found at a lodge. The team whiled away the evening roaming around the cabin, playing pool, smoking smelly cigars, and the cocktails were never ending. When Katie excused herself to go to her room at eleven o'clock that night, the team, led by Alan, was just getting warmed up, the dining hall now converted into a poker room.

Exhausted from the long day, Katie lay in the center of the king-sized bed looking up at the speck of light on the ceiling, a reflection of some light source coming from somewhere. It couldn't be from outside she considered; it was as dark as black ink outside. Quiet . . . with all the ruckus of twelve drunken people in the cabin, it was amazingly quiet in her room. The only sound was her breathing. She rolled on her side, pulling the sheet and blanket with her, and shoved her arm under the fluffy pillow. The sheets felt cool to her already cool skin, the air conditioning set a little lower than she would have liked. She stared at the light glowing from beneath the bathroom door, left on to serve as a night light in the otherwise black room, except for the lone mysterious speck of light on the ceiling.

It had been a long day, first with the drive to Alan's cabin, and then playing hostess to a team of attorneys, on cue for any errand large, small, or insignificant, for her boss. Alan's bedroom, two doors down from Katie's assigned bedroom, had been part of the tour prior to the arrival of all the attorneys, that and she had been in and out of his room during the afternoon and evening fetching folders and boxes of fun team building material, which were really prizes for the poker game. As the man in charge, Alan could not be bothered to run his own errands. As the only non-attorney, low person on the very expensive totem pole, Katie was errand girl, and she felt it in the muscles of her calves from running up and down the wooden stairs for a good part of the day.

Katie rolled onto her back and flung her arm above her head, the tiny speck of light on the ceiling catching her eye. She blinked a few times, and then her eyes remained closed as she fell into a sleep plagued by dreams of a teenaged girl, and a the memory of boys shouting.

Sunday morning, Katie, expecting a deserted kitchen on the second floor, was surprised to find Alan, his back to her, flipping pancakes on an electric griddle. The scent of coffee hung pleasantly in the air.

"Good morning," she said brightly.

"Good morning!" Alan said. He turned toward Katie and offered her a beaming grin.

"You're up awfully early," she commented as she poured coffee into a blue mug. "Have you been to bed yet?" she asked, certain his response would be no.

"Oh, sure! I had my four hours of shuteye," he commented, gleefully.

Raising her eyebrows in surprise, she commented, "Four hours . . . I need at least eight. I don't know how you can function on just four hours of sleep."

She stepped closer to Alan and peeked at the golden pancakes on the griddle. "So, you're a chef as well as an attorney. Smells good."

Flipping a pancake, he commented, "Oh, I have lots of talents, and cooking is something I enjoy doing. I cook a pretty mean steak on the grill, too."

Alan leaned toward Katie, and pressed his hip against hers. "How'd you sleep?" he asked.

Feeling the warmth of him through the fabric of her Capri pants, Katie shifted her weight away, their bodies no longer touching. "Wonderful," she said. "Like a baby nestled in her mother's arms."

Alan looked into her eyes and thought, she had the most interesting way of seeing life.

Smiling, she continued, "It's so quiet here. So peaceful. It would be a great place to get away from the city. To just be. To find one's center. You know, not during a team building exercise weekend, but a time when no one was here . . . a *quiet* weekend."

Placing the spatula on the counter, Alan draped his arm across her shoulders, tugged her toward him.

"You should come down to the cabin some weekend," he insisted.

Laughing uncomfortably, Katie said, "Well, it would be pretty lonely here rambling around in this huge place alone. It would be a great couples get away though. Brad would love it . . . hiking during the day, and sitting by the fire in the evenings."

"We should plan a weekend—have Nancy and Brad for the weekend . . . a little hiking and wine tasting in front of a roaring fire," Alan suggested.

"Morning!" a voice boomed behind them. "You got the coffee brewing, Alan?"

Katie jumped, and Alan's arm fell away from her shoulders.

"About time you're dragging your ass out of bed, Scott!" Alan said. "Grab yourself a cup of coffee. You're gonna need it after the night you had!" Alan laughed.

"I think I'll take my coffee, and mosey on out to the deck," Katie said. "I'll let you *gentlemen* discuss business." Katie walked away from the obscenity language-filled kitchen. She left behind the scent of strong brewed coffee, pancakes and hangovers.

It was going to be another busy day, Katie contemplated as she took a sip of her steaming hot coffee. If Alan intended to stick to his agenda, it would mean a team hike at eleven, too early, in Katie's opinion, for many of the hung-over attorneys. As far as Katie was concerned, the hike was going to be the high point of the long weekend. Most of the other team activities would be in the cabin, she reflected, with a group of people—attorneys— she had little in common. The attorneys would spend most of the weekend smoking cigars and drinking, which she knew was a typical weekend for many of them. As a nobody, a lowly paralegal, she would pretend she wasn't offended by the discussions of tits, asses and, who they'd like to screw, just as she had pretended not to be offended last night. It had been as if they had forgotten she was in the room, that or as if she'd morphed into one of their good old boys, she thought with a roll of her eyes.

A cool breeze caught at Katie's hair, blowing it across her face. Deep in thought, she set her mug of coffee onto the wooden table next to the rocking chair where she was relaxing, and crossed her arms.

"Hey . . ." Alan said softly, as he sat down next to her on the companion rocking chair. "You okay?"

Tucking the rouge strand of hair behind her ear, Katie responded, "Of course. I was just enjoying the peace and serenity before beginning my day."

"Nice, isn't it?" Alan remarked. "I love sitting out here on the deck enjoying a cigar and scotch, with a view of the lake on one side of the deck and the mountains on the other."

Katie glanced at the lake, where it had been kissed by the sun, sparkling so brightly in places it appeared as if diamonds had been sprinkled along its smooth surface.

"You okay if we go over a few things for today? I hate to intrude on your serenity," he teased.

Katie laughed, and said, "It's your weekend, boss. I'm at your disposal."

"Alan, will do. No need to be formal. We're all on equal footing on these trips. I'm just plain old Alan for the next few days," he chided.

Katie smiled skeptically as she leaned back against the wooden rocking chair.

"After breakfast," Alan said, "I thought we'd get everyone alerted and ready for the hike. A few hours of hiking should satisfy the exercise nuts in the group, although I saw Stan take off in his running shorts an hour ago. Then a late lunch in the dining hall, as you call it." He grinned, and leaned toward her. "Since it's a work event, I should get a little work in, so I'll give a presentation as we're wrapping up our meal about where we're headed this next year, our new clients and the cases we wrapped up last year. And I'd like for you to give an update about the staff at the firm—share details about new employees, potential issues, concerns . . . end your talk on a positive note. You know . . . share how the employees are motivated for a new year at the firm, and fired up to support the attorneys on staff in any way they can."

Erin's face swam before Katie's eyes as she glanced over at Alan. End her talk on a positive note, she thought. Well, she considered, there was one employee at the firm that was *not* happy.

"Sure," Katie said. "I'll take a little time to throw something together after I finish my coffee."

Standing, Alan glanced down at his wrist, and said, sheepishly, "Oh, hey, when you finish up, would you mind . . . I left my watch in my room. I can't function without knowing what time it is. Would you mind going to my room and grabbing it for me. It's on my nightstand." He oozed as much charm and sincerity at Katie as he could muster.

"I . . . of course," she stammered. "I need to run upstairs anyway."

"You're the best, Katie," he beamed as he squeezed her shoulder. He walked into the cabin filled with noisy attorneys milling around the great room with cups of coffee cradled in their hands.

And so begins my day of fetching, Katie thought irritably.

Moments later, Katie sidled up to Alan, touched his arm, and offered him his watch.

Squeezing her shoulder and smiling down at her, Alan said, "Thanks, Katie." Leaning toward her, he said softly, "It's nice to have you here . . . to have someone I can depend on to make sure everything runs smoothly."

"No problem," she whispered back.

"Katie!" Steve, one of the senior attorneys, boomed. "Would you be a dear and get me a refill? I'm resting up for the hike." He grinned at her from his comfortable position on one of the oversized leather chairs.

"Steve, there is *nothing* I would rather do right now than fetch another cup of coffee for you," she said sarcastically. "And don't forget to tip your waitress."

The room erupted in laughter as Katie walked toward the kitchen with his large white coffee mug in her hand.

Jesus, she thought irritably, I *cannot* wait until this weekend is over!

15

The fire crackled in the fire pit and smoke hung lazily in the air as the team of attorneys and Katie sat cozily outside the cabin enjoying a cooler than usual summer evening. The team was worn out from the late night before, that and the early start to the day and team hike. After the long morning hike and morning meeting, the attorneys had spent time in the hot tubs on the decks at the cabin, and then gorged themselves on a heavy dinner. And throughout the day a river of cocktails had flowed.

Katie sipped her way through a glass of wine after dinner and now the lids of her eyes were surprisingly heavy. At nine o'clock in the evening, she was more than ready to call it a day and crawl into her king-sized bed.

"Katie," Steve said. His voice sounded farther away to Katie, than the few inches his lawn chair was positioned next to hers.

"Hmm?" she murmured, noticing the bottle of wine he was holding in his hand.

"More wine?" he asked.

Sure," she mumbled softly. "But just a smidge, please." She watched the older man fill her plastic cup full of red wine.

Smiling, she thanked him, and sank back into her chair, one leg tucked beneath her. It had been an okay day, she considered as she looked at the team of men and one woman sitting around the fire.

Alan, she thought, had been a great host so far for the event. He'd shown surprising stamina during the three-hour long hike. For such a portly, older man, he hadn't broken a sweat on the hike, that, after downing a few beers, and with only four hours of sleep. Glancing at him sitting next to her, she wondered how he managed to keep going, while most of the team were beginning to wilt. If anything, she observed, he seemed to be catching a second wind from somewhere.

Well, she thought with a yawn, if I had a second wind, it blew away after Alan's speech in the dining hall.

"How you doin', kiddo?" Alan slurred.

Amused, Katie considered, Alan might just have to call it an early night himself, that or pass out drunk around the fire pit.

"Tired. I'm sorry, but I think I'm going to have to call it a night. Do you mind? Is there anything you need me to do first?" she asked, hoping his response would be, no.

Wrinkling his nose, he said, "No. You go on ahead inside. Just relax, you deserve it."

Shifting closer to her, his mouth close to her ear, close enough for Katie to smell the alcohol on his breath, he said, softly, "You were a great help today. I really appreciate all your hard work."

Smiling sleepily, she responded quietly, "You are quite welcome. And if there is nothing else, then I'm going to turn in for the night." Unsteadily, Katie rose to her feet.

Steve grabbed her wrist to steady her.

"Careful there, girl," Steve said playfully. "Don't want you falling into the fire . . . might have a lawsuit on our hands!"

Laughter exploded in Katie's ears as she walked toward the cabin.

"Katie!" she heard from behind her. She turned back toward the fire pit and the Weaver team.

"Katie," Alan called after her. "Would you mind bringing my box of cigars down to the lower deck? I'll meet you there to get them so you don't have to come all the way back out here."

"Sure. The ones in your room?" she asked irritably.

"Yeah. On my dresser," Alan said.

Yawning as she walked slowly up the steps to the third floor, Katie considered . . . perhaps I could just throw the box of cigars off one of the decks, and hit you in the head. She chuckled as she envisioned the wooden box chunking off the side of her boss's head. She opened the door to Alan's bedroom, and spying the wooden box she knew was filled with expensive cigars, Katie walked across the room to retrieve them, her last task for the evening.

"Oh!" she exclaimed when she felt an arm wrap around her waist, and felt hot breath on her neck. "God, Alan! I didn't hear you. I thought you were outside." She was surprised to find that she wasn't alone, and alarmed to be in the arms of her obviously drunk boss.

"Alan," she said as she tried to wiggle from his embrace.

"Come on," he slurred into her ear. "You know you want it. You've been practically begging for it since this morning, coming on to me with those big doe eyes of yours."

As Alan pulled her with him to the bed, she noticed that he had shut the door behind him. She was alone in the monster-sized cabin with her boss, in his bedroom, and even if she hadn't been, no one would come to her aide if she cried out for help. The sleazy attorneys would assume she was crying out in fun, that or they wouldn't care in their drunken states, and she doubted they would care to help her even if they were sober.

Katie toppled backward onto the bed, on top of Alan, feeling his hard-on pressed against her back. His hands were everywhere, rubbing and tugging at her body. He shoved his hands beneath her blouse, slipped a hand beneath her bra, for a moment cupped a breast. Roughly, he flung her off him, then rolled on top of her, the weight of his body pressing her into the bed, taking her breath away.

"Alan . . . *Alan*," she said breathlessly. "Stop. *Please*."

He nipped her throat with his teeth, and then his lips were on hers—soft and wet—then pressing hard against hers with urgency. One large hand tangled in her hair, pulling painfully, while his other hand grasped her hip. He thrust his legs between hers.

"Be patient . . ." he groaned.

"No," she sighed, barely able to breathe under his weight. "No . . . you have to stop. Please. STOP!" With tears burning her eyes, beginning to panic, she struggled to dislodge him. "I can't breathe," she sputtered. "Get *off* me . . ."

He slid his hand between their bodies, between her thighs, then slid up toward the button on her pants.

She thrashed about, trying to buck him off her, but the sheer massive size of him was unmovable. Exhausted, she tried to reach him, "Alan, what about Nancy, and Brad? This *cannot* happen . . . at all . . . and . . . and please, *Alan.*"

She felt his body go limp, his body a boulder of a dead weight, and panting with the struggle, she was able to wiggle out from beneath him.

Pulling her blouse together she scrambled to her feet. Trembling from the shock of what had just happened, she looked down at Alan, still lying on his back, the front of his dress pants spotted with the evidence of the last few moments.

He stared up at her.

She rushed toward the door and yanked it open.

As she stormed down the hall toward her bedroom, she heard Alan's voice shout to her, "Come back, Katie. Don't leave me."

Slamming her bedroom door behind her, Katie turned the lock, locking Alan out. Her hands shaking, she grabbed her suitcase out of the closet; no longer tired, and finding her third wind, she began cramming her clothes inside of it. Within five frantic minutes she had everything she had brought with her on the trip, packed and zipped into her suitcase.

She feared at any moment Alan would knock on her door. With one hand clenching the handle of her suitcase, she paused at the door of her bedroom, holding her breath. As quietly as she could, she opened the door and peered down the hall. It was empty. Alan's door was closed. Katie rushed as quickly and quietly as she could down the stairs, and out to the garage to her car. Katie threw her suitcase on the backseat, quietly closing the door, then climbed onto the driver's seat, easing the door closed behind her. Then, holding her breath, using the garage door opener, she opened the door, and hoping no one noticed, she drove down the long winding drive toward the road, closing the garage door as she drove away.

16

Numb from shock, Katie began the three-hour drive home. Her knuckles were white and her fingers stiff from clutching the steering wheel as her emotions ran the gamut. What happened, Katie wondered. Was Alan right, had she come on to him? No, she thought, hysterically. What the hell was wrong with her for even considering such a thing? He was flipping drunk, she realized, but . . . but had Alan assaulted her because he was drunk, or in retrospect, had he been leading up to his actions at the cabin. Had he been planning some sex-fest with her all along, with his requests for hugs, brushing up against her, and . . . and touching her, she thought bitterly.

"My boss . . . a nice man . . . he was supposed to be a nice man," Katie wailed to the windshield. "This wasn't supposed to happen to me. Not to me. I didn't do anything to deserve . . . any . . . of that." Her voice trailed away. "What he did to me. I . . . I'm nice," she reasoned. "I'm not some whore. How could he do that to me? He treated me like . . ." she cried, tears of disgust burning a path down her cheeks.

She sobbed on the long drive home, but by the time she pulled the highlander onto the driveway at the home she shared with Brad, her tears had dried up, and an eerie sense of calm had settle over her. The physical battle with Alan, and the emotional war that had waged within her on the long drive home, had exhausted her.

Not wanting to wake Brad, Katie didn't bother to pull her car into the garage. As quiet as possible, she unlocked the front door, and then hiked her suitcase into the entryway of the house. Guided by the nightlight plugged into the outlet in the hall, Katie slipped off her shoes, then walked across the plush carpet to the living room—a room rarely used except by her as a reading room—and flipped on the small reading lamp. She walked back to the entryway, grabbed her suitcase, carried it to the small reading room, and placed it against a wall. She glanced down at her wrist watch and read, 2:05 a.m. She was too tired to unpack. It could wait till morning, she considered as she yawned an ear popping yawn.

She flopped onto one of the chairs in the small room, rubbed her face with the balls of her hands, and sighed softly. Looking up and across the room, she stared blindly at the small table that held a collection of portraits of those most dear to her. She sighed again, dreading the explanation she would have to give Brad in the morning for her early and unexpected return home from her trip. He had no idea she'd be arriving home, had arrived home, early because she hadn't called or texted him. The few hours of solitude on the drive home had been needed to calm her frazzled nerves and had given her time to decide what to tell him—why she was planning to quit her job.

Mid-way home, Katie had come to the conclusion that nothing could make her go back to the firm. Nothing could force her to face one more day of Alan's bullshit. One quick trip to pack up her office was all she'd be able to stomach, and that was going to be tough. The timing was right, Katie reasoned. Stacey would be home for good in a few weeks. Friends had helped her sister find a realtor, and offered to let Emily and Stacey bunk with them until she found her own permanent place. In a few short weeks, Brad and Katie's lives would be back to normal, well, Katie speculated, minus her well-paying job. Brad would understand, Katie reassured herself, but . . . just what he would understand she wasn't sure, because she didn't understand what had happened, or why it happened. Why had Alan hurt her like he did?

She walked over to her suitcase and then drug it toward the center of the room, unzipped it, and rummaged through the contents until she found a tank top and boxer shorts, then she dug for her toiletry bag. After brushing her teeth, washing her face, and changing into her night clothes, Katie folded the pair of black pants—dress pants she intended to throw away to try to rid herself of tonight's memory—and white short-sleeved blouse she'd been wearing that evening and placed them on top of the now zipped suitcase.

After flipping the lamp off, bathing the room in darkness, Katie tiptoed up the steps toward her bedroom on the second floor, wondering just what reason she would offer Brad for quitting her job. That was her most pressing problem right now. As a millionaire, what would Alan do if she told anyone, including Brad, what he had done to her? A reminder from her past burned in her gut, and she knew that if she told, Alan would hurt her, and not just shout profanity at her like he did his legal team, but hurt her physically, or worse. He'd hurt Stacey, Emily or Brad. She *couldn't* tell . . .

As quietly as she could, cloaked by the cover of night, Katie walked across the master bedroom toward the master bathroom. Softly, trying not to make a clicking sound with the light switch, Katie, using the dimmer switch, cast the room in a muted glow. It would be just enough light for Katie to see when she walked into the bedroom to pull down the covers on her side of the bed and fluff her pillow.

The hand towel by her sink caught her eye. Absently she walked over and removed the half-folded towel, noticing it was damp, then replaced it, now folded in half on the rack. Strange, she thought, that Brad would use my sink and my towel.

Wearily, Katie allowed the dim glow from the bathroom to light her way as she stepped into her bedroom. She paused. She wrinkled her forehead. She held her breath for a moment, and then continued toward the bed. Feeling as if fingers had brushed her spine, she shivered. She sniffed. Something wasn't right—a smell, sound—something. A moan came from the bed. She glanced toward Brad's side of the bed hoping she'd not woken him. In the soft light, she made out his form lying on his side. Katie sucked in her breath when she saw a bare arm fling across his waist and heard a feminine moan. She froze. Held her breath. Then, in a daze, as quietly as she could, she shuffled back to the bathroom and carefully, quietly, turned off the light, both rooms in darkness once again.

Her mind was a dark, blank, nothingness as she stood with her fingers lingering on the light switch. Finally her mind began to process what she had seen, didn't want to believe what she'd seen. Katie wanted to laugh hysterically at her over-active imagination. Girl, she thought, you are losing it. *All the Alan bullshit has you seeing things.* Then she heard the moan again. She began to perspire, and hot tears sprang to her eyes. It couldn't be . . . it couldn't be, her mind protested.

Pulling her hand away from the light switch, Katie slipped from the bathroom and tiptoed back down stairs. Not bothering to turn on the reading lamp, she slumped onto the chair she'd vacated not fifteen minutes ago. Tears burned her cheeks as she ran her hands through her tangled hair.

What to do, she wondered, frantically . . . what was she supposed to do?! After changing back into the now wrinkled clothes she had arrived home in, Katie zipped her nightclothes back into her suitcase. Her eyes fell on her purse, and she darted toward it. Grabbing her cell phone, she clasped it tightly in her hand as she made her way back up the stairs toward her bedroom. She just had to see, just be sure that what she thought she had seen was real.

Katie flipped the dimmer switch on in the bathroom once again, but this time she turned the switch up, bathing the bathroom in bright light. The light cast a glow mid-way into the bedroom. She crossed the room swiftly, and holding the phone in front of her she pressed the camera function button, and then clicked. The room exploded in bright light from the flash of her phone.

As if at a play, Katie watched the flurry of action unfold on the bed before her. Brad, startled, jerked toward the source of the flash. He shielded his eyes from the next series of flashes from Katie's cell phone.

Katie heard a familiar woman's voice shriek, "My, God!"

"Stop!" Brad boomed, as he tried to shield the woman huddled next to him from the camera and the light.

"For the love of all things holy, Katie! Stop!" Brad shouted.

Tears of anger blurred Katie's vision, as she shouted, "Get out of my bed you whore! Get out of my house! Show your fucking face," she insisted, as she ripped the sheet from the woman's grasp. She wanted to see her face, to see what woman had the nerve to warm her bed while she was away on her disgusting, nightmare trip with her son of a bitch boss!

The light caught the woman's profile. Katie knew her. It was a woman who worked in the same office as Brad. She released the sheet, as the woman snuggled against her husband.

"How long . . . ?" Katie asked.

"Jesus, Katie! What did you expect? You're never here, and when you are here, your head's not here. It's as if your mind is off somewhere else. And when you do seem to focus, it's just on Emily. You don't have time for me . . . you haven't since she moved in."

She couldn't believe what she was hearing. Her fault. Brad was telling her it was her fault there was a woman in her bed—that he was *sleeping* with some other woman in *her* bed! Trying to shake away the day, Katie shook her head. She had to get out of here . . . get away, get away from everything, everyone.

It sounded as if a swarm of bees were buzzing inside Katie's ears as she ran back down the stairs. Grabbing her suitcase and her purse, she rushed to the door, to her car, and not knowing where she was going, sped back down the road.

Stomping her foot on the brake, Katie came to an abrupt halt. She screamed, and pound her fists on the steering wheel until her hands felt bruised. Her throat raw from tears and shouting, and her body limp, Katie slumped back against the seat. All the energy from her very screwed up day was gone. Wiping snot on her arm, and brushing her tears away on the palm of her hand, Katie turned the steering wheel, accelerated and headed toward the highway. Exhausted, she needed to find a hotel to hole up in, to just curl up in a ball, and tuck away from the world.

Tucked under the white sheet on the king-sized bed in her rented room at the Hilton Hotel, in Florence, Kentucky, Katie stared at the clock on the bedside table, watching as one minute absorbed into the next. At five a.m., unable to sleep, she slid out of bed, grabbed her clothes from her luggage, got dressed and headed for the office. It was her hope and expectation that on a Monday morning, by the time she arrived at five-thirty, the law office would still be deserted. Most of the attorneys and paralegals were probably still asleep at the cabin, she suspected. Any of the office personnel—clerical, accounting or the receptionist—would not arrive for a few more hours. Plenty enough time to box up the personal belongings in her office and make her exit, unseen.

Promptly, at five thirty, the air muggy and yet cool to her skin, Katie walked across the parking lot toward the office building that housed Alan's law firm. The passcode to the security system allowed her purchase, as it had for the past ten years, to the section of the building that led to the Weaver law offices. Knowing time was of the essence, Katie rummaged through one of the break rooms, and then a closet for a discarded box and garbage bag to pack up the various items she had accumulated during her time at the firm.

She was in a hurried frenzy, intent on packing her belongings and then locking her office door—planning to leave her office door key and the garage door opener for the cabin on Alan's desk before the first employee arrived. Unconcerned about breaking knick-knacks, or photo frames, Katie tossed odds and ends into the box. She scanned the room, all evidence of the prior occupant, now packed away.

God, what was she doing, she wondered as she turned and looked around at the bare walls. Was she doing the right thing, running away . . . again?

Shaking her head, Katie heaved the box under her arm. She placed the box on the floor in the hall so she could lock her office door, then she sought out Alan's office, cautiously—as if he might at any moment, jump out at her—opened the door. The room was dark, as she knew it would be, as she walked across the room. She paused in front of his desk, stared down at its bare polished surface, then looked across the room at the cabinets along the wall, at the various trinkets he had acquired over the years. With a sigh, placed the key on top of a yellow post it note on which she had written in a black permanent marker, "I Quit!"

"Well," Katie said to Alan's chair. "That's it. Ten wasted years of my professional life." With shoulders slumped, Katie walked back across the room and quietly closed the door to her professional past, and the nightmare of the last few months behind her.

Six-fifteen, Katie registered as she glanced at the watch on her wrist, then grabbed the box from off the floor, and walked briskly toward the exit. As she slid the box on the back seat of her vehicle, Katie sighed with relief. Coffee, she thought groggily. She needed to find several very large cups of coffee. Caffeine and a plan was what she needed.

A half hour later, hunched over a cup of coffee at Starbucks in Crestview Hills, Katie tried to sort out the last twenty-four hours of her life, but it was too much to sift through. Resting her chin on the palm of her hand, she knew what she needed to do, desperately . . . *run*. Thank you Jesus, that Emily was no longer a concern . . . that Stacey would soon be home.

Pulling her cell phone out of her purse, Katie noticed that she had eight text messages and three calls from Brad. They could wait, she thought angrily. Leaning back against the wooden backrest of her chair, Katie looked out of the window and watched the employed people scurrying like mice towards the shop for their caffeine fill-up of the day. Brad would be joining the work throng in an hour, she considered.

For the next hour, Katie barely registered the small groups of people, sometimes alone, sometimes in groups of five and six, mill about the cash register as they ordered coffees, most often to go. When she knew Brad had left for the office, she ordered a refill of coffee, and headed for their home.

With a click of the garage door opener, the heavy door yawned open. After pulling her car into the two-car garage, Katie turned off the ignition, and then clicked the little box again, this time shutting the heavy garage door. For a moment longer, she remained leaning against her seat, taking in the silence.

Katie entered the home she shared with Brad. The air inside the house felt different, now that she knew her marriage was a lie, had been for . . . she had no idea how long Brad had been living a lie. Standing in the entryway, she saw walls that merely housed a few of her personal belongings, nothing more, no longer her home. She wandered aimlessly through the rooms on the first floor of the house. Then, exhausted, more from her knotted emotions than from lack of sleep, Katie collapsed onto her favorite chair in the reading room. Placing her chin on the palm of her hand, Katie gazed around the room. She sighed heavily and leaned against the back of the chair, her head resting against its high back. A collection of photographs resting on a small table caught her eye, one in particular. For a few moments, Katie continued to stare at the photograph of an older woman—dressed in summer casual shorts—her arm draped around a woman of similar age; frothy waves crashing in the background.

Katie rose from her chair, walked over to the small table, and picked up the photograph held securely in an ornate metal frame. Caressing the image of the woman, Katie walked back to her chair. The image brought back memories of long ago, when she was a teenager, some memories good, and many the stuff of nightmares; memories she'd locked away long ago.

Nan was the woman in the photo, her mother's younger and only sister. For a year, Nan had been a fill-in mother for Katie, providing a haven, a place to get away from a nightmare no young girl should ever experience. Katie's spirit had been shattered the summer before her senior year of high school, and Nan had lovingly and gently helped Katie collect her many shards and helped her to fit the pieces of herself back together.

Katie's memories took her to a time far removed from the house she shared with Brad, to a driveway attached to a small house—the house Aunt Nan owned, years ago, in central Kentucky. As teens, Stacey and Katie had clung to one another in the driveway of their aunt's home the weekend her family had driven her from their home in northern Illinois to the central part of Kentucky. Katie had remained with Nan at her home in Kentucky, healing, as much as young girl could from the events that had transpired, returning to Illinois only when necessary. During her senior year, long hours had been spent on the phone with her sister and parents, and then once a week they would make the drive to Kentucky to visit her. It had been a seemingly endless year, but somehow Katie managed to focus just enough to complete her last year of high school.

A broken heart took Stacey and Katie's father the summer after Katie graduated from high school. He'd always been her strong protector, but he'd been helpless against the dangers that lurk for little girls and women. He'd felt helpless after that summer, and never lost the feeling he'd failed her by not being able to protect her.

After their mother's accident three years later, Stacey remained in Illinois to attend college, but spent most of her summers at Nan's house, with Katie, in Kentucky. Nan had been the loving arms that had caught her nieces when the weight of the world had pressed down on them.

Katie never returned to Illinois but instead attended college in Kentucky. The memories of what had happened in Illinois when she was in high school, were still too raw. The only time she returned to Illinois, was for her father and then her mother's funeral, and then last year, to help with funeral arrangements for Stacey's husband, and most recently to take Emily to her grandparents.

Nan had been a widow as long as Katie could remember. Vaguely she remembered her uncle, a tall man with a kind smile. With no ties holding her down, after Katie married Brad, Nan moved to North Carolina to be near a high school girl friend where they opened a quaint shop together. They served the best coffee and pastries within a one hundred mile radius, and also offered a small lunch menu catering to the locals and tourists.

The walls of their shop were strewn with local artist's work—artists within a few hundred miles—and occasionally on weekends they opened shop for gallery night for artists to share their works. Katie's favorite feature of the shop was the back room. It was a mysterious, cozy room that served as a library and book store, where plush leather couches and chairs were placed in front of a fireplace. It was the area used when writers visited the shop for an occasional book signing and reading. Many notable authors had graced the room for over eight years.

"Oh, Nan," Katie said to the photograph. "What should I do? Where should I go? Where *can* I go?" She hugged the picture frame to her chest.

For the next few hours, Katie worked quickly, sorting through her closet and Emily's, both bedrooms, and the basement, packing away their treasures in plastic tubs. She'd decided since Stacey would be home in a few weeks and school would not be in session for at least another month, it would be best for Emily to remain with her grandparents in northern Illinois, however, Katie wondered, where would *she* go?

"The last room," Katie said to herself as she stood in the reading room. She placed the framed photographs in her last remaining box. Pausing, she stared down at the photograph of Nan. She sighed heavily. "Where am I going, Nan?" she asked, as if the woman with kind eyes in the photograph could convey what she should do with her life.

After she'd drug all the boxes into the reading room, Katie collapsed onto her favorite chair and slid the bar on her cell phone. "Quite the collection of text messages and calls from Brad old boy," she said sarcastically. "Asshole."

She knew she was going to have to speak to him eventually. "But not just yet," she said to the room as she dialed a different number.

On the third ring, Katie heard a familiar woman's voice, and responded, "Nan."

"Katie," Nan said in her soft voice. "Honey, I've been thinking a lot about you lately. I even had the *strangest* dream about you last night. Remember the morning glory flowers we had at the house in Kentucky, years ago. We'd sit in the garden for hours and while away an afternoon talking and sipping glasses of ice-cold lemonade. Remember, sweets?"

Smiling, with tears in her eyes at the memory, and sudden rush of emotion she felt, Katie whispered. "I sure do."

Katie loved the special name Nan had given her, sweets, what she had called her since she was a little girl—all because she'd loved the home made sweets her aunt baked.

"In my dream last night, you and I were sitting in the garden, but this time you were all grown up, and instead of glasses of lemonade, we were sipping glasses of wine. I could hear the robins calling each other in the background. But, sweets, you were cryin' in my dream. Somethin's wrong. I can feel it. What's happened?" Nan, asked, worry making her high pitched voice deeper.

"Oh, Nan," Katie cried. She broke into tears. Sobbing, she shared with her aunt what had happened at the cabin with Alan, and then walking in on Brad and *that* woman, finding them sleeping in her bed.

"Okay, *now* I'm ready to call you," Katie said angrily as she placed her cell phone to her ear and waited for Brad to answer his cell phone. She'd had a long talk with Nan two hours ago, and since then she'd done a lot of thinking about the past, and her future.

His voice exploded in her ear, "Why the hell didn't you call me back?"

Pulling the phone back, she smiled knowing she'd pissed him off. Good, she thought angrily.

"Why didn't I call you back?" she asked indignantly. "You're lucky I'm calling you at all, you maggot!"

Part 2

17

~

On the road for over an hour, Katie glanced out of the window at what seemed to be an endless white fence for one of Kentucky's horse farms. Beautiful, she mused as she turned her attention back to highway 75, the road leading her away from life with her soon to be ex-husband and the law firm.

The evening after Katie caught Brad in bed with one of his co-workers, they'd met at their house and had a heated discussion about his needs, which no longer included her. Brad felt life had grown stale with Katie. He needed more in all areas of life, much more than she could give him. He wanted to live—he'd said—to recapture the feeling he'd had years ago when he'd entered college—vitality and freedom. He wasn't getting any younger, he'd told her, and needed to grab life by, in his case, the tits apparently, she thought, sourly.

What did *she* want she wondered, as she passed an SUV, noticing a man and woman sitting in the front, and two young children sitting in the back. A family, perhaps driving together to some summer vacation getaway, she mused with a sigh.

It had been too much, the months at the law firm dealing with Dale, Alan's indifference to Erin's feelings, the attack she'd endured at the cabin, and then seeing Brad in bed with another woman. After Katie caught Brad in bed with his co-worker, she'd driven away from the house they'd shared, in shock, the day's events slowly sinking in. At the hotel, Katie had begun to absorb the wave after wave of past few months, and before she talked to Brad later that night—hearing his empty words—she'd known it was over, felt an overwhelming need to put as much distance, emotionally and physically, between her current life and her as possible.

It hadn't been a long discussion, if you could call their shouting match a discussion. Brad and Katie had stood in the reading room at their home, he shouting at her that he needed to grab life before it was too late, that she was a good woman, just not right for him at that time in his life. She'd wanted to shut it all out, his voice, and the pain from the past year—pain from men for far too long. She'd seen through her husband's tired and worn veil of deceit and *assholeness,* and wondered how she'd never seen it before, that he was a self-serving, needy little boy. A man—he was not. She realized at this late stage of his life he would never be a man, at least not a man that could live life on a deeper level—living and loving, or even know what that meant.

In moments, the world had come crashing down, at least for Katie, for Brad it crashed when Emily moved in. After their talk, Brad had packed a few of his things, left their home and gone to stay with the woman that would begin his journey of grabbing life. And for two weeks, Katie had sorted through her life—the life she'd shared with Brad. She'd made an appointment with an attorney and had gotten the ball rolling for a divorce, both of them wanting to move on with their lives as soon as possible. It was so easy really, she considered, that a life she'd taken so long to build was severed so easily, within just a matter of weeks.

It was amazing, Katie thought, how little she'd accumulated over ten years of marriage—clothes, jewelry, photos, and books. There were few items in the house that she cared to take with her, the memories associated with any furniture or dish an unpleasant one. She'd kept a few of her father and mother's things tucked away over the years, her mother's favorite throw blanket that she snuggled with when watching TV, and a wooden box that her father had kept odds and ends in. She also had a favorite pillow, blanket, and a small box of crafts that her niece had made for her over the years.

Not a lot to show for her life, she reflected. Now, her highlander was packed with everything she cared to take with her into her future. Nan had asked her to come stay with her while she figured out what she wanted to do with her life—take a time out to just be. To just be, Katie contemplated . . . *just be.* Glancing at the clock on the console, Katie approximated she would arrive at Nan's house by two that afternoon. It was a six and a half hour drive and she was in no hurry, having no plan once she arrived. If she felt like stopping along the way—for coffee and to stretch her legs—there was no one to cater to any longer. There was no one and nowhere, she reflected, that required her time, or her, really.

Several hours later, Katie stopped for gas, and then decided to take a half hour to browse through a few of the town's shops. She bored quickly with the antique shops—more junk than antiques. Standing on the sidewalk in the hot summer sun, she squinted down the deserted street wondering where the town kept its coffee shop hidden. Every town had a coffee shop, didn't they, she wondered hopefully.

Katie stood with other sightseers at an overlook in Tennessee. She was the only single in a crowd of families and couples she noticed, feeling alone, and rather like an alien amongst the happy faces of strangers who seemed to have everything they could possibly need in life. Trying to ignore the giggles of children and the parents that looked at them adoringly, Katie sipped on over-priced, bitter coffee.

When she'd stopped for gas, she'd ventured around the small town, and found that the town hid its coffee shop on the edge of town near a K-Mart and a bank. All your shopping needs, Katie thought with a roll of her eyes. The coffee shop had been an experience—and thus far the highlight of her drive—where the colorful locals hung out, all two of them. Two mangy old men were fixtures, it appeared, who propped up the restaurants old counter, chewing away on pie and tobacco, spitting in their empty coffee cups, empty but for their brown spit. The coffee shop had seen better days and so had the woman working behind the counter. Katie had begun walking toward the grease smudged door the second her fingers touched her to-go coffee cup.

She snapped a few shots of the picturesque valley below, with small towns so small from her vantage point, they looked like toy towns her niece would have loved playing with. It was a stop she'd made several times before—always stopping at the same overlook—when she'd driven to visit her aunt. Then, it had been happier times. Emily and Stacey's world had been intact, and Brad had been hers . . . and the firm. Katie sighed, and with tears of bitterness burning her eyes, walked back to her vehicle, giggles taunting and ringing in her ears.

18

Late afternoon, as the brilliant sun prepared for evening, Katie pulled into the town of Marion, North Carolina, where her aunt Nan lived. It was an old town, established in 1844—historic and quaint, nestled against the Blue Ridge Mountains. The town was large enough to sustain itself economically. A large part of the commerce driven by tourists. While husbands golfed at one of the lavish country club golf courses, or the more laid back courses the locals preferred, wives spent their money at the unique shops in town, and spas at the country clubs.

The locals broke tourists into two categories—country clubbers, and the bed and breakfast crowd. Country clubbers drove polished black Mercedes and Porsches, and stayed at hotels in one of the nearby cities like Asheville, while the bed and breakfast crowd drove SUV's and trucks, and were content to stay at one of the many bed and breakfasts in town, spending their time taking in local nature, hiking, or hitting a few rounds of golf at one of the less pricey golf courses outside of town. The mild climate, beauty of the mountains, and varying degrees of complexity, terrain, and price of the golf courses, drew tourists to the town during most of the year, all but a few months during winter. The result of which was the quaint town of Marion was filled with boutiques, coffee shops, art galleries, and restaurants always hopping with business. Marion had most of what the towns people needed, but if the locals felt a need for the lights of the city, they needed only drive forty minutes and they'd be in Asheville, North Carolina, where shopping, festivals, and wine tasting awaited them.

It looks the same, Katie reflected with a small smile as she drove past the town square. There were black wrought iron tables placed outside of restaurants on concrete patios or sidewalks, where customers could enjoy a lazy late afternoon glass of wine, iced tea, or coffee. Women and young girls— dressed in pastel sundresses—strolled down wide sidewalks, shopping bags clutched in their hands or flung casually over their arms, as Katie continued toward Nan's house—away from the hustle and bustle—at the outskirts of town. Nan's house was nestled into the countryside, a view of the mountains from the back of the house, and a view of a white steepled church perched high atop a hill, from the driveway. At one time, Nan's two-story farmhouse sat alone outside of town, but that had been eighty years ago, when the house had been built. Now, she owned the cozy farmhouse. The old house had a wraparound porch, wide enough for several wicker tables, straight-backed chairs, and rocking chairs. The front porch had a bed and breakfast feel to it . . . welcoming. The inside of the house was as welcoming as the outside, with a living room, den, kitchen, and half bath on the first floor, and three bedrooms and two bathrooms on the second level.

Katie parked her highlander in the driveway, leaving room for Nan to access the two-car garage when she returned home later that evening from the coffee shop. She climbed the porch stairs, and unlocked the front door with the key found, not so creatively hidden, under the doormat that said *Welcome*. A large spacious entryway met Katie when she walked across the threshold into the house, and Hunter, Nan's seven-year-old yellow lab. Hunter barked, but the wag of his tail let Katie know that he remembered her, as she leaned over and patted his back.

Straightening, Katie stood for a moment, allowing the front door to hang open as she admired the stained glass window at the top of the landing that led to the second floor. She walked toward the room on the left side of the entryway, her favorite room, the den. A large window overlooked the front porch, and beyond, to the deserted road and further to a field of tall grass and wild flowers. The den had a large old cherry stained desk placed in the center of the room. A couch, chair and coffee table were placed against the wall near the fireplace. It was a beautiful room—dark and mysterious—reminding Katie of an old library, a room where she'd love to sit and read. The mysterious room with beautiful furnishings had been intended to be used by Nan as an office for her business, however she preferred to take her laptop to the kitchen and do business overlooking her garden from the kitchen window, with all her paperwork strewn across the island.

Katie walked toward the window in the den, overlooking the porch and yard, pressed her forehead against the warm glass, and sighed.

"Hey, Hunter."

Katie turned her attention to the dog pressing his muscular frame against her thigh. She reached down and patted the gentle giant on his back. "How are you doing?" she asked.

He licked her hand in response.

"Good dog," she said softly.

She walked toward the entryway, then into the living room.

Nothing had changed since her last visit; the comfortable furniture had not been rearranged, nor any of the tables. She walked into the large kitchen—massive in size—a room with a cozy feel, made more so by the rustic stone fireplace. Katie noticed the only change in the room was the wild flowers in the green metal vase placed in the center of the island. The kitchen was one of Nan's favorite rooms in the house, where she spent hours cooking and visiting with friends.

Nan had had a larger than usual window installed above the sink, allowing her a view of the distant mountains, the view also from the island at the center of the kitchen. It was a room as wide as it was long. There was an old wood table—nicked from years of use—large enough to seat ten people placed at the far end of the room next to the fireplace. The kitchen had a warm glow about it; the beauty of nature outside felt inside, enjoyed from the large window. A door led from the kitchen to the lush, aromatic flower and herb garden, where benches were nestled near flowering bushes and trellises' heavy with rose bushes. One of Nan's favorite of all the flowers in her garden were the morning glories—rich purple and soft blue flowers on winding vines.

All the floors in the house were the original wood, buffed to a shine. Rugs with warm colors were placed around the house, large ones in the living areas, and small ones in the hallways. None of the furniture was new, but Nan had taken good care of her home and everything was still in good condition. It was a home where visitors and owner felt comfortable.

Nan had left a note on the island in the kitchen for Katie, telling her to make herself a cup of tea and get settled in. She was to use the larger of the two spare bedrooms, the one with a partial view of the mountains at the back of the house. After unpacking her two suitcases, Katie shoved the four boxes she'd brought with her into the closet and then shut the door, not ready to go through her memories just yet. Nan had opened the curtains in the bedroom, realizing that if she didn't, the light from the outside would not shine into the room for a while.

Suddenly, Katie felt the weight of the past few weeks settle over her, and she collapsed onto the queen-sized bed. She smoothed her hand over the satin fabric of the blue comforter. It was cool to her touch.

In a daze, she stared out of one of the bedroom windows, seeing only a blur of green from the leaves on the trees in the backyard. With a ragged sigh she stood up, walked to the closet, and opened the door. She opened one of the boxes and rummaged through it. Finding what she was looking for, she walked over to the two windows in the bedroom and pulled the curtains closed—throwing the room in darkness—then she walked back to the bed, climbed to the center, and curled onto her side. She pulled the soft blanket she'd taken from the box over her body, and tried to inhale her mother's scent, long since faded away.

It was dark when Katie woke several hours later. She sniffed. The air had a tangy scent. Nan was home she realized, and by the delicious aroma hanging in the air, it was obvious she was in the kitchen cooking. But Katie was too exhausted to stir and fell back asleep, her body jerking as she fell into a nightmare of hands tugging at her.

19

Katie opened her eyes. She blinked a few times as she tried to get her bearings, then she remembered . . . Brad in bed with another woman . . . Alan holding her down on his bed . . . and the long drive yesterday to Nan's house in North Carolina. Stretching her arm, she reached for the digital clock on the night table, turning it so she could read the time. One o'clock, she read. P.M.!

"My Lord!" she exclaimed. "I've slept through the evening and night . . . and morning!"

She rolled over onto her back, groaning with fatigue. She was as tired now as when she'd closed her eyes yesterday.

Slowly, she sat up, tugging at the rumpled clothes she'd been wearing since yesterday morning. She ran her tongue over her grimy teeth, unbrushed since the morning before, and ran her hand through her hair. She needed a shower . . . and coffee.

After showering and changing into a pair of baggy running shorts and over-sized t-shirt, with Hunter leading the way, Katie wandered downstairs to the kitchen—destination caffeine. Nan had set out a coffee mug next to the coffee pot, and next to the mug was a fluffy cranberry scone. Sweet, sweet, Nan, Katie thought, appreciatively. Perched on one of the stools at the island, Katie nibbled on the scone and sipped on hot coffee.

"Okay," she said to the garden beyond the kitchen window, "I'm here. Now what?"

Pushing the plate and mug forward, Katie rested her head on her arms and moaned, "What am I supposed to do with my life now?" Lifting her head, she rested her chin on the palm of her hand and stared unseeing out the window. "I'm in my forties for Christ sake. How can I start over?" Laughing hysterically, she wailed, "I don't know if it's possible, or even what that means."

After clearing away her mug and plate, Katie wandered through the house, pausing at a window to peer out into the world, and then moved on to the next room and a different window, seeking inspiration. Finding none, Katie climbed the stairs to her bedroom, and fell back onto the bed where she remained until hours later when Nan knocked softly on the bedroom door.

"Hey, sweets," Nan said softly as she crept into the dark room.

Katie was awake, resting on her side with her mother's blanket nestled beneath her chin.

"Hey, Nan," Katie said in a raspy voice, raw from tears shed for her parents, the death of her marriage, and her career—grieving for who she had been.

Katie gave Nan her best smile, watery though it was, as she glanced at her, still wearing her coffee shop uniform of a black blouse and slacks, smelling like a sugary pastry and dark brewed coffee.

"Why don't you come down and sit with me in the garden?" Nan suggested. "It's a beautiful evening. You don't want an old lady like me to have to sit all lonely-like in her garden all by herself, do you?"

Katie knew perfectly well that Nan loved her time alone in her garden in peaceful reflection. Nan was worried about her, Katie knew.

"No, I wouldn't want that," Katie answered.

"It's a nice cool evening," Nan said. "I was thinking about cracking open a box of wine."

Unable to hold back the smile, Katie thought, Nan and her boxes of cheap wine.

"Now, I know you aren't much for drinking," Nan said, with a pat of her hand on Katie's arm, "but a nice glass of red wine does a girl good every now and again. I'll go get changed into some leisure-like wear, and meet you out back. Okay, sweets?"

Katie wandered through the garden barely registering the beauty all around her, flowers teaming with life, a butterfly flitting about, bumblebees seeking nectar from a cluster of flowers, and birds chirping a song. Deep in the heart of the garden there was a sitting area with chaise lounges and tables, and it was there Katie stopped and flopped onto one of the cushioned chairs, rolling onto her side into a defeated fetal position. She closed out the world in the only way she knew how, by shutting her eyes.

Nan placed their glasses of chardonnay on the small table next to Katie and then slid onto the wide lounge chair next to her niece. Gently, Nan brushed aside the hair that had fallen onto Katie's face.

"Baby girl," Nan said.

Katie rolled toward Nan and leaned into her, her arms wrapping around her aunt's waist, and Nan leaned into her broken niece, wrapping her arms around her, kissing her hair. A long time passed before Katie struggled to sit up, scooting over to make more room for Nan to sit comfortably next to her, which was not difficult as the two women were similar in their petite size.

"You're gonna be okay, sweets," Nana crooned.

"When, Nan?" Katie murmured. "When...?"

"Just give life time to do its job, to smooth out the wrinkles of pain," Nan said wisely.

Nan reached for Katie's glass of wine, and said, "Here, sweets," and handed the glass of red wine to her niece. Then she picked up her own glass and took a sip.

Still snuggled close to her aunt, Katie took a sip of her wine and reflected, "Your garden is lovely this year . . . as it always is."

"There's something about digging your hands in the earth, turning it over and then tending to the shrubs and flowers . . . something about it that's mighty peace-inspiring," Nan shared. "I'm inviting nature into my life by growing this garden. My small world. A world that I grew, and I don't invite anything but beauty into it. Sweets, there's so much to be learned from the animals and insects that pay my garden a visit. Take that robin over there, up in that tree. Hear him singing?" Nan asked, as she gestured toward a chubby brown bird perched on a branch of a tree nearby.

"I see him," Katie said lazily, knowing Nan was trying to help her see her vision of the world. "And I hear him singing to us," she said.

"I have yet to see one of the robins that visit my garden stressed out about life's worries. No . . . it's always the same thing. Perched on a tree, singing a soothing, peaceful song to anyone who cares to pause long enough to hear. Not many do that these days," Nan said as she looked down at Katie. "Pause long enough to hear a robin sing, or notice the world around them . . . the important things in life."

The fog of the past two weeks lifted a little as Katie focused on Nan and her garden, the colors, smells, and sounds, suddenly more vibrant.

The two women continued to sip their glasses of wine snuggled comfortably together on the chaise lounge, surrounded by the sounds of nature, and cooled by the evening summer breeze.

20

⁓

The next morning, Katie, still wearing her boxer shorts and t-shirt, sat hunched over a cup of coffee at the island in the kitchen as Nan busied herself preparing for her day at the coffee shop. Nan was wearing a black blouse with ruffles around the neck and a pair of black capris. Half Nan's closet was filled with black clothing for what she felt was appropriate apparel for the coffee shop.

"Why don't you come by the shop today and have lunch with me?" Nan suggested. "It'd do you good to get out of the house for a few hours, and Lynn would love to see you."

Lynn was the co-owner of the coffee shop, and had been Nan's best friend for as long as Katie could remember. Her real name was Lynda, but everyone shortened her name to Lynn, and she didn't seem to mind . . . it was the only name Katie had ever called her.

"Maybe," Katie sighed.

"But if you don't mind, change out of those drawers first," Nan said playfully. She planted a kiss on Katie's forehead.

"Oh, I don't know," Katie teased. "If I wrap a pretty scarf around my neck it would dress the outfit up mighty nice."

"I hope to see you for lunch, dear, say . . . one-ish," Nan said casually, trying not to apply pressure to her fragile niece. Nan had not forgotten the other occasion that had broken Katie. When Katie was a senior in high school, Nan feared young Katie would never have the courage to venture back out into the world. She wouldn't have blamed Katie if she'd become a recluse, unable to try, unable ever to trust the world again. Nan often wondered how she would have responded if it had been her instead of Katie who had endured such a brutal attack.

"I might pop in," Katie said unconvincingly, not sure if she was ready just yet to face the world, even her aunt's friend. Still feeling bruised and battered, and very much a loser without a job, and a husband that, well . . . not even good enough to hold onto a husband . . . and no job to support herself. God, she wondered, could life pile any more shit on her?

"Maybe," Katie mumbled as Nan walked out of the kitchen and headed toward the garage door, her car, and the world outside of the safe walls of her comfortable home.

Looking down at the dog staring up at her, Katie asked, "So, Hunter, my fine yellow colored friend, what have you got goin' on today?"

The yellow lab shoved his head onto Katie's lap and licked the palm of her hand as she reached down to scratch the back of his neck.

"Don't suppose you have any words of advice for me, do you, friend?" she asked sarcastically. "How's your boss been treating you . . . and your spouse? Any nasty goin's on . . . like, I don't know . . . maybe someone assaulted you lately . . . violated your personal space, or . . . dog space?"

Sighing, Katie pushed her stool back and squatted down next to Hunter.

"What am I saying? Nan's your boss and friend. She'd never hurt you like all those assholes hurt me, would she? No—No—she'd never hurt you, would she?"

Rising to her feet, Katie looked down at Hunter, and commented, "All righty. Maybe Nan has a point. I'm asking for advice from a dog. Nothing personal, Hunter, you're a great dog. I just think maybe I need to talk to some people . . . or at least see some for a few hours . . . or half hour."

Hunter padded along behind her as Katie climbed the stairs to get dressed.

After pulling on a pair of jogging shorts and t-shirt, Katie walked over to the window in her bedroom that faced the mountains—the side of the house facing away from town. She pulled the curtain aside and let the light of the day into her room. She pressed her forehead against the glass, and stared blindly—the yard, trees, and mountains not registering. Then, with a heavy sigh, she turned away from the window and the unacknowledged scenery. Rummaging through her makeup bag, Katie found a ponytail maker and cinched her hair back tight.

She sprang down the steps. After downing a glass of water, Katie called out to Hunter. "Hunter. Hey, boy. You wanna to go for a walk?"

Hunter jumped, and let out a bark in the affirmative.

Nan's house was at the edge of town, the last house at the end of the street that lead out of town. The road running past Nan's house was rarely used, just by the few houses situated on the road. Years ago, the town had rerouted the road allowing for what they considered a more efficient flow of traffic in and out of town. Now, as Hunter and Katie walked away from Nan's house, and away from town, she didn't bother putting a leash on the dog, knowing they wouldn't meet another person or a car on their walk.

It was a beautiful morning—dew droplets still clung to lone weeds where the sun had not yet dried them. The sun's rays were not yet blistering hot. A light breeze lifted the tendrils of hair on her neck and the leaves on the trees as she passed by. Hunter remained close, not running ahead, as if he knew she needed him close to her.

Several hours later, after she'd showered and changed into a pair of jean shorts, a nicer t-shirt, and pulled her air-dried hair into a low ponytail, Katie climbed into her vehicle. Nervously, she drove to the coffee shop.

A few minutes later, Katie stood in front of the door of the coffee shop. For a moment she stood where she was and looked through the window, at the people inside—smiling faces that seemed so at home, belonging to someone, and to somewhere.

Taking a deep breath, she reached for doorknob of the coffee shop. Her heart beat erratically. Sweat pooled in the pits of her arms. Her hand trembled. Attempting to calm the panic she felt, she gave herself an internal shake and thought, I need to purchase more effective deodorant, and then, squaring her shoulders, she walked into coffee shop, noisy with lunch rush customers. As usual, there was a large crowd of tourists and regulars seated at almost every table in the dining area of the shop.

Nan and Lynn's coffee shop was a popular place in town, for both breakfast and dinner. Nan had not only a green thumb, but also a gift as an exceptional cook, and it was her culinary skills that drew in the large breakfast and lunch crowds, that and the friendly home-like atmosphere of the coffee shop. Her scones were in high demand in town, and her home-made soups, salads and various kinds of sandwiches sold out every day.

Lynn was the first to see Katie enter the coffee shop, and wiping her hands on the green apron she had tied around her waist—over her black pants and black short-sleeved t-shirt—Lynn rushed over and pulled the younger woman into her arms. To Katie's embarrassment, tears sprang to her eyes as they hugged each other tight.

"Men are pigs," Lynn insisted in Katie's ear, and then pulling away, she said, "Let me get a look at you. Just as pretty as ever . . . maybe a little thin, but your aunt Nan will fix that with all her good cooking." Lynn nodded, confidently.

Lynn and Katie's aunt Nan couldn't have looked more different. Lynn was six inches taller than Nan—her hair dyed black, where Nan's hair was dyed a subtle shade of blonde. Lynn was a little on the heavy side, but not in a way that she seemed unhealthily so, where Nan was a just a sprig of an older lady—both in their mid-seventies. Socially, they were well-matched. They both loved life and people, and people and life loved them back. They were both outspoken, and those that knew them loved them for all their quirky, forward-speaking, and forward-thinking ways. They were certainly not what you would think they would be for women from their era. As children, they'd been fortunate to have parents who supported their dreams no matter how big they might be, and as women, they'd had husbands that encouraged them to be all they wanted to be, not allowing their status as women to hold them back.

Knowing what Katie had experienced as a teen, and now as a woman, was difficult for both older women. It was difficult to stand by and watch her struggle, but Nan and Lynn knew Katie had to find her own way on her precarious, fragile journey—a journey of finding her inner strength as a woman, but they intended to be with her for every step she would allow.

"Oh, Lynn," Katie said with an embarrassed smile. "I'm *not* thin, I assure you. It's the baggy t-shirt and shorts." Brushing the comment aside, Katie marveled over the older woman's youthful energy and appearance. "You look amazing, Lynn. As you always do. Whatever magic pill you're taking, please give me one."

"Oh, girl," Lynn crooned, "no magic pill here. Just good clean living!"

Katie had no doubt about the genuineness of Lynn's words. Katie knew few people with the deep love and commitment for others. Lynn and Katie's aunt were two very special women . . . just as her mother and father had been.

"Sweets!" Nan exclaimed as she contained her urge to rush over and pull her niece into her arms giving her a bear hug. Instead, she cleared an abandoned coffee cup and discarded napkin from a table, and then walked to the sink in the back room. Then casually, she walked over to Katie and embraced her tenderly.

"How was your morning, dear?" Nan asked.

"Okay," Katie said. "Hunter was kind enough to accompany me on a walk."

"He's such a good companion," Nan said with a grin. "Better than most husbands."

"Ain't that the truth!" Lynn said as she walked behind the counter to help a customer.

Katie grinned, knowing Lynn had been blessed to have a dear husband for over thirty years. He had doted on Lynn, and she on him. Lynn was a jokester, rarely serious even about the love of her life. When Earl had passed away several years ago, it had been a dark time for her. Aunt Nan had helped her find her way—helped her get out of bed each day, and eventually, helped her create a new life.

"So, what's edible on the menu today?" Katie joked.

"Did I hear that child right?" Lynn asked. "What's edible? Careful, girl. Your aunt will put you to work for insultin' her menu." Lynn winked at Katie.

"We've got your favorite," Nan said, "a vegetarian sandwich with tomatoes, red onions, cucumber, a little guacamole, and a slice of provolone cheese, all on wheat bread. We have your favorite soup too, black bean garnished with green onions."

"MMMM," Katie murmured. "Tasty."

"You want to eat in the library room?" Nan asked.

"Of course," Katie said with a hint of a smile.

The library room was the large room at the back of the coffee shop, beyond the nook room. The nook room was where specialty items were placed on antique bookshelves—scarves, jewelry, jeweled compact mirrors, and other items—that Lynn had selected from various vendors throughout the state, to display and sell to customers. Each of the coffee shop's rooms, even free wall space in the library room, displayed various types of artwork—photography, oil paintings, watercolor—by artists living within a two hundred mile radius.

While Nan's dream had always been a quaint café, Lynn's had been a specialty shop, and the back room—the library room—to Katie, pulled the entire shop together. The library room was a large room—the wood floor covered by a richly colored ruby red rug, and dark leather couches, coffee tables, and side tables were placed before a stone fireplace, cozy when in use during the fall and winter months. The walls were lined with shelves, stacked full of old books and new. Customers could spend an entire day—curled cozily on one of the overstuffed chairs or couch—at the shop reading one of the books, or they could take a book home and swap it on their next visit. Or, if a customer chose, they could purchase a book they could not part with.

There were several people in the library room seated on the over-sized chairs. Lamps glowed nearby on side tables. The room had an old library feel—a room that inspired quiet reflection by its visitors.

Katie walked toward one of the empty couches in front of a coffee table and settled in while Nan prepared their lunch. Barely had she sat down, when a sensation of panic crept over her . . . a feeling that had her wanting to run out of the room. It felt as if the room was closing in on her, as if she were sitting in a small closet with no air conditioning on a hot summer day. A cold sweat washed over her body. Her heart raced, and her body trembled uncontrollably as she pressed her body deep into the couch. She closed her eyes, drew in a deep calming breath, and crossed her arms across her chest—hugging herself tight—in a defensive gesture.

Five minutes later, Nan walked into the library room and found Katie still leaned back on the couch, her eyes shut—her face, dirty dishwater gray.

"Katie," Nan said, concern cracking her voice.

She placed their trays of sandwiches, soup and tea on the table. When Katie did not respond, Nan sat down next to her and placed the back of her hand to her niece's cheek. Her skin was cold.

"Sweets," Nan said softly, "are you okay?

Opening her eyes, Katie gulped in a deep breath. "I'm okay," she said shakily. "Just had the weirdest feeling come over me, but . . . but I'm okay now."

"Here," Nan said as she handed her a cup of hot tea. "Sip on this."

As she sipped the green tea, a little color returned to Katie's cheeks.

"Good," Katie said with a weak smile.

Feeling a little better after she'd eaten half of her meal, Katie asked Nan, "So what's been new around town?"

Nan was relieved the color had returned to Katie's cheeks. She shared, "Busy with tourists and regulars here at the shop. Lots of tourists staying at the B & B's in town. Wine evenings on the weekends have been a big hit here at the shop. Wine evenings give the golf clubbers a bit of culture, that and we invite several artists to come in and talk about their work, you know, for special showings. Lots of my breakfast and lunch regulars come in. It's like a big ol' extended family getting together in an evening. My great food, great wine, and great company . . . it's what life's all about."

"How's Stu doing?" Katie asked. Stu was a gentleman friend who was sweet on Nan.

"He's just fine I should think," Nan said easily. "He was in early this morning for his regular cup of black coffee, and egg and cheese sandwich."

"Nan, why don't the two of you kids just get married, that or shack up?" Katie said mischievously.

"Well, for heaven's sake, Katie. I see that soup made you feel better. You're just full of sass, aren't you?" Nan joked. Avoiding the question, Nan said, "I better get back to the coffee room before Lynn has a meltdown." Nan knew perfectly well that Lynn could handle the entire shop herself, but wanted to avoid the topic of Stu for now.

"Okay. I think I'll head back to the house. I must be coming down with something because I still feel exhausted," Katie confessed, the glimmer of headache from an hour ago, beginning to pound with her heartbeat. She'd hoped lunch would ward it off, but it hadn't.

"Go on home and get a nap," Nan insisted, trying not to show how concerned she was. "If you're feeling up to it, I'll cook us a nice dinner tonight."

"That sounds nice, Nan," Katie said wearily. "I'll see you at the house later."

After letting Hunter out to do his business, Katie sought something to relieve the pounding in her head. After washing the pill down with a glass of water, rubbing her temples with her fingers, she walked to her bedroom. She shut the door to her bedroom, pulled the curtains closed—shutting out what seemed to be brilliant white light—and then got into bed, snuggling her mother's throw blanket under her chin.

Five hours later, Nan checked on her niece and found her still sound asleep. She stood above her for a few moments and watched the steady rhythm of her breathing. Tenderly, she glanced her fingers across Katie's cheek. The blanket, still tucked beneath Katie's chin, caught Nan's eye. Her fingers touched the blanket, knowing it had been her older sister's, and now it was cuddled beneath her niece's chin, the only way she could reach out to her mother, taken from them too soon. Bending over, Nan brushed a light kiss across Katie's forehead, a kiss from her, and from Katie's mother, then she walked out of the room, carefully closing the door behind her.

21

At eight thirty, Katie walked downstairs to the living room where Nan was watching TV.

"Well good morning, er, I mean evening, sleepy head," Nan said with a smile, relieved to see her niece out of bed. "How's your head feeling?"

"Much better," Katie said. "I don't know what hit me. I sat down at the coffee shop and just all of a sudden felt awful. I took an Ibuprofen when I got to the house, and then I crashed. I think I fell asleep, literally, the moment my head hit the pillow."

"Katie, I think you're wrung out from all the stress and changes you've experienced in the last few months, and from the trauma from the night at the cabin. By itself, what happened at the cabin is bad—and would break any woman—but with what happened to you when you were in high school, it would've been like a wave crashing into you. Then, you found your husband in bed, in *your* bed, with another woman. Well, either of those situations would be enough to send most women over the brink, or, well, most women would be furious, shouting and destroying her husband's things. And as far as your boss, lots of women would've called the cops, or had their husband kick his ass, which of course, you didn't have that option with your husband's head, literally, somewhere else. You've had a time of it, sweets."

Raising her eyebrows, Katie said, "Well, that was a graphic picture, Nan, but . . . I suppose you're right. I just feel like I've been on automatic pilot. I've thought about it all . . . but, it sounds strange, but I don't think any of it has really sunk in yet."

"No, I don't think it has. It will though, and when it does, it won't be pretty. It's *okay* to yell and cry, Katie, but you haven't done that yet—haven't really dealt with what happened—and until that happens I think you should take it easy. Just give yourself time to heal," Nan said, thoughtfully.

"But I have to work, Nan. I walked off my job two weeks ago. I'm going to need a paycheck eventually. I have a little money in savings, and I'll be getting half of the marital assets from Brad, from the divorce settlement, but I'd rather not dig into any of that. I've never *not* worked before. I'm going to have bills . . ." Katie's voice trailed away as she sat down on the couch.

"Are you hungry?" Nan asked. "How about I make you a fat ham sandwich with all the fixin's, and we can discuss your future."

"Sounds great," Katie said, still thinking about how she was going to live—pay bills—without money, without a paycheck. "I *am* actually kind of hungry . . . which is a first for me in a while."

Nan sat next to Katie at the island in the kitchen and watched as she dug into the sandwich. Katie ate without saying anything, washing down bites with the water Nan had placed in front of her. After she finished the sandwich, Nan offered her a cup of hot tea.

"Have you considered what you might *want* to do, as far work goes?" Nan asked. "Not right now, but when you've given yourself time to just be for a while. You know you're welcome to live here with me for as long as you like. You can retire here with me if you like," Nan grinned. "You won't have to worry about payin' rent . . . my house is paid for, just a little bit of taxes every year, but that's nothing. Eventually, you can chip in a little bit for groceries."

Katie smiled at the thought of living with her aunt into her retired years, not what she'd planned for her old age, not at all. Old and dependent upon her elderly aunt. Lord, she was such a loser, she thought, miserably.

"Honestly, Nan, I haven't even thought about what's next for me, personally or professionally. I don't know, Nan." Katie said, miserably.

"Well, let's talk about it for a minute. How 'bout a law office? Most of your experience is at law firms," Nan said, reasonably.

"No—No. I don't want to go back to that kind of work. I know too much. I know what those men are like, what rich men—powerful men—are like," Katie said firmly as she shook her head, a frown furrowing her brow.

"Well, that's a start. You know what you *don't* want to do," Nan said, encouragingly. "I tell you what, while you're figuring it all out, why don't you come help me at the shop . . . part time or full time, which ever you want. You can start whenever you want . . . tomorrow, next week, in two weeks . . . or a month if you want. I think it'd be good for you to get out a bit. Be around people."

The room was quiet for a moment.

"Take time to think about it," Nan said. "The offer will be out there for you."

"No. I don't need to think about it, Nan," Katie said with determination. "You're right. I need to get out there—stop hiding in the house—and do something, and I really appreciate the offer. I'd like that, but maybe I can start next week, after I rest up. I'm just so tired still, and felt so awful today. I think you're right. I'm just worn out."

"Well, alright then! It'll be us girls—you, Lynn, and me at the shop, and a few of the part timers," Nan said as she patted Katie's knee.

Nan was relieved Katie had agreed to work at the shop, believing the interaction with people would help her healing process, help her move forward and begin figuring out who she was, and where she was willing to let life take her. Right now was just a stopping off place for Katie, a place to hide out until she decided to live again, and figure out what kind of life she wanted to live.

"Why don't you do some writing over the next week?" Nan suggested. "In college you used to love to write. Remember how you said that one day you were going to write a novel? I believe you could," Nan coaxed with a smile, more than just a little serious about the idea. Her niece was a gifted writer and anything she set her mind too, she could accomplish. She just needed a little spark to get her going, and Nan intended to help her find that spark.

"Write, huh?" Katie said, wrinkling her brow. "What would I write about?" the idea of writing an intriguing one.

"I'm sure you have a few great stories that are just asking to be written. The best stories are the ones straight from the heart, often filled with pain, love, loss, and longing. You've got lots of those in you," Nan assured her niece.

Katie placed her chin on the palm of her hand and mused, write . . . write about what?

Over the next few days, Katie thought about what Nan had suggested—*write.* While she took long walks with Hunter, and lazed about the garden sipping iced coffee, Katie considered what she might write about.

Nan had offered her the use of her den and Katie had eagerly accepted, setting up her laptop at the desk. She just needed to figure out what to write, needed inspiration. Then, one night, woken by a nightmare, her t-shirt soaked with sweat, and her heart pounding, the dilemma about what to write about was solved. She had her answer . . .

22

One morning, three days after Nan suggested she write, Katie closed the door to the study behind her, pulled the curtains closed, clicked on the small desk lamp, and brought her computer to life. The screen of the laptop glowed, waiting expectantly for her to share her most secret thoughts. For the next several weeks, Nan saw very little of her niece, and one evening, worried, she poked her head into what was now Katie's writing room. Katie had been so engrossed in wherever her story was taking her, that she hadn't noticed Nan. Nan closed the door gently behind her, taking comfort in the knowledge that her niece was finding her way.

Once Katie had begun writing, she found it difficult to stop. She began writing early in the morning—sipping on cups of coffee, taking breaks only when her stomach screamed at her and she had to rid herself of all the coffee she'd drunk—and wrote late into the night. Some nights, when the house was quiet as Nan slept, Katie sought out the boxed wines her aunt kept chilled. Those were the crying nights. As she sobbed and downed glasses of wine to sooth the pain—forcing herself to remember—words flowed from Katie's fingertips.

"Hey, Nan!" Katie surprised her aunt one afternoon when she appeared for lunch at the coffee shop. "What do you have that's good for lunch?"

Nan looked up from her stooped position behind the counter where she was grabbing napkins. "Well," she said, pleasantly surprised to see her niece. Holding on to the counter, she pulled herself to her feet, and said, "For you, sweets, anything."

Nan examined Katie, noticing that she'd grown thinner since she'd arrived almost a month ago.

"I could use a cup of iced coffee, for now," Katie said with a tired smile.

It had been another late night writing session. She'd written the last chapter of the book . . . a journey of agonizing proportions. But still, the writer of the story had no idea where the next chapter of her life would take her . . . where she wanted to go.

"Let me get us some coffee and I'll join you in the library room," Nan said. "I'll be just a few minutes."

"Sounds good," Katie grinned, and then walked toward the back of the shop, through the crowd of happy tourists and lunch regulars.

"Hey, shugs," Lynn smiled.

"Hi, Lynn," Katie smiled back.

"Nice to see you. Hope you stay out of your writing cave for a while and hang out with us here at the shop. I miss seeing your pretty face," Lynn said, hopefully.

"Yeah, I think I'm ready for a break from the cave," Katie admitted.

"Good," Lynn beamed.

Katie shuffled passed a few shoppers in the trinket room and then continued down the hall toward the library room. She was a little disappointed to find the room was not completely abandoned. There was a man in the room sitting on one of the plush chairs, his nose buried in a book, a cup of coffee next to him on a side table. As she walked past the man with dark hair, Katie had the feeling she knew him; there was something familiar about him.

She couldn't place it—the scent of his cologne perhaps, or the way he was casually seated. It must be one of the regulars, she mused as she stared at the tall bookcase filled with books. She walked to the bookshelf section where her favorite books were located—the mystery section—and considered that it might be nice to sit in the garden and get lost in a good book. After pulling several books off the shelf, Katie found one that piqued her interest, and book in hand, she curled up onto her favorite spot at the far end of the couch.

"Katie? It *is* you!" A deep voice said.

Hearing a familiar voice say her name, Katie's heart began to pound. She snapped her head in the direction of the man with dark hair, now standing and smiling down at her.

Stumbling to her feet in surprise, Katie whispered, "Jack," stunned to see Jack Andrews, a man from her past, from life at the law firm. Hesitantly, Katie placed her hand in his outstretched hand.

"What are you doing here?" he asked.

Jack knew she'd left the Weaver law firm. There wasn't much in the legal world, that wasn't known—shared between the net of other attorneys. He'd heard the rumors about Katie, about a woman walking off the job at one of the largest firms in the tri-state area and knew it was her. He suspected he knew the reason she'd left the firm. Katie had seemed to him to be a bright, genuine woman when they'd met at the firm. She'd greeted him when he arrived for his interview with Alan Weaver. At the time of their meeting at the Weaver firm, it had surprised him that she'd work for an attorney like Alan, a man known for his disrespect for his female employees, and women in general. Men like Alan put on a good act for the women they had their sites on, and rumor had it, his sites had been *locked* on Katie. After a grave miscalculation on his part, she'd bolted from the company with not so much as a good-bye to a single employee leaving Alan high and dry as his assistant and his human resources manager. And here she was, hiding out, it would seem, in North Carolina.

"I'm—I—my aunt owns this coffee shop," she stammered, with a swoop of her hand.

"Well, it is certainly is a small world," he beamed.

She was leery of Jack, a man from her past, someone associated with Alan Weaver.

"Why are you here . . . in North Carolina?" Katie asked. "Why aren't you in Kentucky?"

Jack detected the chill in her tone, and realized the rumors swirling around her departure from the Weaver firm were very likely true. "I'm working in the area," he said kindly.

"So you *didn't* take Alan's generous offer to work for his firm?" she asked, wrinkling her brow skeptically.

"Hell no!" Jack laughed. "About five minutes into the interview with Alan and my gut was telling me that it was not the place for me. Alan's firm wasn't my only consideration. I had several other offers, one in California, one on the east coast, and one in Chicago. When I got the call from you, I wasn't looking for a different firm. I had a great job at a firm where I was comfortable, but when I began receiving requests for interviews, I realized it was a sign that life wanted me to make a few changes. It was time to take the leap—take on new challenges that would stretch and expand my mind and life. It's what life's all about, the continual process of change that grows us."

The more Jack talked the more at ease Katie became. It had been a shock to see him—the flood of unpleasant memories of Alan and her old life crowding her mind—and suspiciously she suspected Alan had sent Jack to find her, to hurt her in some way. It had seemed odd that Alan had allowed her to walk away with the damaging secret she now held. If she chose to disclose that her boss, a multi-millionaire, had sexually assaulted her, it could ruin him, and her as well. Alan wouldn't hesitate to hurt her, Katie feared. She shook her head, dispelling old memories of a similar situation.

All of sudden, Katie became aware of her rumpled appearance and reached her hand up to smooth her hair, and then smoothed her t-shirt over her shorts. There was nothing she could do about the lack of makeup and bags under her eyes, she reasoned, as she smiled up at the six-foot-two man with dark brown hair and eyes the color of a brilliant summer sky.

Jack noticed Katie smoothing her hair and t-shirt and smiled a worried smile, as he noticed how thin she'd become since he'd last seen her, and noticed the dark smudges beneath her eyes. Pain that only a woman's soul could know, he knew, would break the strongest of men, something he'd learned a great deal about when he was a young boy. As he looked deeply into Katie's eyes, he saw the ghost of pain he'd seen many times before in other girl's, and women's eyes.

"Here we are," Nan said in a singsong voice. "Lunch is served!"

Nan watched as Katie and the attractive tall man—she estimated to be a few years older than her niece—turned toward her. She had the distinct feeling she was interrupting something, and by the looks of Katie's flushed cheeks, and the way her hand kept smoothing her hair, she suspected this was not the first meeting between these two. Intriguing, she thought with a small smile.

Pretending she hadn't noticed the steamy situation, Nan continued, "We were out of black bean soup, sweets, so I brought you chicken noodle instead." She set their trays on the coffee table in front of the couch.

Katie had been so engrossed in her conversation with Jack—surprised that her past had manifested before her in a physical manner—that the sound of Nan's voice had startled her.

Tucking a stray strand of hair behind her ear, Katie, said, "Nan, lunch looks great. Thanks."

There was a moment of silence before Jack extended his hand toward Nan, and introduced himself. "Hi, I'm Jack."

"Nice to meet you," Nan said, accepting his hand in her firm grasp. "I'm Nan, Katie's aunt."

"Sorry," Katie said, embarrassed that she'd neglected to provide an introduction. She was still taken aback that Jack was standing in the library room of her aunt's coffee shop. What were the odds, she wondered, that of all the coffee shops in the world, Jack Andrews would have found Nan's, and was standing next to her, as if they were the oldest of friends.

It was the first time since arriving in North Carolina that Katie seemed engaged in something, Nan noticed. She made a snap decision.

"Katie, would you mind if I cancel our lunch date? Lynn is swamped," Nan lied. "We just had a large crowd come in, right after you walked back here."

"Oh," Katie said. "No—No, that's okay. We can chat tonight at dinner."

Nan patted Jack on his masculine forearm, and said, "It was real good to meet you, Jack. Perhaps I'll see you again soon. Do you live around here?"

"Asheville," he said with a smile. "I was just telling Katie that I moved to the area about a month ago."

"Oh," Nan said. "Well, isn't that nice. What is it you do?"

"I practice law," he said.

Darn, Nan thought. *That's not going to endear him to Katie, not with how she felt about lawyers these days.* But she kept that observation to herself.

"What type of law do you practice . . . at some large fancy law firm, I suppose?" Nan asked.

"Not a large firm. I've hung up my fancy law firm brief case. Now I'm handling cases for women and children who've been victims of violent crimes. I've been involved in legislation for human trafficking victims . . . helping with those types of cases for a few years now," Jack shared.

Nan could tell by the way he talked—the way his face took on a serious look—that he was passionate about what he was doing. She might just see the handsome young man again after all, she reflected.

Katie looked up at him in surprise, having written off all attorneys' as low life scum—men that used their legal power to hurt women; they certainly didn't help them. She realized she wanted to learn more about his work. Not for any personal reason she assured herself, but strictly because of her own history.

"Welcome to the area, Jack," Nan said brightly. "Stop in next time you're in town. Are you over this way often?" she asked sweetly.

"I do get over this way occasionally," he offered.

"Well, kids, if you'll excuse me," Nan said. "I need to get back to work. I'll see you later, Katie," she said, with an innocent expression, and a wave of her hand.

"I'll be out to see you soon," Katie said to her aunt, as Nan walked out of the room leaving them alone.

"Don't let me keep you," Jack said, gesturing toward Katie's lunch.

"Would you like to join me?" Katie asked. "I'd like to hear more about your work. Such as . . . how in the world did you ever get into the field of law that deals with trafficking? I've heard about it, but few attorneys want to touch it. Not a lot of money in it, and it's relatively new. Besides that, helping women . . . again, not typically going to make an attorney a lot of money. Real money—big money—is in the representation of corporations, saving them money by getting employees to settle harassment and discrimination suits. Of course, there's money in ambulance chasing—going after what might pan out to be a big-ticket case, but the real, solid steady money, is in corporate defense. Why not just stick with what you know, what you've done in the past? Why the change now, at your age?" she asked, with a note of accusation in her tone.

Katie still wasn't sure she believed Jack's excuse—that his new life had brought him within thirty minutes of Nan's house. And representing women, what kind of cockamamie story was that, she wondered skeptically? It made no sense to give up a position as a top attorney with a prestigious law firm making, she was sure, a high end salary for . . . he had to have taken a tremendous cut in pay. She doubted he was making even half of what he made at his old firm.

Jack waited for Katie to be seated and then folded his tall frame onto the couch next to her.

He chuckled. "Let me see if I can answer your many questions." He paused for a moment, and glanced up at the ceiling as he decided where to begin, how much to share with her about his life.

He looked at her—measured her up.

"You seem to find it difficult to believe anyone, especially an attorney, would give up a very generous salary—*lots* of money," he allowed, when he noticed the incredulous look on her face. "I did give up a very generous salary. You're absolutely right, and that seems to surprise you, and I can understand why you find that surprising. A great many people believe attorneys go to law school with the intention of making a butt load of money, so they can spend a butt load of money—on cars, boats, houses . . . women." He looked at her with a question in his eyes. "Is that your assumption of all attorneys?"

When she did not respond, he continued.

"Katie, men—people for that matter—are all different. Our pasts shape us into who we are. My childhood formed me into who I am, just like yours did you. My life wasn't always as easy as it seems now. Time grows us in the ways it should, if we let it, always watchful of the signs and cues, such as the one I had recently. The various opportunities I was faced with was a sign that I was to move on . . . to consider something different with my life. I knew the human trafficking work I was doing, as an attorney on my own time, was part of that change. I have made my money. I have plenty of money saved and invested, so to continue on the old path would have provided a shallow growth-less existence—no meaning or purpose. It's like your life now . . . a new growth journey," Jack said softly.

Katie looked down at her hands, embarrassed by her current situation.

"My journey right now is nothing like yours. I, unlike you, did *not* have a multitude of offers . . . job offers. I left Alan's firm with nothing lined up, and on top of that, I left my husband," she said, bitterness adding a hard edge to her words. "I left my entire life behind, so our life journeys—the signs you are talking about—do not seem to apply to me."

"I think you're wrong about that," Jack insisted. "You were presented with options, any choice leading down a different path."

She tried to contain her anger at his arrogant words. As if their lives were anything alike, were *ever* anything alike, he with his life as an attorney, able to pick and choose where he wanted to work. She had just been practically raped by a man like him . . . an attorney.

Her lunch untouched, Katie abruptly rose to her feet.

"I have to get going, Jack. It was nice to see you," she lied.

He knew he had angered her, and that she still saw him like Alan, nothing more than a user. But he intended to show her she was wrong. Not all men were like Alan Weaver.

"Maybe I'll see you again. I'm over this way quite a bit. I'll stop back in, and hopefully you'll be here," he said with a warm smile, trying to soften the words he'd spoken about her life choices.

"Maybe," she said with a tight smile.

Katie, with Jack following her, walked toward the front of the coffee shop. She breezed through the busy lunch crowd, and looked over her shoulder at Nan.

"I'll see you later tonight, Nan!" Katie said, briskly.

Once outside, Katie walked down the sidewalk toward her vehicle, hoping Jack would not follow her.

23

The conversation with Jack had lit a fire under Katie, so hours later, too distracted to write, she stormed into the kitchen, and while sipping a glass of wine, cooked the anger out of her. By the time Nan arrived home several hours later, a much calmer Katie, grilled salmon, salad, and pasta, met her in the kitchen.

"Well, what's been goin' on here?" Nan asked happily, taking in the place settings on the island, and the glass of wine waiting for her. "MMMM. Smells good, sweets," Nan said, appreciatively.

Hunter bumped against Nan's leg, and she bent over and rubbed the soft spot under his chin. "Good boy," she said.

He answered her with a contented bark.

"Did you have a good rest of the day?" Katie asked brightly. The effects of the glass of wine she'd sipped while cooking dinner made her eyes sparkle brightly.

"Why, yes—yes, I did. Stu stopped in for a bit just to bug me. That man is such a pain in my ass," Nan said absently, as she popped a cherry tomato into her mouth.

"Oh, Nan," Katie giggled. "That man is nothing but sweetness with you."

"That man is not sweetness!" Nan lied, and took a sip of her wine.

Katie shook her head, knowing her aunt was head over heels in love with Stu, and he with her. She didn't understand why they didn't get married or at least shack up. Their relationship had been a topic Katie and Nan had discussed over the years, and it was always the same answer when Katie asked. Nan wasn't ready to settle down yet, which always made Katie smile. Not ready to settle down, at her age, Katie wondered; if not now, then when?

After dinner, Nan and Katie took the half-empty box of wine and their wine glasses to the garden, and sitting in their favorite chaise lounge chairs, giggled like school girls as they talked about Stu, and Nan's first husband, Katie's uncle. Nan's first husband had been her high school sweet heart, Nan shared for about the two-hundredth time. Katie never tired of the story. When she'd been a little girl, Katie had sat raptly as her mother or Nan shared their schoolgirl love stories, which always led to stories of her father and her uncle. Her uncle, father, and mother, long since gone, to wherever loved ones went and waited, Katie thought, with a sigh.

The ladies had travelled beyond tipsy, when Nan grinned, and said, "So, tell me Katie . . . tell me about the luscious man I met this afternoon. Jack."

"That . . . Jack, Nan, is no luscious man. He's an attorney. No different from any other man, or attorney!" Katie swung her half-full glass of wine in the air as if she were toasting a crowd, sloshing wine on her leg. She rubbed at her leg as she licked her lower lip.

"Oh, hell, Katie! Men aren't all alike, even the attorney ones. Men are men, that's for sure, but just because they all sport a penis don't make them all alike!" Nan cackled.

Katie snorted, and almost rolled out of her chair.

"Nan!" Katie shrieked. "You said, *penis*!"

Nan laughed so hard she sloshed most of the wine in her glass onto the ground.

Katie's mood turned somber. She took a large gulp of her wine, and said, angrily, "They're just a bunch of *dicks*."

The memory of the side of Alan's face, his rumpled hair, and the smell of his alcohol wreaking breath as he'd held her down on the bed at his cabin, stormed through her mind. Then she thought of Brad, the night he'd looked at her as his arm shielded the whore lying next to him in their bed.

"I hope Alan burns in hell," Katie slurred. "I *pray* he dies a miserable death, and then *burns* in hell screaming in agony for all of his eternity, and Brad . . . he made a promise to me. He promised to love me and be here for me—not abandon me when I was helping a child, *our* niece, for Christ sake. Not—not have sex with some random woman when things got a little tough . . . in *my* bed!" she cried. Tears flowed down her cheeks, and she swiped at the snot running toward her upper lip. "I felt like that girl . . . you know, when I was in high school. I knew what was happening, but I couldn't move—then . . . then I passed out. When I came too, I felt the pain, heard them laugh—felt something being poured on me. They stripped me naked, Nan, and some of the kids knew what they planned to do to me, but they let them do it to me anyway." Katie shook her head, and smiled bitterly. "But God had a little mercy, didn't he." She laughed hysterically. "He let me pass out again as the other three boys took their turn at me . . . taking something I could never get back. Then they dumped me down the road from mom and dad's house, and dad found me the next morning when he was on his morning walk. Daddy found his little girl half naked, bloody and passed out in the dirt," Katie sobbed. "They—they killed my daddy."

Nan swiped at her own tears streaming down her cheeks. In all the years since that horrific night, this was the first time Katie had talked to her about it. Katie had shared what happened that night with the nurses at the hospital where her frantic mother and father had taken her that morning, where Katie had been physically examined in a humiliating fashion. They had poked and prodded her, and taken pictures of various parts of her body, and then she'd reported what she could piece together to the police.

Since that summer, Katie had been silent about the attack, trying to forget. The evening all those years ago had begun with an excited teenaged Katie, excited to be attending an end of the summer party with friends from school. A few weeks before Katie was to start her senior year of high school, one beautiful summer evening—she had been a very different Katie then, trusting—she had taken great care with her outfit, selecting a lavender colored summer dress to wear to the party. Early the next morning, her father had found her unconscious, thrown like a rag doll along the side of the road a block from their house, her dress in tatters.

The night of the attack, Katie's classmate's parents had been home for the first few hours of the party, but in a small town like theirs, where everyone knew everyone, the parents felt they could leave the large group of seniors alone for a few hours. When the parents left, it was to a group of seemingly wholesome church kids enjoying a warm summer evening, playing volleyball and corn hole, sipping on pop and listening to music. The parents left at nine that night, and then the tone of the evening changed. College kids crashed the party. The college boys shared the beer they had stashed in the trunks of their cars, garden games forgotten as kids began downing alcohol. Music blared, and kids snuck off into dark corners inside and outside the house.

That night, feeling dizzy, Katie told her girlfriend she wasn't feeling well, and one of their classmates hearing their conversation, offered to give her a ride home. The tall boy helped her walk to a car where four boys waited inside. She passed out in the car, and the boys drove her to an abandoned building located at the edge of town. They carried her inside, and as she wavered in and out of consciousness on the cold, dirty concrete floor, the boys continued to drink the beer that their college buddies had given them. Then, one by one, over a four-hour period, they took turns raping her. As one boy raped her, another held her down—one of her wrists broken by the intense pressure of the weight of the knee pinning her down. Her struggles to be free were met by a searing, burning pain when one of the boys punched her, breaking her jaw.

When they were done with her, they considered dumping her at her house but lost their nerve, unable to approach the home of their childhood friend—a house where just a few years before they had eaten chocolate chip cookies Katie's mother had baked. Katie's father found her the next morning, and frantically her parents drove her to the hospital. She remained at the hospital for several weeks, undergoing surgery for a broken jaw, shattered wrist, and tears to her vaginal wall. It had been the most brutal assault the team of surgeons had ever seen.

At the hospital, it was confirmed that traces of a date rape drug was found in her system. The investigating officer estimated it had been around ten o'clock, the night of the attack, when Katie was drugged by the boys she'd known throughout her childhood. That night, Katie had done the one thing all girls were told never to do . . . she had walked away from her drink. She hadn't drunk alcohol, or even a soft drink that night, but she had been sipping on water, and it was in her water bottle that the drug had been introduced into her system.

It had been a grueling ordeal, but Katie's family had been a loving, strong source of support every painful step of the way. The night of the end-of-the-summer party, changed Katie's life and the lives of her family forever. One shocking, devastating, impact of reporting the assault was that Katie lost most of her friends, and when school started her senior year, even teachers treated her differently. Katie had to move away—leave her school and family—because of harassment that escalated to the point her family feared for her physical well-being. She was bullied while at school— pushed in the halls when she changed classes, called degrading names, and even the family home was vandalized. Her parents had taken Katie to Nan's house to stay, where she finished healing, inside and out, and completed her senior year of high school.

She pressed charges against the five boys who had raped her, and after a short hearing, lasting only a few days, the boys had each received a sentence of one-year probation. Although it had been a horrific crime, the boys were all under the age of eighteen, so law dictated a mere slap on the wrist, and a promise that no one would ever know what they had done. Juvenile offenders were protected by law, their crimes sealed from public knowledge.

Seeing his little girl broken by a nightmare he could not protect her from—rape—and the cruelty from their community of friends, unable to protect her, or give her justice, had broken Katie's father's heart. Nan knew, just as if those boys had driven a dagger into his heart; they killed him. But Katie had blamed herself for his death, thinking that if she hadn't gone to the party, she would have been safe, and her father would not have died from a heart attack. Her mother had explained to Katie that was not the case and that a girl or woman should not have to hide in their house to be safe from rape, but she had never forgiven herself for his death.

"My God," Katie wailed as she looked up at the stars. "Is there even a God? I—I just don't know, Nan. Maybe not for me."

Carefully, Nan placed her glass on the table next to her and looked intently, if a little unsteadily, at her niece. She considered her for a long moment, wondering what to say to snap her niece out of her land of anger, bitterness and distrust of men. It was understandable, Nan knew to be hurt, angry, and bitter after what the boys and men Katie trusted had done to her. They'd cut into the very core of her as a woman. But she didn't want to her niece to take up permanent residence in the land of spiritual un-living, the place Katie seemed to have gotten lost in after the rape had occurred. Nan watched as Katie flung her legs to the side of the lounge chair, plant her elbows on her knees, and her face in her hands.

"What have I done to deserve this?" Katie cried. "First, what happened in high school, then dad, mom, Stacey's husband . . . then Alan . . . and Brad? Am I cursed, Nan?" she asked as she looked across at her aunt, demanding an answer.

Considering her niece, Nan offered, "Maybe you're lookin' at this all wrong, Katie. You know, the entire universe isn't here plotting against you. Everyone has a journey—separate from you. Your parents, Alan, Brad, and even the boys that raped you."

Katie felt as if Nan had slapped her. Raising her voice, she said, "The *hell* you say!? *I* need to think differently about *rape, infidelity,* and *death*?!" She's flipped out of her drunk little mind, Katie thought angrily as she stared at her aunt in amazement and anger.

"That didn't come out quite right," Nan said in a rush. "Just hear me out."

She placed her hand on Katie's knee. From the look of Katie, Nan thought, at any moment she was going to jump off her chair and storm into the house, the opportunity to rattle her enough to wake her up, gone.

"Katie," Nan continued in a pleading voice, "life is a journey."

Christ with the flipping journey talk again, Katie thought irritably.

"We're all on a journey, and as much as it pains me to say this, because I know it hurts, sweets, I know, but maybe your season with Brad was over . . . it *was* over . . . *is* over. It was time for Brad to move on. He needed something else . . . was ready for the next phase of his journey."

"Really . . . so he had to *fuck* some woman in my bed to get to that next phase. What? Was she his next phase transport? So long, Katie! Hello whorish phase!" Katie said dramatically, throwing her arms into the air.

Well, at least she hasn't walked away from me, Nan thought.

"Now, I admit he went about it all wrong," Nan said. "He should have manned up and divorced you, and then moved on, but it doesn't change the reality that the next stage of his life journey is with someone else. And when a man steps out on a woman, my sweet niece of whom I love with a big piece of my heart—who has been more a daughter to me than a niece—his hearts already gone." Nan grabbed Katie's hand and squeezed it, feeling it tremble. "And as far as Alan goes, well that is one miserable son of a bitch . . . the lowest of the low," Nan snarled in anger.

Katie leaned her head against Nan's shoulder, and whimpered, "God, Nan . . ."

Nan smoothed Katie's hair, calming her as if she were a child again.

"I can't help but think, Katie, that what happened at the cabin was what was gonna happen. The first day Alan met you—the day he interviewed you for your job at his law firm—whether he consciously knew it or not, what happened in his bedroom at the cabin was what he wanted all along. He wanted you," Nan said, her gut telling her that Alan had been planning and hoping Katie would jump at the chance to be his on-the-side for a while.

"But I'm not like that, Nan . . . the whore-around girl," Katie said softly.

"Well, I think he knows that now, and I suspect he's already moved on to find a woman that will be," Nan said in disgust.

Sitting up, Katie wiped the tears of pain, self-pity, and aloneness from her lashes. Curling back onto her lounge chair, she took a deep breath, and said, "Fill 'er up, sweet-sweet, Nan," indicating a refill of her wine glass. She stretched her short frame, crossed her legs at her ankles, and propped her arms on the chair.

"Here you go," Nan said as she handed Katie her glass filled with red wine. "It's natural to be angry—to feel anger. Not to, would mean there was something wrong with your soul, but eventually you have to begin that journey of letting go. To hold on to all this will consume your spirit and destroy you." Nan shared wisdom that is grown only through a great deal of living life.

"But, Nan, they all got away with the things they did to me, and who knows who else they've done these things to. How many other girls have there been, and how many more women will there be? The monsters win." Katie said angrily.

"That's where you're wrong," Nan insisted as she trickled the last of the wine from the box into her glass. "They did *not* win . . . unless you let them destroy you each and every day by the memory of it all, then they *will* win!"

Nan knew Katie hadn't pressed charges for the sexual assault at her boss's cabin, and she understood why, why most women don't, but especially Katie. She'd already experienced how horribly sexual assault cases could go for girls, and women too. But she wanted to make sure Katie knew it was an option.

Nan asked, "Have you considered reporting Alan to the police?"

"Oh, God, Nan!" Katie said, her head whipping toward her aunt. For a moment she looked at Nan as if she had two heads. "Jesus! Remember how that went when I was in high school?"

"I remember. But they *didn't* win. You stepped forward. You challenged, not only those five boys, but also a lot of people who had some very twisted ideas about how girls should be treated, and the lengths they will go to protect miserable, dark spirited boys. They didn't win," Nan insisted.

"But they destroyed me," Katie said. She leaned her head against the headrest of the chair and closed her eyes, shutting out the stars and the rest of the world for a moment.

"They didn't destroy you. You were just broke for a while. I heard a quote once, some Japanese thing. It goes something like this—they say when old pottery's been damaged it becomes more beautiful. They use gold to mend it, making it even more beautiful than it was before."

"Nan . . . that's beautiful," Katie said with a smile. "But I'm afraid I'm not pottery and you can't put me back together with melted gold. It would really hurt," Katie snickered.

"Oh. You know what I mean, sassy britches. It's life. Living life's troubles makes us who we are, makes us beautiful," Nan chided. "And maybe it didn't go as you wanted, as maybe it should have gone, but you stood. You took a stand," Nan said firmly as she watched the war of memories wash over Katie's face.

Her eyes still closed, Katie said softly, "I couldn't this time . . . stand I mean. It was too close to home . . . too similar to last time, in high school. I trusted them, those boys, and Brad . . . Alan. I trusted them not to hurt me. This time, with Alan and then Brad, it was just easier to run away . . . just . . . just run away." She sighed heavily.

"Maybe it wasn't running away," Nan said thoughtfully. "Maybe that *was* your stand. Leaving. It was certainly a clear message to Alan. Maybe the thing with Alan and Brad, maybe it was your inner self telling you it was time for you to begin living instead of un-living. That's what you've been doing, you know. Since all that happened when you came to live with me, when you were in high school, you hid a part of you away. Maybe that part of you is ready to live again," Nan said, and believed. "Katie," Nan said intently as she leaned forward toward her niece. "I know you're writing, and I believe it will cleanse your soul—that it's part of your path—but about what you're writing, I think there's more for you to do with all this. And I think there's more to your journey than thinking about or hanging onto memories about some seriously sexually disturbed, miserably married rich asshole, and your husband breaking his promises to you, and your heart. My heart tells me there is so much more for you. You have a real message for women with your writing. And one day—when you're ready—you'll allow a good man to love you, and you'll be brave enough to love him back."

The two women listened to the air breathe around them for a moment—the leaves rustled, the grass swayed, and frogs called to one another.

Katie rolled onto her side, and shared, "I *have* been writing. Not about the firm. I can't imagine ever writing about that night. I try not to think about it . . . the cabin . . . Alan, and Brad. But I have nightmares about it. When I got home, after driving hours away from what that jerk did to me, I needed the safety of my husband's arms. I did *not* need to arrive home from the cabin to watch my husband put his arms around another woman . . . comfort *her*." Resting her head on her arm, Katie said, "If I ever wrote anything about the law firm, you know, things that happen to women at work, I'd be known as the woman who couldn't take a dirty joke, as I was *sued* by Alan for violating his precious privacy for writing a book about what he did to me. God, it is *so* screwed up!" Katie said in frustration and bitterness. "He's—he's a maggot! That's what Alan is . . . a god damn maggot!"

"Don't give up, sweets. If you do ever decide to write about it, you don't have to write it so they know it's them. Just, well, just write it in a way so they can't sue you." Nan considered her niece, and said, "Christ in heaven, Katie, stop being afraid of the world. Once you stop holdin' on so tight to all that fear, you'll see that the world really isn't that scary. Fear of fear is often scarier than the boogie man. Help yourself, and help other women while you're at it!"

Nan was flaming mad, her anger directed at all the men that slaughtered the spirits of women who couldn't fight back . . . were too broken to fight back.

"What else you got goin' on . . . your gig at the coffee shop, which don't get me wrong, Lynn and I love having you. You've got one book almost done, and I don't even know what it's about. But sweets, you have *got* to find a way of getting this toxic shit cleansed out of your soul. Maybe if you write about it, the pain will flow out onto that computer screen of yours—forever gone from your precious spirit."

Nan watched Katie pucker her brow, and continued, "Katie, maybe this is God or the universe—that's how all the kids are sayin' it these days—opening a new door for you. It closed the old one, saved you from those ugly people. Now it's holding a door open for you . . . just waiting for you to walk through it to your destiny."

Nan turned in her chair and reclined, taking the pressure of the day off her legs.

"Nan, I—I just can't. I'm trying hard NOT to think about it all. My God, writing about it . . . that would mean reliving it. I don't think I have the strength to go through it all again. I just—I just can't, Nan," Katie cried, feeling as if the weight of Alan's body was pressing her down, constricting the air in her lungs.

"I want you to think about something over the next few days," Nan insisted. "Let your spirit connect with what I am about to say . . . find the truth in my words. You've lost so much—your innocence to those boys, in the most violent of way, your father, mother, husband, brother-in-law, and you lost your niece abruptly when she went home to your sister. You lost your sister to her world in Chicago. You lost your job, and all the people you knew, even Alan who you thought was a friend."

Nan turned her head toward Katie, and said softly, "Come on, let's go in and finish our talk. A mosquito is nibbling me. Must be tryin' to suck the wine out of my blood."

Carrying their glasses and the empty box of wine, the women walked toward the glowing light in the kitchen.

Katie settled onto a stool at the island in the kitchen as Nan disposed of the wine box.

"Sweets," Nan said as she pulled out a stool and sat next to Katie, "you've had a lot of loss in your life, and I don't just mean people went away. You also had loss on a spiritual level, as a woman. The loss of yourself to those boys—a woman's core is her spirit, a gift to be given in a loving, gentle environment. It's supposed to be a sacred special time for a woman. That night all those years ago, your most sacred self was brutalized. It wasn't a celebration of sharing part of yourself, a choosing, a saying goodbye as you offered your gift to a man you loved. And you haven't been whole since. Your spirit's mourning this sacred loss because it was lost through violence and not given with love.

"Then, your parents both died of broken hearts. In both situations you were unable to say goodbye, their passing sudden and unexpected, which often happens in life, but in this situation their hearts were battered by the brutality of what happened to you. They left this world broken, and even if you had said the words goodbye, it wouldn't have been a goodbye to the spirits you had known, but some darkness that had taken residence within them. Even your brother-in-law was taken by an act of violence, again, such unrest around his passing."

Nan paused for a moment, and watched Katie's still form.

She took a deep breath, and continued, "Those boys, your parents, your brother-in-law, Emily, Stacey, Brad, and even Alan, all represent something on a spiritual level. All lost due to tragic and traumatic ends. Your spirit won't let go . . . *can't* let go. The spirit of the young girl inside of you—the part of you who has never faced the rapes in high school—can't face saying goodbye to all those people. Katie, if you can face what happened to you—being raped when you were a girl, embrace the younger you, and all that pain, you'll finally be able to say goodbye to the pain from that time in your life. You'll be able to let people in, really let them in, and open up enough to trust, and love. Trust that the world will not only provide the occasional pain, but also pleasures that are part of our earthly existence. You need to open your arms to the part of you that you pushed away that night. Begin the journey of goodbye—let it all, them, go."

It was quiet in the kitchen, but for a cricket that had ventured in from outside.

Gently, Nan continued, "Don't be afraid to live, Katie. *Love* you. That includes loving that scared, lost teenaged girl that was you. You know, it's what your mom and dad would want for you . . . for you to embrace life . . . to *live*."

162

Katie's tears dropped to the surface of the island, and Nan stood up and wrapped her arms around her shoulders, pulling her toward her. She pressed her lips to her niece's forehead.

"I'm afraid, Nan," Katie confessed. "It seems like everyone leaves me, that maybe I'm not worth keeping, or I'm worth so little that I'm not worth *not* hurting. If I was something, you know, someone else, life, and those in it, would love me enough to stop hurting me . . . to stop leaving me."

"I'm not going anywhere," Nan said.

It scared Katie, knowing that Nan was wrong. One day she would leave her as everyone did. Old age had a way of taking people you loved.

Katie looked tenderly at her aunt, examining the small features of her face, so young for a woman in her seventies. She smiled, letting her love be her response, not wanting to say aloud her fear that one day even her aunt would leave her.

"Your parents didn't want to leave you, Katie, and Brad loved you, it was just their time, their time for the next phase of their spirit journeys. And as far as Alan—things aren't always what they seem. We each have our own reality. For you, it was painful and disrespectful what that man did to you . . . what he wanted to do, maybe based on what those boys did to you, maybe because your spirit is older and wiser than his. I think it was wrong and hurtful too, but that's the spirits that *we* are," Nan said, trying to pour her life experience into her words in the hope Katie would see the world through her eyes of aged, wisdom.

Nan watched Katie run her finger along the top of the island, wondering what was going through her mind.

"I'm not excusing Alan, but you have no idea what was going through his mind or his life," Nan said.

Katie interrupted, "Nan! I know all I need to know. Sex! That's it . . . that's the depth of the man."

"Well, maybe that's what he learned when he as a kid, that sex doesn't mean anything. Or, maybe, just maybe he had feelings for you and it exploded out of him that night at the cabin, especially as much drinking that was goin' on, like you said. It was obvious he let you see a side of him he wouldn't normally have shared. And even drunk, on some level, he had to have known he was taking a tremendous risk by touching you . . . letting you know he wanted something more with you. He had a lot to lose that night . . . and I'd say Alan was the one that lost this time," Nan said insightfully.

Speechless, Katie looked up at her aunt and considered all she had just said, and then smiled. She couldn't be all bad, she supposed, not if this beautiful woman was so intent on fabricating ideas to make her feel more than she was. It was true, Katie realized, her mom and dad had not left her, at least not intentionally, and Brad . . . she sighed. Maybe he was meant to move on to someone else. As she sat in the warmth of Nan's kitchen, an idea niggled at her . . . perhaps she had chosen Brad because he was safe, and knowing that, she knew there was someone else for him, and hoped this time he found a woman for more than one season of his life. But Alan, Nan hadn't convinced her that he'd lashed out—hurt her—because he cared. If he really cared, she thought sadly, he would have known she could never give him what he'd wanted from her. No, her gut told her that he was a miserable asshole, just like Dale, and she hoped Karma kicked his ass one day.

24

*

"Whatya have?" Katie asked the man standing at the counter, appearing to be dressed for a day at one of the many golf courses outside of town.

Two weeks had passed since the boxed wine evening, and the things Nan said had settled over her, weaving into her thoughts, and through her memories. After that night, Katie had become stir crazy. She was a social person—loved being around people—and suspected staying hidden away all day, every day, at Nan's house wasn't helping her in the journeying forward process. Since then, Katie had been helping Nan and Lynn at the coffee shop. She'd caught on fast, even picked up the lingo the two older ladies used when taking orders.

Nan hadn't insisted on a structured work schedule for Katie, so she'd created her own. She chose to work the early shift so she could use her afternoons to work out chapters of her book. She took long walks with Hunter, and then shut herself away in her writing room for hours to capture all that was pressing on her mind.

"Here you go!" she said to the man dressed in blue and orange plaid shorts. She handed him a tall cup of steaming hot black coffee. Not very original, she considered as she watched him walk out the door.

Jack had made good on his promise to stop by the coffee shop on his way through town. On most of his visits, he arrived at the coffee shop with his computer bag draped over his shoulder, and ordered a cranberry scone and tall coffee—sitting for hours at his favorite table against a wall out of the way of walking traffic, reviewing legal files and cases. Katie would watch him from the counter, trying to figure him out—figure out who he was . . . figure out who any man really was for that matter. Just what went on in the nasty, tiny minds of men, she wondered as she banged a coffee mug on the counter harder than intended. She was still struggling with distrust and bitterness where men were concerned, and that included, she thought, the man walking toward her with a smile and an empty coffee cup.

"Hey," Jack said as he sauntered toward her.

"Refill?" Katie questioned with a raise of her eyebrow.

"Yeah," he said with a grin. "Your powers of perception are astounding."

"Funny man." Katie smiled. She filled his cup with hot black caffeinated liquid, and then handed it to him.

"Good memory," Jack commented.

"Excuse me?" she said.

"The coffee. You remembered what I was drinking," Jack said easily, with a mischievous twinkle in his eye.

"Oh," Katie said. "I—I guess it's just—just what you said. A good memory."

"So how's the writing going?" Jack asked as he studied her face, wishing he could get behind the uptight, untrusting wall that she'd built around herself.

"Oh, boring stuff. You know how women are . . . the things that go on in our heads. Boring," Katie said.

"No woman or person, for that matter, is ever boring. And you, Ms. Katie, are a fascinating woman," Jack said warmly.

"Get back to work," Katie said as her cheeks burned with embarrassment. "You're holding up caffeine progress. Ralph, here, needs his coffee fix. Isn't that right, Ralph?" Katie joked with one of the coffee shop regulars.

"I don't mind waitin' for my coffee. Sounds like you were havin' a real interestin' conversation," Ralph said, his eyes twinkling with humor as he watched Nan's niece and the man she was trying so hard not to notice. But it was obvious to the regulars that Katie noticed the handsome young attorney, especially considering the fire truck red of her cheeks right now. Love, wasted on the young, he thought as he sighed and grinned.

All the coffee shop regulars were casual kind of small town folks, never in a hurry to get where they needed to go, seemed as if the entire town operated that way. The town of Marion was one of those lazy towns where its residents milled about on the sidewalks checking in on one another—keeping their fingers on the pulse of their neighbors. Everyone knew everyone.

Ralph was a sweetheart, Katie thought with a smile that lit up her face. All right, so there were a few men in the world she could trust, she reflected, such as Nan's old men friends.

"You are such a stinker, Ralph," Katie said, offering him a warm smile.

At the coffee shop, and at Nan's house, Katie had begun to breathe— begun the process of letting go of her old world.

Katie stretched her arms above her head and glanced at the clock on the wall behind the counter. Another half an hour and I think I'll head home, she mused. What to do to busy myself until then, she wondered as she scanned the dining area. Most of the crowd, besides a few regulars, had cleared out. The only occupants at the tables were Janice—a lady who came into the coffee shop almost every afternoon for coffee and Wi-Fi—and Jack. Late coffee shop workday, she considered.

Not the most glamorous job, Katie reflected as she scooped up discarded paper napkins and wiped off empty tables, empty but for the plates, cups and trash left behind by customers. But at least it's peaceful, she thought, happily. Softly, she hummed a soothing tune as she moved from table to table whisking away evidence of the various patrons from the day.

"Oh!" she exclaimed when she bumped into someone, and turning, saw Jack towering over her. "I didn't see you. Sorry."

He placed a hand beneath her elbow to steady her.

"No harm done," he said smiling down at her. "From the sound of the song you were singing, I'd say you were far away, in a nice peaceful somewhere."

It was obvious to Jack that he'd startled her, more than a person should be startled from bumping into someone in a coffee shop. Whatever had her running away from the Weaver firm, he mused, still had her jumpy . . . scared. He smiled a small gentle smile at her.

"You okay?" he asked.

"Yes—of course," she stammered. "I . . . I'm fine." She felt ridiculous and embarrassed that she'd been caught by surprise, and that he knew he'd flustered her. She needed to feel in control of her world, and for a brief moment, it hadn't felt that way.

He dropped his hand. "Okay," Jack said.

Katie realized she was still standing next to him, staring up into his eyes. Giving herself an internal shake, she took a step back, wiped a hand on her green apron, and adopted an air of uncaring attitude. She noticed the computer bag draped over his shoulder.

"Well, you have a good day," Katie said.

Katie heard Nan's voice behind her mumble, "Oh, good grief."

Jack pressed his hand gently to Katie's shoulder, and smiled down at her, wanting to say something, wanting to know what had happened in her life, at the firm to turn her into the skittish woman she was, like so many women he had known, knew. He paused for a moment, and then slowly walked away from her, walked to the door of the coffee shop.

Katie stood rooted to the spot as she watched him walk to the exit of the coffee shop—noticed the ease of his gait, the broadness of his shoulders, and the muscle in his forearm as he reached for the door.

Suddenly, unexpectedly, he turned away from the door, turned in her direction, and walked back across the room toward her. She inhaled sharply, nervously, and fidgeted with a button on her blouse. As he drew closer, Katie looked up into his face, lost in the depth of his eyes.

Jack stopped, close enough to touch her if he'd wanted to. He looked into her upturned face. "Forgot my cell phone," he said quietly. Not turning from her, still looking into her eyes, he leaned toward the table, grasped his cell in his hand, and held it up in the air.

Katie's face burned with embarrassment as he turned and walked back toward the door.

After the door closed behind him, Nan asked, "Now what was *that* all about?"

"Excuse me?" Katie said distractedly, as she walked behind the counter, avoiding Nan's eyes.

"So when are you going to give that boy a chance?" Nan asked.

"Nan, sometimes you make absolutely no sense at all, like now, for instance," Katie said as she placed the rag on the counter.

"That boy's sweet on you," Nan said, grinning. "Such a nice boy, too."

"First of all, he is *not* a boy. And secondly, I think your old age is rattling your brain!" Irritably, Katie considered that surely her aunt was beginning to feel the effects of cognitive decline.

"I felt sparks in this room! And it wasn't because the air is dry in here. It was the sexual friction coming off you two. Seriously Katie, one of these days you're gonna have to lay that shit suitcase down somewhere . . . leave it behind and move on. Let someone in!" Nan said.

"I am," Katie said, and offered her aunt a fake grin. "I let you in."

"That's not what I meant and you know it," Nan said disapprovingly.

Nan shifted her body so Katie couldn't walk away, and asked, "You think women have a shelf life on feeling? That once you become a certain age, that as a woman, you no longer have the right to feel, hurt, or to fear? Never be ashamed that you feel . . . and that some man scared you . . . or that even those *boys* scared you."

"No—No. I am *never* letting anyone back in. I cannot—will not—lose everything again, Nan. I'm not taking that chance. Jesus," she hissed, so Janice, the part-time employee wouldn't hear, "I lost my marriage, my home, and my job . . . I lost *everything*."

"*No*, from where *I'm* standing," Nan said, pointing her finger at Katie, "I'm beginning to see you lost what you needed to so you could gain something better. You just need to *see* it. And you will. When the time's right."

"Ugh, Nan! Where do you come up with this stuff?" Katie laughed. She leaned forward and gave her aunt a tight hug, the woman of un-ending hope. Surely some of that hope was bound to rub off on her eventually, she speculated.

"I'm headed to the house. Do you need me to pick up anything?" Katie asked as she untied her apron.

"Oh, I don't know," Nan mumbled. "Maybe a nice young man so Stu and I can have a double date." She swatted her niece on her behind. "Pick that up for me," Nan joked, and then walked back into the back room.

Closing the door to the coffee shop behind her, Katie entered the muggy afternoon, a smile titling the corners of her mouth, shaking her head at what her aunt had said. Oh, Nan, she thought. Such a romantic . . . in love with the idea of love. *And even if I were ready for love, if it were real . . . if there was actually a man in the world that was capable of something more meaningful than some cheap sex thrill . . . the ink is barely dry on my divorce papers.*

Katie glanced up at the sky before she climbed into the highlander, noticing the dark clouds in the distance. "I need to hurry home if I want to get a walk in before it rains," she said to herself.

"Come on, boy!" Katie said to Hunter. "Let's get going so we can make it back before the rain starts, although a nice cool rain shower would feel good as hot and sticky as it is outside."

Hunter barked, and wagged his tail in response when Katie opened the door leading to the driveway and the muggy afternoon. After her walk, Katie wanted to get in a few hours of writing before Nan got home. Lately she'd been spending entire evenings plucking away at the story she was proud was shaping up nicely.

As she walked down the road away from the house, Katie noticed it was even muggier now than when she'd left the coffee shop, and the sky was gray—no peeks of brilliant blue sky from earlier in the day. Although there was a wind blowing, within minutes the heat and mugginess of the day had her t-shirt clinging to her sweaty body.

As she walked, Katie's thoughts turned to Brad, remembering the day of their wedding. He'd seemed so happy, she reflected, and so had she. Such a solid man, not the type to hang out in bars after work with the guys. No, she thought bitterly, apparently while the guys were at the bar, Brad was hanging out with one of the women at work. Stealing time with the skank during romantic dinners at some infidelity restaurant—the Cincinnati hookup place. She walked faster as she envisioned a dark, secret place in Cincinnati where the extra-marital nasty happened. She shook her head to dispel the memories of the early days with her ex, and thoughts of his cheating.

"Stay out of my head!" Katie shouted.

"Haven't thought about that day in a while," she said to Hunter, "and I won't ever again."

Long grass blew across the road in front of Katie as her thoughts wandered, as they always did during her walks. She shoved her hands in the back of her blue jean shorts pockets and allowed her thoughts to take her.

Lately she'd thought a lot about her senior year in high school, that night . . . the glimpses her mind would allow. As she walked, her mind echoed with the laughter of teenage boys, and the few words she could make out. "You know what you're good for?" the boy had slurred "Fucking. That's all any girl's good for. Girls are lucky, they ain't got nothin' else they gotta to do in life but lay back and take it." Then she passed out again, to the vision of one of the boys that had been to her house when they were small children, above her, and the pain he was causing her. Unconsciously, Katie rubbed her wrist.

She was so engrossed in her thoughts that she hadn't notice that the wind had picked up, and that Hunter was whining at her. The pelting rain brought her thoughts out of the abandoned building in Illinois, and back to the country road in North Carolina. When the cold rain spattered her forehead, she looked around in surprise, getting her bearings . . . looking at the grass in the field to her right swaying crazily in the wind. A crash of thunder made her jump in surprise. Hunter barked.

Let's turn back, Hunter!" Katie shouted over the wind. She turned around in the middle of the road, and began walking against the wind as Hunter jumped around her expressing his urgency to get back to the house.

The wind howled around them, and the rain felt like needles as it stung her arms, and pelted through her peach colored tank top. For half an hour, Katie walked bent into the wind whipped rain, soaked through to her underwear; her tennis shoes disappearing as she stomped through puddles of water. Thunder boomed, lightening cracked in the distance, the wind blew the tall grasses, the branches on the trees, and whipped her hair into her eyes, blinding her. She felt alive—electric! She couldn't remember ever feeling so alive and free.

She stopped along the side of the abandoned road, and closing her eyes, lifted her face to the sky, welcoming the cleansing rain.

It was then, with the wind howling around her, and the rain beating down on her, that she was overcome by a sensation of peacefulness. She felt her father's presence, felt the warmth of his arms as they embraced her, pulled her close.

"Dad," she cried, the wind carrying her words away. "I miss you! I miss you and mom . . . and . . . I'm so sorry I hurt you, that I broke your heart. I'm so sorry," she sobbed.

She stood in the middle of the country road, the wind howling around her, and the rain beating at her body, unfelt as she found comfort in her father's presence. A calm came over her, just as it had when she was a little girl, when her dad hugged all the bad in all the world away. He was there with her . . .

As suddenly as the storm had begun, it ended. Katie opened her eyes and looked up into the sky, watching as a rainbow spread above her head. Rainwater dripped off her hair, skin, and clothes—like a baptism—as she looked up into the sun and the brilliant watercolor washed sky. Her father loved the smell after a rain, and as she sniffed in the scent of the earth, she smelled the scent of his cologne.

"Dad . . ." she said, and smiled. She stood for a few minutes more, her arms hugging her waist—pressed against invisible arms hugging her—then she opened her arms, and let go . . . saying goodbye.

25

Jack leaned his blue jeaned hip against the counter at the coffee shop, and smiled down at Katie. She looked youthful, much younger than her age, in her black shorts, black t-shirt, and green apron that matched her eyes.

"Katie, go to dinner with me, or coffee, or just a walk some night," Jack said in his most convincing voice.

It wasn't the first time he'd asked Katie to dinner, and each time she had created an excuse. She had to help Nan with something, or work on her book, or . . . wash her hair, he thought with a smile. What she didn't realize was that he wasn't going to give up on her. He'd met few women like her. She was a keeper, the kind of woman a man walked with down a leaf covered sidewalk hand in hand, made gentle, and then passionate love with, spent years lost in comfort and love in a garden—shared one another's world.

Was it her imagination, or were his eyes a deeper shade of blue today, like the morning glories in Nan's garden, Katie mused. She blinked.

"I'm sorry—what?" she asked, embarrassed that she'd missed what he'd said. Sighing, she thought, I must be a little stir crazy today, that would explain my lack of focus. She blinked a couple more times, hoping that would clear her head.

"Sorry, I was thinking about . . . um . . . inventory," Katie said. "Nan and Lynn need me to help them do inventory this weekend." Well that was a big fat lie, she thought, as she saw Nan out of the corner of her eye give her a look that meant she'd heard her fabrication.

Grinning, Jack leaned his arms on the counter, making himself comfortable in the unusually slow coffee shop. He was taking it slow with Katie; she was like the skittish ponies he'd known as a teen. Slow, Jack, he thought, go slow with her.

"Coffee, Katie, just a cup of coffee?" Jack asked. "It can even be here." He swooped his arm in an arc towards the mostly empty chairs and tables in Nan and Lynn's coffee shop.

As Katie stared at the handsome man leaning against the counter, features strong, yet boyish at the same time, long sleeved dress shirt rolled casually to his elbows exposing his muscular forearms, she heard her father's voice whisper, as if he were standing right next to her . . . "Don't be afraid to live, Katie." She blinked, and then gulped down her fear.

"Well, technically," she smiled, "we *have* had coffee together," and held up the cup she had stashed behind the counter. She took a sip. "See."

He played along, and said, "Well, true, but I was thinking we could actually sit at a table together while we each drink a cup. Talk, get to know one another better . . . see what's going on in that beautiful head of yours."

"Scary," Nan mumbled, as she walked from behind the counter to clear off a table.

Katie looked after her aunt, shook her head, and said, "Woman, don't you need to clean the library room?"

"No," Nan said sweetly. "It's nice and tidy in there. It's what's happening in this room I'm worried about."

"Just coffee," Jack said, and grinned. "Something to eat. I know this quaint little restaurant right here in town . . ."

"Okay," she whispered. Then louder said, "I'll have dinner with you."

"Tomorrow night?" he asked, watching as Katie stood a little taller. He knew a stance of defiance and bravery when he saw one. It was a stance he'd seen in girls when he was a teen . . . the sign they weren't giving up . . . they weren't letting life beat them. She was fighting, he noticed proudly.

"I'll pick you up at Nan's, and then we'll go to the little Italian place across from the town square," Jack said gently, with a kind smile.

Panicking, she said quickly, "I'll meet you."

"That's fine. Say . . . seven?" Jack responded easily, with an encouraging smile.

"Sounds great," she said breathlessly.

"I'll see you then," he said, trying to appear calmer and cooler than he felt.

"I'll see you." Katie fiddled with the hem of her black t-shirt, and watched as he walked to the door of the coffee shop.

After the door to the coffee shop closed behind him, Katie released the breath she'd been holding, and jumped when Nan said, "I'm proud of you girl." Nan gave her niece's shoulder a tight squeeze.

"Jeez, Nan," Katie said in a rush. "It's just dinner."

"I was afraid I was gonna have to knock you from the nest," Nan said under her breath, as she walked away from the counter. She walked toward the window, and stood watching as Jack drove away.

"What's that you say?" Katie asked.

"Oh . . . nothin'," Nan replied sweetly.

The next night, dressed in a yellow sundress made of soft gauzy fabric, a three-quarter length sleeved sweater covering her shoulders, and her feet slipped into a pair of white flip flop casual sandals, Katie walked nervously into the Italian restaurant where she'd agreed to meet Jack. The restaurant was located at the town square, in the center of town, just a few blocks down from the coffee shop. It was one of the nicest places to eat in Marion, with an outside dining area, a patio with elaborate flowering plants—flowers trailing over the sides—placed about, creating a garden feel. The air was heavy with perfumed flowers and it was there that he was waiting for her.

Jack looked handsome in a khaki-colored slacks and a light blue colored short-sleeved shirt, casual with one of the buttons on his shirt open, Katie noticed. He stood when he saw her walk into the garden area, and then walked toward her. Placing his hands gently on her elbows, he leaned forward and brushed his lips against her cheek.

"You look lovely," Jack smiled admiringly.

"You two," Katie said, and then blushed as she realized the words that had slipped out of her mouth.

Jack's eyes twinkled, and he chuckled, as she stammered, "I-I mean, you look nice."

"I was fine with looking lovely," he chuckled.

Gallantly, he pulled the heavy wrought iron chair out for her, and then scooted her and the chair in closer to the table, a comfortable distance so she had room to cross her legs, and swing her purse onto the back of the chair.

After they ordered wine, Katie cleared her throat, and fiddling with the silverware near her, she said, "Tell me something about yourself."

"What would you like to know . . . you read my resume," he smiled.

Katie laughed as she realized how silly she seemed. She knew more about Jack than many women knew about men they dated initially, at least professionally, and academically.

"Touché," she said as she raised her glass.

"So you want to know about Jack the human being, not just Jack the evil attorney," he said. He smiled, shifting his eyebrows in a mock villain fashion.

It wasn't in Katie's nature to be so forward. Caution was the underlying component of who she was. While she was trying to do what Nan had suggested, and what her parents would want—be brave—not afraid to live, she still needed to embrace life on her terms and that meant being sure who Jack was, as sure as she could be.

"Alright," Jack said as he leaned back in his chair. Getting comfortable, he rested his ankle on his thigh, and draped a long arm across his knee. "But this is a two way street here . . . you have to give a return on this conversation. Deal?"

Smiling, Katie shook her head in the affirmative, not sure exactly what she would be able to tell him. What she could say about her past that wouldn't scare him off, she pondered. She doubted the big man attorney had ever personally known a woman who had experienced what she had. Not possible, she thought as she stared at his crisp shirt, her gaze travelling to his brown casual shoes. *Not possible,* her eyes returning to his handsome smiling face watching her intently.

Katie took a sip of her wine, ready to hear his story of wealth and excess as a child, assuming his parents were people of consequence, his father an attorney like he was, his mother a homemaker, or perhaps an attorney as well. She suspected his childhood home was a three story min-mansion, and already knew he had attended the best schools—the best his parent's money could buy.

"Let's see," Jack said as he looked at a point above Katie's head. "Like you, I have a mother and father . . ." He paused for a moment, and took a sip of his wine, and then he began again. "For several years," he said, "as a teen, I lived at a private school."

As I suspected, Katie thought. With a smile she said, "One of those fancy kinds in Europe?"

"Well," he said as he gave her a measured look, "it wasn't real fancy. I'm sure there were other schools that were fancier." He tipped his glass of wine back and gulped down the remainder of the contents, then continued. "It was a children's home. The school I lived in for a few years, was a home for unwanted kids." He looked into his empty glass, then looked up, and smiled, his smile not quite reaching his eyes.

Katie felt as if the air had left her lungs as she stared at him, speech-less, not knowing what to say. In her wildest imaginings, she had never considered that Jack's life had ever been different from any other spoiled rich attorney, and the childhood that created them. She felt like an ass for the way she'd treated him, for the assumptions she'd made because he was an attorney, for assuming he'd had the same beginnings as Alan and many of the other men at the Weaver law firm.

Raising her eyebrows, unable to meet his eyes, she said, "Oh my God, Jack. I—I honestly don't know what to say to that. I'm sorry. I mean, why, if you don't mind, I mean, if you can share," she stammered as her cheeks turned a bright red.

"Katie," Jack said as he leaned forward and covered one of her hands with his much larger one. "It's okay. It was a long time ago, and it really wasn't so bad. Kid's homes get a bad rap, but they're really not that bad," he assured her, trying to calm the shock from her eyes. "I was just one of those kids . . . like thousands of other kids who had parents that couldn't take care of them, should never have had kids." He sighed and continued, "My dad was a druggy. Other kids in class were playing ball with their dads, but my life with my dad was a little different. I spent a lot of time, when I was a boy, helping my mom put my dad to bed after he passed out from using."

Jack took a deep breath, and said, "When my dad wasn't passed out drunk or from using, he was angry . . . shouting and knocking my mom around. She ended up in the emergency room a couple times from broken bones—a broken nose, ribs—but she never left him. Most of the time we didn't have food. The neighbors knew how it was, and sometimes they'd feed me," he said, his thoughts far away in a small, dirty apartment in Northern Kentucky. "Anyway, I was twelve years old when my dad died of a heroin overdose. And my mom wasn't much better than my dad was. She didn't use drugs, but she was an alcoholic, and after dad died, she attached herself to whatever scumbag she could find at the bar she hung out at. She cycled through half dozen men in the year after dad died." Jack gestured to the small scar by his right eye, and said, "This was a Christmas gift from one of them. My face caught his beer bottle." He smiled to take the sting out of his words, and childhood reality.

"Jack," Katie said sadly. She envisioned him as a little boy—the little boy he might have been—enduring so much sadness, so different from her life at his age. She was disgusted with herself for making assumptions about him for no other reason than he was an attorney. She had lumped him into a similar category as Alan and Dale, believing that he'd been some rich kid—spoiled and without human capacity to care for other human beings. It was an eye opener for her—that was for sure—realizing that all attorneys did not necessarily start out as spoiled children without a care in the world.

"It's okay, Katie," Jack assured her. "You didn't know. It's not common knowledge. I made a decision long ago—for professional reasons—to hide the details of my childhood from people, to protect me. Most people have pre-conceived ideas based on prejudice about kids that come from addicts. Most people think, because of well-intentioned people, that kids that come from addicts will grow up to be addicts themselves . . . and they write them off. But I wanted more. It just burned in my belly to make something of myself. But I knew if anyone found out about my parents, and that I lived in a children's home for a few years—not because I had done anything wrong, or had been a bad kid, because I wasn't—that I'd never make it. I never would have made it as far as I have. It was tough being a foster kid—trying to prove to everyone that I was as good as other kids, prove that I was worth something."

He rubbed his chin, and glanced at Katie. He saw the intensity, like embers, smoldering in her eyes.

"There just were not a lot of foster homes that wanted teenagers," he explained. "It took two years to finally find a family that would take me in. They were great people. My mom—yeah, I call her mom," he said, when Katie looked at him quizzically. "Mom was a high school teacher and dad worked at a factory as a manager in the computer department. They couldn't have kids of their own—loved kids—so they took in foster kids. I was their last one. When they accepted me, we clicked. I lived with them throughout high school. They gave me a safe place, a quiet place, where I could study, and soon I caught up with my classmates, and then I passed them all up, graduating valedictorian. My foster parents taught me how to trust that life wouldn't always hurt me, that there would be bad times but good times would always follow."

Katie was dumbfounded—speechless.

"I learned a lot while I lived at the children's home," Jack continued with a painful expression on his face. What he remembered still hurt him. "The kids at the home . . . we were all we had. We got to know each other pretty well, and some of their stories, their lives, were the stuff of night-mares. You can't imagine," he said as he slumped his shoulders, and folded his hands together in front of him, as if in prayer. "Some of the kids—boys and girls—had been sold for sex by their parents. One kid had been three-years-old when she'd been sold."

He clenched his jaw for a moment, and looked down at the table, as his memories took him back in time to the home, to his brothers and sisters of the state.

Placing her fingers over her mouth, as if to hold back a cry, Katie closed her eyes as her stomach rolled and her eyes burned with tears for the pain she felt for those children, and for Jack. She swallowed, took a deep breath, opened her eyes, and examined Jack, seeing him differently than just moments ago . . . with compassion, and reached her hand across the table and touched his hand.

Jack was startled by the warmth on his hand, and looked up, and then over at Katie.

"I didn't tell you any of this, Katie, so you'd pity me," he said with a sad smile. "That's the last thing I want from anyone."

Embarrassed that she'd hurt him, Katie began to extract her hand from his, but he grasped her hand, and held it gently.

"I just want you to know, that while I don't know what it's like to have lived through what you have, I do understand pain, longing, and loss, and—and," Jack stammered, "I would *never* hurt you, Katie."

Katie reached over and lightly touched her fingertips to the top of his hand, his hand now sandwiched between both of hers. She was surprised by what she was about to admit.

"I believe you, Jack." She bent her head. Her heart felt heavy as she said, "God, I feel like such a jerk."

"No. Don't feel that way," he said. Gently, he squeezed her hands. "You had no idea, and even now, it doesn't change what *you* went through. My past does not impact what happened to you at all. We each have our own pasts that have shaped us, and I like to think it makes us the kind people that we are. Meeting all the kids at the home, and even the things that happened with my own parents, shaped me, gave me a passion to make an impact on the world. It's why I opened my law practice in Asheville, and am focused on women's issues—why I give my time to help human trafficking organizations."

A light clicked on in Katie's mind as she groaned, "Oh. Now it makes sense—why you declined Alan's job offer and all the other job offers." She pulled her hands away from Jack's grasp and pressed them to her burning cheeks. "I am so awful," she groaned. "Can you forgive me for being such a bitch to you?" she asked.

"Katie," Jack said firmly, and tugged her hands from her cheeks, weaving his fingers loosely through hers. "No apology needed."

Smiling at her, he gave her fingers an encouraging squeeze.

"Now . . . your turn," he said.

Leaning back on her chair, Katie bit her lip, and tucked a foot beneath her. The memories from high school rushed through her mind like a raging river after a thunderstorm. Fidgeting, she smoothed the hem of her sundress, then tucked a strand of hair behind her ear as she collected her thoughts.

"Like you," she said, as she glanced up at him, "I have, had . . . have . . ." She sighed, and started again. "I grew up in a small town in northern Illinois with my mom, dad and little sister."

For a moment she smiled as memories of the bedtime stories her mother used to read to her and her sister, and the hugs from her father as she impatiently tried to pull away to run outside to play with the neighborhood kids, played through her mind.

"I was lucky," she remembered with a ghost of a wistful smile tugging at the corners of her lips. "I had a beautiful family."

Jack, with his attorney's mind for detail, caught the 'had' in her statement, and leaned forward on his chair listening attentively.

"Like most kids who had a childhood like mine, I took my family and my life for granted, expecting my family to always be there, you know, because nothing bad ever happened to us, or really in our town. Then, one day my world changed . . . one night." She shuddered as if the fingers of a cold wind or a ghost from day's sadness past had touched her. Her flesh crawled with goose bumps.

Wanting to touch her, to let her know she was safe, Jack raised his hand to reach out, then thought better of the idea, fearful she might bolt like one of the ponies at the home tended to do. He forced himself to sit back on his chair, giving her room for her memories.

"It was the perfect summer night," she shared with a small smile. Absently, she picked up her almost empty glass of wine and ran a finger along the rim. "A friend was throwing an end of the summer party, celebrating the beginning of our senior year. Most of the kids I had known since first grade were there. Susie's parents were there, at first, cooking hamburgers and hot dogs on the grill for us, like parents do at parties like that," not realizing that for many kids, like Jack, her life was a foreign concept, their lives so very different.

"Just a bunch of kids horsing around, playing yard games, giggling— you know, just kid stuff," Katie remembered. "Then the parents left and the tone of the party changed. Some college kids showed up and brought alcohol with them, lots of beer and hard liquor, stuff older kids had bought for *them*. I guess it had all been planned . . . the beer and older kids showing up, but I hadn't been in on that planning committee," she said sarcastically. "It's not that I'd never drank before," Katie confessed. "I'd sipped beer before," she said, and wrinkled her nose, remembering.

Jack smiled at her youthful comment and attitude.

"Anyway," she sighed. "All I drank that night was bottled water. But about an hour after Susie's parents left, I started feeling sick . . . dizzy. The world was spinning. I thought I was going to be sick, you know, throw up. I had gotten a ride to the party with my best friend, but one of the boys we knew offered to drive me home. Nice kid . . . I thought he was a nice boy," she reflected softly. "By the time we walked to his car, he had to help me walk because I was so out of it. It was as if I had lost control of my body, my legs barely able to hold me up, and my vision was blurred. He helped me into the car. It was dark and everything was foggy, not crisp, like it should have been. I saw other boys I knew in the car. Nick helped me get into the back of the car, where three of the boys were sitting. I can still hear the laughing . . . their voices," she said as if dazed. She raised her hand to her ear and then brushed her hair back.

Jack saw the waitress approach and he waved her away, knowing this was not the time for Katie to be interrupted from her deep thoughts.

"The noise . . ." Katie said, closing her eyes. "God, the noise in the car . . . the music was so loud—the laughing and shouting." Opening her eyes, Katie leaned her elbows on the table, and rubbed her shoulders, trying to rub away the pain her body remembered. Sitting up straight, unconsciously she rubbed her wrist and continued in a rush. "The boys that I'd known since childhood, had drugged me and then they . . . they took me to an abandoned building and raped me, each one of them. They held me down . . . and raped me."

She touched her lips with the fingers of her left hand, and stared unseeing in front of her. The face of the boy that had told her what girls were good for, his face fuzzy because of the drug they'd given her, and his voice sounding as if it were an echo—a never ending echo, rippled through her mind.

"I remember the smell of them and the taste of them as . . ." She shook her head slightly as tears burned her eyes at the memory. "They broke my jaw," she said as she placed the palm of her hand against the side of her face." She paused for a moment.

Never in his life had Jack felt as angry as he did at that moment, at the same time wanting to pull Katie into his arms and take the bad memories of the world away, keep her safe. He wiped at the tears hanging on his lashes with the back of his hand, and sniffed.

Looking away, she said, "They tore me up inside." She ran her fingers through her hair, and said softly, "I had to be stitched up . . . you know . . . inside." Blinking, she exhaled and continued, "When they were done with me, they dumped me, bleeding, half naked, with beer poured all over me, and . . . and . . ." She raised her hand as if warding off an attacker. "They were all over me, they had . . ." She couldn't say what they had done, instead she said, "They dumped me a few houses from my house. Dad found me the next morning." Wiping at the tears that blurred her vision, she said, "My dad found me, bloody . . . and they had taken some of my clothes . . . so he found me almost naked."

"Jesus, Katie," Jack exploded as he ran a hand over his hair. He sat back looking up at the top of the umbrella that was sheltering them from the evening sun. Jack had known girls at the home that had been raped, had listened to their stories, and knew that the rape was just half the battle. Court proceedings also caused trauma to the victims—a different way of being raped again . . . emotional rape.

"I pressed charges, and all those people I thought were my friends turned on me saying I should have kept my mouth shut. I was no one to them, but the boys, well, they were the star football players from school. People were more concerned for the boys that raped me—about their futures, about their sports scholarships, than me, their victim."

Katie was quiet for a moment as anger rippled through her.

"Not one person supported me except for my family. *God* . . . it was like being raped all over again. I mean, not—not physically, but—to have all those people I knew all my life shouting at me, calling me names like 'slut' and saying I wanted it, and that I actually let them do those things to me. I had never experienced such cruelty in my life . . . and mom and dad, it broke their hearts, first having those boys do that to me. I think daddy blamed himself because somehow he thought he should have been able to protect me from every bad thing in the world. But how were we to know . . . how can a girl know all the bad stuff and bad people waiting for her?"

Katie looked at Jack, and laughing bitterly, she said, "We lost all our friends. Our house was vandalized. Someone smeared shit on my car." She explained, "I used to park my car in the driveway at my parent's house, and one night someone smeared shit on the windshield and the doors. And dead, bloody animals were put on our porch. After that, Mom and dad moved me to Kentucky to stay with Aunt Nan to get away from it all. But they stayed there . . . in that town." Katie paused and shook her head . . . remembering it all.

"All five boys . . . all the boys there that night that raped me, each of them were sentenced to one year probation . . . just one year of probation because of their age. They were all under the age of eighteen."

Katie inhaled deeply as she tried to calm the shakiness that had come over her. She exhaled.

"I was eighteen when my dad died of a broken heart, because he couldn't protect me," she said. "Couldn't protect me from something that should never happen to any girl or woman. After dad died, a lot of the life left my mom. She was just never the same after all that happened. A few years after my dad died, she passed away. She slipped on the basement stairs. Fell down most of the steps and hit her head." With a big sigh, Katie said, "And that's *my* childhood."

"God, Katie. I want to apologize for all men on this planet, for what happened to you. No girl or women should ever have to endure that. We live in such a sick society, where men think that brutalizing women make them men. It doesn't. It makes them monsters." He shook his head and leaned forward on his chair. "You're so strong, Katie, such an amazingly strong woman for being able to journey through all that, and be here, now."

"Oh, I'm not that strong, not really," Katie stated. "It's not as if I took a stand and vowed to kick some legal ass. I was broken, and part of me will always be broken by what they—those boys and the town—did to me. Not so strong." Katie sighed heavily, and shook her head dispelling the webs of memories. "What do you say we order something to eat? You didn't ask me to dinner to hear me whine about my childhood!" she exclaimed.

Knowing she needed to put her memories aside, Jack picked up the menu, and with no appetite, made a quick selection.

An hour later, Katie and Jack left the restaurant.

"Walk with me?" Jack asked, wanting to keep Katie with him a while longer.

"Sure," she said as she smiled up at him.

It had been difficult to share what she had with Jack, Katie pondered, but sharing with Jack had seemed so natural, maybe because of the childhood he'd lived. If there was a man that could connect with her about pain and loss—understand the darkness of those days—it was Jack, she realized.

As they walked down the sidewalk—past shops glowing with evening light, restaurants, and other couples—their hands brushed together. They spent a half an hour walking off their meal, and then found themselves standing in front of a majestic water fountain—backlit by bright light, water spewing high in the air. Mist from the fountain cooled their warm skin.

"Wish?" Jack asked as he pulled a coin from his pocket.

"A wish," she grinned as she took the coin from his fingers. "A wish . . . okay. I've got it!" She grinned mischievously, and tossed the coin high in the air, losing sight of it as it fell into the lighted spray of water.

Raising an eyebrow, he asked, "Your wish was . . .?"

"Now you know I can't tell you. It won't come true," she kidded.

With her hand tucked into his arm, the couple walked back the way they had come, laughing and making small talk about silly things.

"How 'bout that coffee?" Jack asked, as they walked past a small shop that served sandwiches and cheap coffee.

Smiling, she said, "Sure. Just don't tell Nan I went in here," gesturing toward the small eatery.

Jack laughed heartily as he followed her into the restaurant.

Two cups of coffee later, Katie told Jack why she had left the Weaver law firm. As he listened, he considered, it was even worse than he had suspected. Anger broiled inside him just below the surface, for a second time that night, at all she had endured at the hands of men.

"Sometimes I think I blew it all out of proportion, you know—Alan wanting me to have sex with him on that retreat. I'm not stupid," she smiled shyly. "I know people all across America are having affairs, having sex with their boss in his office, or in board rooms, or with co-workers. But—oh—I don't know. I guess I just wasn't in the mood!" she joked.

"Not everyone, Katie," he commented, grimly. "Not everyone is doing the wild thing at the office, and not all bosses are miserable excuses for human beings, expecting their employees—trying to force employees—to participate in that behavior with them. But you're right, there are plenty of them out there that need to be taken down. Those types of bosses, men like Alan Weaver, need to be fired *and* sued."

Rolling her eyes, and shaking her head, Katie laughed.

"Ugh! This is the first time I've been able to joke about what happened the night at the retreat. It wasn't funny—it still isn't. But as often as women are attacked at work, sexually, I wonder if I should just get over myself and adopt the attitude that, it is what it is. There's nothing I can do about it. Being devastated doesn't change it or make it better. I just don't know how to just . . . just be okay with it. As far as having sex with Alan, Jack, I don't want to be one of those people that screw around on their spouses." Shaking her head and smirking, she said, "I guess I'm just not as fun as a lot of people in the workforce, and why," she laughed, wryly, "I am *not* part of the popular crowd!" She waved her hand in an arc indicating the absence of a large crowd of friends.

"Well, I'm right there with you," Jack said. "And no! You did *not* blow what happened at the firm out of proportion. Men like Alan, are scum. They prey on women, and keep hammering away until they find one weak enough to give themselves away. Scum," he repeated.

"No woman should ever have to put up with what you have, as a young girl, or as a woman at the Weaver firm. Everyone deserves, and should expect to be treated decently," Jack said sincerely.

"Sometimes I wonder if I did the right thing by leaving," Katie said thoughtfully, "if instead I should have stuck it out. It's not going to be different anywhere else. Men are men, and companies are companies, just different faces and names."

"No. You did the right thing. *I* think anyway, you did the right thing by leaving," Jack assured her. "Maybe that was part of what you were *supposed* to experience on your life journey, to learn that it's okay to let go. You were supposed let go of the bad, and journey forward to something better . . . something wonderful." Gently he took her fingers in his, and said, "You deserve so much better."

"Thanks," she said with a smile as she leaned forward on the orange bench seat. "For tonight. It's been nice. But, I should warn you about something. Be straightforward with you. With all this talk about sex, I don't want to put ideas in your head . . . give you the wrong idea."

Jack shook his head as he considered the beautiful woman sitting across the table, and smiled. He had his work cut out for him, he realized, before she let down her very thick walls, and gifted him her trust.

"I need you to know that I'm not having sex with you," she stated seriously. "I needed to put that out there." She clasped her hands primly on the table, shrugged her shoulders, and smiled. "Not happening . . . no matter how cute you are."

"Katie, Katie. Who said I was interested in having sex with you. Maybe you're not my type," he joked.

"I—I just. No one!" she laughed, thinking how silly she was. As if Jack would be interested in her in that way.

"Hey, kids," the waitress said as she stood looking down at them. "Sorry to break up your evening like this, but I got to get home. We've been closed for half an hour."

"Oh!" Katie exclaimed, and looked down at her watch and read, eleven-thirty. "I didn't realize it was so late. I'm so sorry."

"Time flys when you're in love, don't it?" the lady said as she smiled and walked toward the counter.

"No—I," Katie said after the woman, then smiled and shook her head. "Old people," she grinned at Jack. "I swear."

After leaving a generous tip, Katie and Jack walked toward the door, saying goodnight to the waitress.

"Have a good night," the lady said with a smile.

Jack looked over his shoulder at the lady and offered her a grin.

"Such a nice young man," the lady said to the door as it closed behind Jack and Katie.

Twining their fingers together, the couple walked the five-minute walk together to Katie's highlander. They paused on the sidewalk in front of her vehicle, neither ready to end the evening. Jack pulled Katie's hand up toward his chest. Looking down at her delicate fingers, he pulled her hand to his lips, and brushed the back with his lips, as she gazed up into his face.

"Goodnight, Katie," he said, his voice husky and deep.

"Goodnight," she whispered.

He stood on the sidewalk, his hands in his front pockets like a little boy, as she slid onto the driver's seat. Katie rolled her window down, smiled shyly at him, and started the engine.

"You know," he said causally. "It's supposed to be a nice day tomorrow. Perfect picnic weather."

"You don't say," she teased.

"Feel like hanging out with the picnic ants, maybe pick up some chicken, something casual, say around . . . four o'clock?" he asked hopefully.

Katie squinted at Jack, as if she were giving great consideration to a picnic.

"I love picnic ants," she said. "And I happen to be free at four tomorrow."

"Would you like to meet me? About fifteen minutes from here there's a beautiful park with hiking trails. Half way between here and Asheville or, maybe I could pick you up at your house?" he asked.

"I'll be ready at four," she said with a smile.

Jack watched as Katie pulled away from the curb, watched until he could no longer see the tail lights of her vehicle, then grinning like a school boy, he walked to his car and drove back to the condo he was renting in Asheville.

26

⁓

"Well, Hunter, what do you think?" Katie asked as she looked down at the yellow lab. Katie had one bare leg tucked beneath her on the wicker-cushioned chair, as a light breeze cooled her skin. She had cast off her navy blue flip-flops under the small glass table on the large wraparound porch hours ago, when she'd begun reading her completed manuscript for the last time. Absently, she tucked a stray tendril of her hair, blown free from the ponytail snugged high on top of her head, behind her ear. A mechanical pencil was pressed against her lips as she considered the manuscript she had spent the last few months writing. Many tears had been shed during the creation of the manuscript. She had literally blown through several boxes of tissues during the writing of most of the chapters.

"It's good," Katie said with a satisfied smile. She caressed the title page of her manuscript and sighed.

Several hours later, as she sat in the library room at the coffee shop, Katie reviewed her manuscript again while she sipped a cup of hot green tea.

"So, now what?" Nan asked from her position behind the couch.

"Hmm?" Katie mumbled, as she flipped a page.

"What's next . . . you know . . . with your book?" Nan asked.

"I'm not sure," Katie admitted.

"Are you gonna send it off to one of those high-falutin' publisher people?" Nan asked.

Smiling, Katie said, "Nan, I'm a nobody. No one will publish my work." Leaning back on the couch, she said, "It was a waste of time writing this."

"Well do it yourself then," Nan insisted. "You're smart. You got a degree. Those words of yours are meant to be read, Katie. Figure it out— how to publish it. Do it!"

"Do it, huh," Katie laughed. "Says the most confident woman on the planet."

As she flipped another page Katie mused, *'do it' . . . why not? I'm an intelligent woman—educated—with all the resources I need, she considered. I've got a computer, internet access and a little money set aside. How difficult could it be?*

"And speaking of your fella," Nan said, with a wicked gleam in her eye.

"What—what are you saying back there?" Katie turned toward her aunt and watched her dust a bookshelf. "What are you saying back there?"

"I was talking about your fella," Nan said slyly.

"Nan, I don't have a fella," Katie grinned. "And we weren't talking about Jack. We were talking about publishing my book, silly!" Oh, that aunt of mine, Katie thought. What was up with the old folks in town trying to pair everyone off, she pondered, as she turned back to the pages she was holding.

Sliding onto the couch next to Katie, Nan said, "We never had a chance to talk about your picnic date."

"Not much to tell," Katie said, not looking up from the page she was pretending to read. "It was a lovely day. The chicken we picked up at a restaurant on the way was yummy and so were the rolls. Coffee . . . delicious. We went on a two-hour hike through the forest and . . . yup, that's about it."

"Has he tried to kiss you yet," Nan asked with a grin.

"Oh my heavens, Nan!" Katie exclaimed as she flopped her manuscript and pencil onto the coffee table in front of her. "You are impossible, lady!" Katie laughed as she looked at her aunt who was putting on an innocent act.

"Well, if you must know," Katie sputtered, "he kissed my forehead."

"Wow!" Nan said with a chuckle. "You two are just moving right along, aren't you? Kind of like a pair of snails."

"Sorry I don't have a rated-R moment to share with you!" Katie laughed.

Lynn walked into the room and watched her old friend, and Katie, as they laughed until they wiped at the tears in their eyes. Now this, Lynn thought, was what she liked to see . . . her girls happy.

"Quiet down in here," Lynn said, feigning seriousness. "Customers are starting to complain about all the noise."

27

~

"So how's publishing coming along," Jack asked as he held out his hand to help Katie climb over an overgrown tree root blocking the hiking path.

Grasping his hand, Katie climbed over the root—twigs cracking under her hiking boots—and huffed with the effort. Sweat trickled between her shoulder blades. It was an unseasonably warm fall day and she was glad she'd shoved a water bottle into the back pocket of her blue jeans. She'd stripped off her t-shirt half an hour ago, and was now wearing just a tank top over her sports bra.

"Good," she grunted.

The path became wider, and evened out. She caught up and walked beside him.

"The most difficult part of all this," she said as she waved her hand in the air as if swatting away a fly, "was editing my manuscript. Fifty times . . . at least!"

"Nothing worthwhile is ever easy," Jack said as he looked over at his lovely hiking buddy. He was pleased that she was able to keep up with him on even the most difficult trail.

They had fallen into Sunday afternoon hiking jaunts at the park where they had their first picnic together. For Jack, he could not think of any way he would rather spend his time—Katie next to him surrounded by nature, the birds singing, a light breeze, and the sun catching in his eyes every so often through the trees.

Feeling a sweaty nasty mess, and knowing she must look like one, Katie looked up at Jack and grinned.

"You really are just that half full glass kind of guy aren't you?" she observed.

Stopping abruptly, halting Katie in the middle of the path, Jack reached for her hand and pulled her toward him. She allowed him to pull her close. He leaned down, and as he pressed his lips against her warm, soft lips, Jack thought . . . the glass to your water.

Wrapping her arms around his neck, Katie pulled closer, and with an urgency that surprised her, she reached up and pressed a hand to the back of his head, pulling him to her, her lips hungry for his. His tongue teased hers, and then he consumed her, she feeling as if a wave was taking her. Long moments later, shaky, his breath hot on her neck, Katie pulled away. He held her to steady her. She looked up into his eyes, lost in the intensity and depth of the sea of blue, as he returned her gaze just as lost, swimming in the depths of her jade colored eyes.

She slid her arms down to his waist and snuggled into him as his arms tightened around her and he nuzzled into her. His hands explored the limited access he had to her softness—the water bottle falling to the ground—and she responded with a moan.

Katie pulled away, passion making her eyes a shade darker. Jack grabbed her hand, pulling her to him for one last tender kiss. Then, hands clasped—water bottle forgotten—they turned toward the path. Walking hand-in-hand they continued down the path, listening to the sounds of fall around them.

That evening, as the day's sun began its decent, Jack began the drive back to Marion.

"Do you want to shower, and then grab a bite to eat?" he asked Katie.

"Sure. That sounds great," she agreed.

"I'll drop you off at *your* place so you can shower and then I'll run home and shower. Meet you back at your house in an hour?" he asked.

Jack found that he'd been losing a lot of time driving back and forth from Asheville to Marion to see Katie, and while a thirty-five minute drive wasn't a great deal of time, with his legal caseload—working sometimes 60 to 80 hours a week—it did make a difference, especially when he was making the trip with increased frequency. He had contacted a real estate agent with instructions to find a house within five minutes of Nan's home. If he had a house near Katie, he reasoned he could work some hours out of his home office, and take breaks for dinner, or weekend afternoons to see her. He'd been pleasantly surprised when within a week he'd received a call from the realtor about a house in the country, just minutes from Nan's.

An hour later, Katie and Jack were dressed in jeans, long sleeved shirts, boots, and jackets, the typical fall wear for a casual evening in North Carolina. The fall season in North Carolina was perfect for outside activities, just warm enough that a jacket was not necessary in the afternoon, and cool enough in the evenings to cuddle up before a fireplace. Katie had been pleasantly surprised when Nan had dug out a couple of boxes from high school she'd saved. Memories Katie had left behind. But as Katie sorted through an old box of clothes, she found there were a few good memories, such as an old pair of brown leather cowboy boots, scuffed and worn from wear. With a smile, Katie thought, the boots were a part of her that needed to be reclaimed.

A change in their dinner plans had occurred when Katie arrived home after hiking that afternoon. Instead of a casual dinner date, Jack and Katie were spending the evening at Nan's coffee shop with many of the other locals and tourists, at an art and wine tasting night with tasty snacks included. When they arrived, classical music was playing in the background to a large crowd, all three rooms filled with regulars and tourists enjoying a night of wine, and meeting local artists.

"Glad you could make it!" Lynn shouted from across the room.

Katie waved at Lynn, and with Jack's hand in hers, walked toward her.

"Awe, aren't they cute?" Nan gushed like a proud mom, into Lynn's ear.

"They sure are," Lynn responded with a grin.

"Hi, guys," Katie beamed.

"Ladies," Jack said with a smile as he bent first toward Nan and then Lynn, brushing his lips across their cheeks.

"Oh, *you!*" Lynn blushed.

A half hour later, standing in the library room sipping on a coke, Jack smiled at Katie.

"I got sidetracked this afternoon when we were talking about publishing," he said. "So how's the world of publishing?"

Blushing, Katie looked up at Jack, and then looked away, still embarrassed by her reaction on the trail that afternoon.

"Good!" she exclaimed. "Who knew publishing would be so easy? I love writing, getting lost in the story, especially knowing the story I wrote will help a lot of young girls find their way, but I was surprised at how much I enjoy the business aspect of writing. The publishing part. It's not that difficult," Katie said.

Jack smiled, hearing the passion in her voice, and watched the animated manner in which she shared her new venture.

"The creative process of selecting designs for the front and back cover of the book, and the design for the inside of the book. I had no idea there were so many details that went into creating a book. Then the nuts and bolts of the process . . . the ISBN number, setting the price and availability for various channels." Seeing the quizzical expression on Jack's face, Katie explained, "A channel is where the book is available. My books are available online. As the publisher, I choose who has access to purchase my books. Not only can a reader order my book on the internet but bookstores can too, and I have it set up so that bookstores in different countries can buy my books and stock it in their stores. My book can travel around the world!" she beamed.

His heart swelled with pride as he heard the excitement in her voice and saw the sparkle in her beautiful eyes. Wrapping an arm around her waist, he pulled her close, and kissed her forehead.

"Katie, you amaze me," Jack said, his voice thick with emotion.

Katie enjoyed the comfort of Jack's embrace, but was uncomfortable with his praise.

"Oh, it's just a book," she protested. "Not as if I am representing a human trafficking victim, or four, like a hero I know. Now that," she said appreciatively, "is something to be proud of. All those kids you lived with at the children's home when you were a kid, would be so proud of you, Jack . . . so proud."

Jack had shared, and she had read on the internet, that a raid had occurred in an upscale neighborhood recently where four girls ranging in age from ten to sixteen, were rescued. Their foster parents, a doctor and his wife, had been trafficking the girls for sex for over a year, and had used their bedrooms as a type of brothel rooms for rich men seeking sex with children. The services had been spread word of mouth throughout the community, johns travelling as far as one hundred miles to use the girls. The FBI had been tipped off by one of the girls' teachers. The ten-year-old little girl's teacher had noticed that the once outgoing and confident little girl, had become increasingly withdrawn, her eyes pointed down at the floor . . . a shadow of what a child should be. One day the teacher released the other children for recess, but kept the little girl in the classroom with her, determined to discover what was causing the change in her behavior. Within five minutes, the little girl was sobbing that she had been forced by her foster parents to have sex with strange men, and sometimes men she knew, during the week and weekends, seeing sometimes as many as six men a night. She and the other girls were told if they did not do as they were told, their foster parents would call their caseworker and report that they had been stealing things from their home. Since they were such a respected family in town, he a doctor, they feared the caseworker would believe them, and place the girls in a juvenile detention center, and from there most kids ended up in jail. The foster parents had asked if that is what they wanted to happen to them . . . to go to jail. The teacher had been horrified by what her student had shared, and called the trafficking hotline immediately.

Jack, the notable attorney in the area for human trafficking cases, had been contacted to represent the victims. He'd been called the morning after the bust had occurred and received a copy of the rescue team's interview files of the victims. Half-way into reading the first file, tears had coursed down his cheeks, overwhelmed by sadness for the victim's lost childhoods, and for past victims he had known. The case was less than a week old, but already he'd put in an abundance of overwhelming emotional hours for the case. It was as if, he thought, his life had come full circle, in a way, representing the spirit of many of the kids he'd grown up with at the children's home. While he couldn't help them when he was just a kid himself, now he could.

An hour into the wine and art party, after meeting several of the local artists, Jack purchased a charcoal sketch of the town square for his home office. And then Jack and Katie said their goodbyes and left the coffee shop.

They paused in the middle of the sidewalk, snuggling together against the sudden chill of the evening.

"Come to my house?" Jack asked.

Katie had been inside of Jack's house several times, providing decorating suggestions, even helping him shop for various art pieces and furnishings, however he had not asked her to accompany him after a date, and as she leaned against him, she hesitated. She pulled back, wanting badly to say yes, but not yet ready to embark on wherever that journey would lead.

"Nothing will happen, Katie. I promise. I won't hurt you," Jack said as he pulled her close and held her in his arms, keeping her warm. "I'll start a fire in the fireplace. We can have a glass of wine or tea . . . talk, watch a movie. I have, I am fairly certain, every corny Christmas movie ever made," he coaxed.

"I *am* a sucker for a corny Christmas movie," she reflected. "Alright, but just a movie," she insisted, pointing a finger at him for emphasis.

"And something to drink to warm the evening chill?" he asked.

"Deal," she agreed.

An hour later, as the antics of the movie Elf played in the background, Katie and Jack sipped on mugs of hot tea, curled next to one another on the couch. Katie, her feet curled beneath her, leaned against Jack, better able to see the pictures on his laptop, of various periods of his life. For the first 16 years of his life, pictures had been almost non-existent, however he had made up for the lack of photo memories during his college years. He was a great photographer, Katie admired, as he flipped through shots of water-falls, and rocky canyons.

"My foster family didn't have a lot of money," Jack explained, "so we did a lot of camping. Red River Gorge was one of my favorite places to go. It has a lot of sandstone . . . and small waterfalls. It's beautiful during the fall with the changing of the leaves," he shared as he continued to flip through the photos. "Have you been hiking down there?" he asked as he glanced at Katie.

Shaking her head, she said, "No. But it looks beautiful."

"We should go sometime," he said, and flipped to another photo.

"Oh . . . that's beautiful," Katie said. "Where's that at?"

"That's the Natural Bridge at Red River Gorge," he said as he placed his laptop onto the coffee table in front of them. "It's a bridge made of sandstone wide enough to walk hand-in-hand. There are no handrails, as you saw in the picture. Just God's bridge jutting out over the forest, far, far below. It's one of the quietest places in Kentucky. You . . . me . . . and noth-ing but God's beauty surrounding us."

Leaning toward her, he asked, "Are you okay? Can I get you anything?"

"I'm good . . . well, maybe that throw over there," Katie said, pointing at the vanilla colored chenille throw blanket she had picked up for him for cozy evenings just like this one.

Katie allowed Jack to take her hand in his, helping her to her feet. He laid down on the long couch, reaching his hand toward her. She laid next to him, in spoon fashion, her back snuggled into him. She scooted closer, liking the feel of his body pressed against hers. He flipped the throw over them, and they settled in, half hearing Elf say something about coffee. Katie felt Jack's fingers as they swept a loose tendril of her hair behind her ear, and felt, as soft as a butterfly, his kiss on her neck. She closed her eyes, enjoying the feel, her breath quickening. His hand felt the groove of her waste, but moved no further. Then with a sigh, Jack reached his arm over her, pulling her tighter against him. He relaxed his arm—forced himself to relax—keeping his promise to her. With the fire crackling, and Elf professing his love, Jack and Katie fell asleep.

28

"Randall!" Erin said. "Look! Katie's in the news. The article is about a book she's written." She read to the middle of the page on her computer screen. "A book for teens. It says . . ." She paused and read to the bottom of the screen. "A work of fiction that deals with complex issues teens face— exposed to social media, reality TV, and even the damaging idea many have about male/female relationships. The reporter quoted Katie saying 'we are lost in a feel good society'."

"Can't argue with that," Erin agreed with a shake of her head. "The article says, 'A society where the most precious gift we are capable of, love, has gotten lost—devalued—and this attitude has created a world of imper-manence in regard to family value, and commitment.' "

Randall leaned over to see what Erin was reading. "Wow!" he exclaimed, and raised his eyebrows. "Did you say she wrote a fiction book? Sounds more like a text book for a psych class," he mused. "Did you know she was a writer?" Erin's fiancé, Randall, asked.

"No. I had no idea," she said, surprised to be reading about her friend on the internet. Scrolling down, she continued to read the online article. Absently, she said, "No, the article says it's a work of fiction, not a psychol-ogy book." She clicked to the second page of the article. "It's a work of fic-tion, a story with all those concerns in mind. Katie 'wrote the book so it's easy to read . . . the intent being for kids to get lost in the story, to identify with the characters. Inspire them to think, feel, and to want more than what society is offering them now. She's hoping after they read her book, kids will be inspired to want long-term, permanent relationships, realizing the depth of loving committed relationships will be the emotional nets that catch them and hold them when life gets rough . . . what they can always come home to, trust.' Hmmm. That's what it says."

Erin leaned back on her chair, smiled, and thought, *you go, Katie. You go, girl.* She sighed. She hadn't spoken to Katie since she'd left the Weaver law firm. No goodbye, nothing. Rumor had it, Katie had left the retreat early, and before anyone had arrived at the office, she'd boxed up all her things in her office. Then, she left a note for Alan that she quit. No one had heard from her since. A few weeks after the retreat, Alan had sent out a memo announcing that Katie had submitted her resignation citing family obligations. The hum in the office after reading the memo had been louder than a swarm of angry bees, no one believing what Alan said . . . that she left for some family obligation.

It wasn't like Katie to leave for a family obligation—not her M.O. She hadn't left after her brother-in-law had passed away and she had to care for Emily. And not to say goodbye . . . that was *not* the Katie, Erin, or anyone else at the firm, knew. Katie didn't turn her back on anyone, and that was how Alan tried to make it sound, as if she'd walked away when the women of the company needed her the most. There had been many informal meetings in the break room with various women at the firm, everyone speculating why she had left. The most likely was that she had gotten into it with Alan, or one of the attorneys had been an ass, like Dale. Katie demanded respect, but not getting it at the Weaver firm, she had walked. Katie was a class act . . . sweet, and Erin thought, no matter why she left, she deserved better than the filth of the Weaver firm. Erin hadn't blamed Katie for leaving, instinct telling her there was a very good reason for her departure, but after she had left the firm, things had only gotten worse with Dale, and eventually it had all become too much.

"Does it say in the article if there's a way to contact her?" Randall asked as he scanned the article.

"Not sure . . ." Erin said as she read to the bottom of the second page. "There," she said, "at the bottom of page two it provides an e-mail address."

"Are you going to contact her?" Randall asked.

"I don't think I really have a choice," Erin said. She copied and pasted the e-mail address into a word document, determined to send an e-mail to the listed address, hoping someone could put her in touch with her friend.

"Do you think she knows what's going on?" Randall asked.

"Maybe . . . maybe not," Erin said. "But I want to make sure she knows."

29

"Erin," Katie said softly. The surprise of seeing the familiar name caused her stomach to burn. Sitting in her writing room at the over-sized desk, Katie's fingers hovered over the mouse as she considered deleting the e-mail before opening it. If she clicked and opened the message, would she be opening a nightmare of memories that would overwhelm her . . . and carry her away? Katie shook her head, and feeling silly, took a deep breath, and then clicked the mouse, opening the e-mail message from a woman she had tried not to think about since she left her job at Alan's law firm.

"Dear, Katie," the e-mail read. "I read the news online that you published a book. Congratulations! I cannot wait to order a copy of your book. It seems you are doing really well. You left the firm so suddenly that I did not have the opportunity to say goodbye."

Not so bad, Katie thought as she continued reading.

Erin explained that she hoped it was okay to contact her . . . knew how difficult it must be to hear from her. She had heard strange rumors about why she had not returned to work after the retreat. The rumors swirling around the firm did not make sense to her, but given her experience with Dale, she could guess what happened and how damaging it was to her.

The message continued to read, "I have thought of you often over the past many months, especially given the lawsuit at the firm…"

"Lawsuit?" Katie said aloud to the computer. Frowning, she read the rest of the e-mail, and then read it again. At the bottom, above her signature of 'hope to chat with you soon,' Erin had provided her cell number.

Katie flopped back against the back of the leather chair she was sitting on, and exhaled loudly. She placed her hands to her mouth, shocked by what she had just read . . . suing Alan. She raised her eyebrows, and continued to stare at the computer screen, wary, as if at any moment the words would come alive and pull her into the world of web. She closed her eyes. So much had happened since she had left. Life at the firm had continued without her.

She opened her eyes and stared blankly at the computer screen, Erin's words blurry ant-like figures. Giving her head a shake, and blinking hard, Katie grabbed a pen and wrote down the cell number Erin had provided, and then clicked the mouse, closing the e-mail. Staring down at the numbers scribbled on the yellow Post-It note, Katie knew she would call her friend, just not today.

"Katie—Katie," Nan said for the fourth time.

"Hmm—what?" Katie said.

"Sweets, where *are* you? I have been talking to you for five minutes and you haven't heard a word I've said, have you? And you've just picked at your dinner. Do you want something else?" Nan asked, doubting by the expression on her niece's face that her distraction had anything to do with the overcooked chicken. By the look on her niece's face, wherever her thoughts were, it was not a pleasant place to be.

"Oh, Nan, I'm sorry," Katie said apologetically. "I—I have something on my mind."

"I can see that," Nan said with a smile. "Care to share?"

Waving her hand above her plate still almost as full as when they had sat down to dinner twenty minutes ago, Katie insisted, "The chicken is fine. It's delicious."

"Something big must be on your mind, because I know that chicken is almost as dry as one of my leather shoes," Nan chuckled. "What's up, sweets?"

Katie sighed, and closed her eyes for a moment. Then she blinked a few times, trying to disperse memories.

"Someone from the firm e-mailed me," Katie said. She looked intently at Nan, attempting to gauge her reaction.

"You're joking!" Nan exclaimed, feeling as if her eyes might bug out of her head. "Who—who in the world would have the audacity to contact you?" Anger began to burn inside her.

Katie scraped her fork across her plate, and asked, "Remember Erin . . . the girl, I mean woman, that I told you about? The sexual harassment case at Alan's firm?"

"Yeah . . ." Nan coaxed.

"Her," Katie said flatly.

"What did she want?" Nan asked, worried that trouble was brewing, just as Katie was beginning to get her North Carolina legs under her. "And how did she get your e-mail address?"

"I'm not sure where she got my e-mail address—oh—wait. Yes, I do know. The article that was written about me in Asheville. Remember? They included my e-mail address. I'd forgotten that," Katie said thoughtfully.

Nan nodded.

"Anyway—that's—she—she and some other women. Alan's law firm is being sued by Erin and some other women," Katie stammered, still in disbelief that anyone had the nerve to sue Alan, and that Erin had contacted her—that the past had reached out and grabbed her.

"Well I'll be damned," Nan said. Her niece's words were not what she had been expecting. Not at all. "So why did she contact *you?* Does she want something from you?" Nan asked suspiciously.

"I'm not sure," Katie admitted. "She provided her cell phone number in the e-mail and asked me to call her."

"Are you going to call?" Nan asked, hoping the answer was no.

"Yes. Maybe tomorrow," Katie said quietly as her fork clattered to her plate.

"Don't let them pull you into anything you don't want to be involved in. But if you want to be involved, I'll support you," Nan said.

Sighing, Katie said, "Thanks, Nan."

As Katie sat in Nan's kitchen overlooking the garden, dark now but for the glow cast onto the bushes in front of the windows, she wondered what Erin wanted. She decided that the next morning she would call and find out.

30

As one hand clenched a coffee cup, and the other clutched the cell phone, Katie said into the receiver, "Erin."

"Katie!" Erin said into her cell phone. "I wasn't sure you'd call me. I'm so glad you did."

"Of course I'd call you," Katie said nervously. "I was surprised to hear from you though." Skirting around the issue of the lawsuit, Katie asked, "How've you been?"

"Better, now," Erin said. "I have to admit, I wasn't doing so well for a while, not at all. I want to talk to you about the lawsuit," Erin stated, "but first I need to explain what led up to suing Alan. I know you're aware of what Dale did, and that Alan didn't care. But something happened after you left, Katie, something that made me realize how serious it all was, and that I had to do something."

Katie took a deep breath. She leaned back on her chair, pushed back from the desk with her toes, and tucked a foot beneath her.

"Okay. I'm listening," Katie said.

Erin filled Katie in on her life over the last few months, about the continued harassment from Dale, and that with Katie no longer at the firm, there had been no one to talk to. Hope for a resolution and safety was lost after Katie left the firm. The stress had been unbearable, never knowing what she would find at work, never knowing from one day to the next if

Dale would lash out at her, or if it would be a good day. There had been no one to turn to, not that she had wanted to share what had happened, even with Katie. Erin shared that it had taken everything in her to report the assault to Katie.

Eventually, she had begun to fall apart. Workdays became a nightmare, taking everything she had just to make it to the end of the day. Then on her way home, she'd stop at a store and buy bottles of wine. But it wasn't long before she needed something stronger to numb the day's events. Sleeping became a battle because when she closed her eyes, her mind couldn't shut out the memories of the day, and when she did fall asleep, she was plagued by nightmares. At one point, she visited her family doctor and asked for sleeping pills so she could get some much needed sleep.

One evening, Erin continued, after calling her over a period of hours, receiving no response from her, Erin's father had driven to her condo to check on her. He found her car parked in her driveway, and as he climbed the stairs to her porch, he noticed all the lights were on. He rang the doorbell, beat on the door, and walked around peeking in windows. Through a crack in the living room blind, he saw her lying on the floor, passed out. Accessing her condo with the spare key she had given him, he tried to revive her, but unable to do so he called 911. He had ridden in the back of the ambulance with her, not knowing what had happened, or if she would be okay. When she got to the hospital they pumped her stomach, and later, when she had regained consciousness, she explained she'd had difficulty sleeping again, and had taken a few sleeping pills with her evening glass of vodka. The near-death experience shook her so badly that she confided in her dad about what had happened at the firm . . . that she had been sexually assaulted. He'd pulled her into his arms and cried with her, that any man could hurt his baby like that.

Tom, Erin's brother, had packed a bag for her, and instead of going to her condo when she was released from the hospital, she decided to stay at her dad's house, needing the comfort that only her childhood home could provide. When she felt well enough, a family meeting had been called. It was then that she'd been encouraged by her dad and brothers to seek advice from an attorney specializing in sexual harassment, and encouraged to report the assaults to the police.

Erin had looked around the living room at her brothers and father, appalled by the suggestion that she go to the police—shocked that they would suggest such a thing. She'd argued that this was the way it was in business. If a woman wanted to work, sexual harassment was something she was going to have to accept and deal with, quietly. Not to do so would make her a crier, the woman who would soon be without a job, and with no future employment prospects. As men, she'd told them, she would think they knew that. They had admitted that women were treated like pieces of sex meat on the job, had seen it happen plenty of times at the jobs they worked at, but it didn't mean they liked how it was.

After witnessing the fallout of what sexual harassment does to a woman—that they had almost lost their sister and daughter because of it—they were taking a stand. From that day forward, each of them committed to a zero tolerance at work. They made a commitment to her that whenever they saw men disrespecting women on the job, they would stand up for her. Not only that, they wanted Erin to feel safe standing up to Dale and Alan, to be an example for the millions of other women that were harassed and bullied at work every day. So, she explained, with her family's help, she had retained an attorney, and had begun a suit against Alan's firm.

Katie listened, stunned by what Erin had shared. Tears burned her eyes as she envisioned her friend lying unconscious, close to death, on the floor of her home. If only she could have done more, she agonized.

Leaning forward, Katie placed her coffee cup on the desk, and then brushing away the tear trailing down her cheek, Katie apologized, "I am so sorry. I was buried so deeply in my own life that I couldn't help you. God, I am *so* sorry, Erin."

Erin, sitting on the couch in the family room at her father's house, smiled, knowing she had come a long way since that conversation with her family. She was stronger, and a better version of herself.

"Katie, it's okay. What else could you do? You did all you could. You *tried*. At least you listened, and I know you talked to both Dale and Alan.

You did everything you were supposed to do. And something tells me, you *had* to leave," Erin said.

Katie placed her elbow on her desk, and pressed her forehead against her hand, and as the memories washed over her.

"Yeah, I had to leave," Katie said sadly. "I'm so sorry."

Understanding more than Katie could possibly know, quietly, Erin said, "Don't worry about it. Leaving was the strong and courageous thing for you to do. You know, Katie, I know the kind of person you are. You put everyone first before you, so I know when you left the law firm it was something you really had to do, to protect you. So don't apologize for protecting yourself."

Wrapping an arm around her waist as she sat back against the chair, fidgeting, Katie could not help feeling that she had let Erin down. She seems to be doing fine, Katie thought, but, maybe I should have stayed and fought for her and for me . . . but . . . it just does not seem like a fight a woman can win.

"You know," Erin said, "since I filed my lawsuit against the firm, several other women, some previous employees and some current, have come forward and are part of a class action suit against Alan's law firm."

Worried about Katie's silence, Erin asked, "Are you still there?"

"I'm sorry," Katie said softly. "I'm still here. I was just thinking."

"Katie, it all works out in the end, at least in this case it has," Erin assured her.

Erin continued, sharing that the loving support of her family had helped her begin the process of healing, and begin the journey to reclaim her life. Once she had shared what had happened to her with her family, her life had begun falling into place. Not only had they encouraged her to take a stand against the male establishment, but also to use her experience to help other women, so she had applied to and been accepted to law school. Her dream was to help victims of violent crimes, both on the job and in their personal lives.

Katie raised her eyebrows in surprise and admiration. She admired Erin's strength and courage, and knew suing a company for sexual harassment was a difficult journey, not one all women could embark, but Katie knew with her family's support, Erin would be just fine. And considering her friend, she knew she would be a strong advocate for women, in and out of the courtroom. Events in life shape us, Katie thought, and although a group of men had almost destroyed Erin, it was what was now spurring within her the desire to help other women. Women like Erin, and her sister Stacey, amazed Katie, their strength and courage, attributes that seemed to have eluded her. Often, she wished she could plant her feet firmly and take a stand, just once, instead of running away.

"Do you remember Shelly, the receptionist you hired a few weeks before you quit?" Erin asked.

"Yeah," Katie said.

"Well, it didn't take Dale long to start in on her too. When you left the firm, there was no one to talk to. It was bad when it was happening to me, but at least I had you. Shelly finally got up the nerve to talk to Alan. As far as I know, he never talked to Dale, or if he did, it didn't do any good. One afternoon, Shelly stormed out of Dale's office, marched to her desk, packed up her things, and never came back. Tanya in accounting remained in contact with Shelly, and she told us that Shelly's husband kicked her out of their house because she quit her job. She had no family—no one to turn to—so she had to take her two kids and move into a women's shelter. This *shit* ruins women's lives, and I don't know, maybe I believe in meant to be. Maybe God placed me there to see all that, to experience it first-hand. God knows I'm a fighter, and I guess the big man knew eventually I would do something about it. No woman should have to lose her job and end up in a shelter while the assaulting bastard is allowed to remain on the job waiting for his next victim!"

Katie wondered sadly what was wrong with the world that men in the business world were allowed to shatter women's lives.

Later that afternoon, the conversation with Erin heavy on her mind, Katie pulled a light weight jacket over her t-shirt, hiked up her black yoga pants, and tied the strings on her tennis shoes. She called out to her walking partner, hoping to walk fast, and far enough, to leave the conversation and memories of the law firm behind her, swirling in the country air.

"Hunter!" Katie called. "Come on boy! You wanna to go for a walk?"

The yellow furry dog jumped up in the air and barked in the affirmative. Yeah, she thought with a sigh, I already feel better.

"Well come on," she said, smiling at the dog. "Let's go!"

As Katie walked down the abandoned road with Hunter by her side, she thought about Erin and the happiness and determination she'd heard in her voice when she'd talked to her over the phone that morning. Katie smiled as she remembered what Erin had shared about Randall, her boyfriend. She shared that she and her boyfriend were back together. One morning Erin had been walking her dog, Max, at the dog park—something she did most weekends—and that when she had thrown a ball for Max to fetch, it had been Randall's dog that had brought the ball back to her. It had been a pleasant surprise for them both, Erin and Randall, when Randall caught up to his dog and discovered Erin and Max. A long walk that afternoon had turned into dinner, and then breakfast the next day. Since then, Randall had been a loving source of support, an ear when she needed to talk, and a shoulder when she needed to cry. When he'd come back into her life, Erin was still fragile, a feeling new to her, but her brothers, dad, and Randall made her feel it was okay to be soft, sensitive and broken. The new fragile side of Erin had taken some getting used to. Erin, their kick-ass daughter, sister, and girlfriend, now needed them to loan her their strength, and they were determined to be her strength for as long as she needed.

"I wish I could have been there for you," Katie whispered to the trees. "I wish I had been stronger for you." With a sigh, she said, "Good for you, Erin. Good for you," and continued walking down the road with Hunter by her side.

31

Katie hung her apron on a hook in the back room of the coffee shop as Nan leaned against the doorjamb, watching her.

"So, what are you going to do . . . join the lawsuit?" Nan asked.

Shaking her head, Katie said, "I don't know. Nan, I don't think anything good would come of me joining that suit."

"Sweets, you would wrap that case up for them, and you know it. The HR Manager of the law firm being attacked by the owner . . . they'd settle for sure," Nan insisted, with a shake of her head.

Katie turned around and faced her aunt. She smiled, placed her hands on her hips.

"Maybe I'm just not the suing type," she said thoughtfully.

"Well, what's that supposed to mean?" Nan asked as she followed Katie down the short hall to the counter. "The suing type? Who *is* the suing type?"

Nan collided into Katie when she stopped abruptly in front of her, and turned toward her, facing her.

"What would be the point?" Katie asked irritably.

"The point? The *point?*" Nan asked as she waved her hand in the air. "The point is to sue the bastard for what he did to you. Because you had to *quit* your job because of that *asshole!*"

"And then?" Katie asked.

"What do you mean, and then?" Nan asked, confused.

"So, I sue Alan . . . then what? Nothing changes. He goes about his same, asshole ways. So what? Nothing would change. But," Katie emphasized, "while his world would remain the same, my face and name would be smeared all over the internet and TV. I would be hurt . . . again," Katie said, her nostrils flaring at the thought. "It's not fair, but it's how it is. You know that, Nan!" Katie flung one hand on her hip and pounded the other on the counter.

Nan looked as if the wind had gone out of her sails, seeing Katie's point.

"But you can't give up," Nan insisted.

Shrugging her shoulders, Katie said, "I'm not. Maybe I just need to find my own way in this mess. Find a way of, I don't know, find my own way to help people—men—understand what they are doing to the women they work with, or the women that work for them—get them to care, like Erin's brothers and dad. Because of her, what happened to her, they will no longer turn their back when a woman they work with is being assaulted or harassed at work. Maybe I can inspire that kind of change," Katie said thoughtfully.

"Well, before you make a final decision, you should talk to Jack," Nan advised. "What did that letter say? When does the attorney want to meet with you?"

A week after Katie had spoken with Erin, she received a letter in the mail from the attorney representing Erin and the other women in the lawsuit against Alan's law firm. The letter had explained who the attorney was, why she was contacting Katie, and provided her contact information. The attorney had explained that female employees—past and present—from Alan's firm, were being contacted and notified about the lawsuit. If any woman felt she had been the victim of sexual harassment and or retaliated by any employee or supervisor employed by the Weaver law firm, then she welcomed them to contact her. Katie had received a separate letter in addition to what she knew was a form letter sent to the other women.

In the separate letter, the attorney requested to meet with Katie, Thursday, which was tomorrow. Katie had agreed to meet with her as long as the attorney travelled to North Carolina for the meeting, as she did not intend to waste her gas and time, driving to a state, or city for that matter, where she did not want to be. She had received the letter a week ago, had a week to consider if she wanted to be part of the lawsuit. Her prevailing attitude was, why subject herself to what she knew would be hell, as the defense attorney did his best to shame and humiliate her on the stand, as he cruelly hammered away at her to share in explicit detail the night at the cabin. She could imagine the taunts from Alan's attorney as he shouted at her that she wanted it . . . the claim Dale had made about Erin.

That's how both Alan and Dale had presented the situation with Erin, Katie remembered. Wanted it, she thought. How was that a viable defense when a rich asshole, or self-entitled boy, made that statement, *wanted it*, in sexual assault or rape cases? It sickened her, the male attitude, and that society supported their abuse of women and girls. Katie shook the memories of her childhood rape hearing from her conscious, shoving it where it belonged, in the deep recesses, safe on a dark shelf of her mind.

Later that afternoon, there was a brisk wind blowing as Katie walked swiftly to her highlander. It felt more like a December wind than November, she considered as she shivered. As she walked, she thought about the hearing she had suffered through when she was just a teen, and the boys that received a slap on the wrist for shattering her life and that of her family. She climbed onto the seat of the highlander and considered, nothing changed by pressing charges. The boys went free, and thousands of boys since then had raped other girls, just like other men would assault and harass other women after the Weaver case was over.

"It never changes," she said aloud as she pulled onto the road and drove home.

"Hi. Come in," Katie said, the next afternoon as she held the door open for the attorney. Katie admired the woman dressed sharply in a pinstriped jacket and skirt, and a smart pair of three inch heels to complete the professional outfit.

Casually dressed in blue jeans and a peach sweater, Katie commanded, "Hunter, stay down," as the overzealous lab wagged his tail, hitting the attorney on her leg. Katie grabbed Hunter by the collar and apologized.

"No problem," the attorney said. "I have a red lab waiting for me at home. How old is he?" she asked.

"Seven-years old," Katie answered.

"He's beautiful," the attorney admired.

"Come on in," Katie said, still holding Hunter by the collar.

Katie led the attorney into the kitchen where she placed her purse and briefcase, with what Katie assumed contained a laptop, on the island.

"Have a seat," Katie said. "I'll be right back. I'm going to put Hunter in my aunt's room for a while."

The attorney nodded and then turned her attention to unzipping and taking her computer out of its computer nest.

"Come on, Hunter," Katie called. The yellow lab followed behind her. She walked into Nan's bedroom, gesturing for Hunter to come into the room with her. "You have to stay in Nan's room for just a little while," Katie said, bending over as if she were talking to a child. "I won't be long, okay?"

Hunter wagged his tail.

"Stay," she insisted as she walked toward the door. At the door, Katie turned around, surprised that Hunter had not moved, still sitting in the exact spot she had left him. "Stay," she said again, and walked out the door, closing it behind her. She walked back down the hall, back to the kitchen where the attorney was perched on a chair, laptop, folders, and documents placed neatly, and efficiently in front of her.

"Would you like coffee, tea, or water?" Katie asked.

"Coffee, if you have some made," the attorney said.

Katie pulled two coffee mugs down from a cabinet and poured steaming coffee into them.

"Cream or sugar?" Katie asked, placing one of the cups in front of the thirty-something year old attorney. Younger than me, Katie considered, wondering how many sexual harassment cases she could possibly have prosecuted in her relatively short legal career.

"No thank you," the attorney said. "Black is fine."

Katie scooted a stool back, and stood in front of it, resting a foot on a rung as she took a sip of her coffee.

"The attorney looked up at Katie, assessing her. "Erin explained that you were the Human Resources Manager working at the firm, the manager in charge who she reported the assaults to. Is that correct?" she asked, wanting confirmation to solid up the basics of her case against Alan's law firm.

"Yes," Katie said, keeping her response short, something she had learned from the attorney who had represented her during the rape trial.

The attorney flipped through papers in the manila folder placed in front of her, and said, "Erin reported two assaults."

"Yes," Katie answered.

The attorney closed the file, looked up at Katie, and asked, "Did you take action, as the HR Manager?"

Katie felt flushed, feeling as if she were on the stand, as if she were being prosecuted, or that perhaps the attorney was not there to question her as a victim but as a person of interest to include in suing. Panicking, she wondered if she had made a mistake by agreeing to meet with the prosecuting attorney.

"Are you implying that I was negligent in my role as an HR Manager?" Katie asked defensively.

"No, Katie. I am trying to get to the facts. As the HR Manager for Alan's firm, you are a crucial part of this case. A great deal of this case hinges on you, on the actions you took after Erin reported the assaults by one of the attorneys," the attorney said, bluntly.

Trying to put Katie at ease, the attorney said, "Erin has already told me she feels you did everything you could, and that's a good thing for you. Had you not done your job, not taken Erin's complaints seriously, we would be suing you right along with Alan and his law firm. So, not only as a woman did you get your role right, but as an HR professional, you got it right. This is serious stuff," the attorney said, as she stared at Katie.

"I'm aware of the legalities surrounding one's role as an HR Manager," Katie said, stiffly.

"Good," the attorney said. She took a sip of coffee, and then asked, "What was Alan's response when you told him Erin had reported that she had been assaulted by Dale in the garden area at the hotel the Saturday at the training event?"

Katie felt uncomfortable answering any of the questions presented to her, and wondered if she should have retained an attorney for herself. She wondered if she was going to need one after all.

"Alan stated that perhaps it was a misunderstanding, that Dale was probably interested in Erin romantically and that she misunderstood his intentions," Katie said stiffly.

"What did you think? Did it seem to you by Erin's description of the events that it was a misunderstanding, as Alan said? Or, based on the report that Erin provided, did she make it clear to Dale that she was *not* interested in him and was in fact offended by his advances?" the attorney asked.

Katie wanted the meeting over as soon as possible, and to extricate herself from the mess. She took a deep breath. *Just tell the woman what happened and she will be on her way. There is no reason to protect anyone, and you do not have to say anything about what happened at the cabin, Katie* thought. *I just need her out of this house, she screamed inside her head in a panic.* She inhaled deeply, and then exhaled trying to calm her nerves.

"When Erin came to my office that day, after the company training event at the hotel, she was a very different Erin. I had never seen her other than professional, calm . . . together. But her behavior that day, in my office, was very *not* like her. She had tears in her eyes, and her body language clearly indicated she was under duress. To me, professionally and personally, that is a clear indicator and message that she did not wish to be touched by Dale. She also told me that she told Dale never to come near her again." Seeing no reason to withhold any information, and wanting to hurry the meeting along, Katie shared, "Of course, I'm sure Erin shared with you the incident at the office. The second incident she reported to me occurred in Dale's office. She stated that he grabbed her again. I reported all of this to Alan. He told me to talk to Dale and I did. Soon after all of that happened," Katie said with a wave of her hand, "I left the company."

"That is the abridged version of what Erin shared," the attorney said. "Now, you're leaving the law firm, that was rather sudden, wasn't it?"

"Yes," Katie said as she stared at the coffee in her cup.

"Why the sudden departure? You were on a retreat with many of the attorneys and Alan, is that right?" the attorney asked, carefully noting Katie's facial and body language.

Katie paused. The attorney watched the emotions war across her face. Just what did she want to tell the attorney, Katie stewed. If she told her what happened, the attorney would haul her into court wanting to use the fuel against Alan. With the information I have, Erin would definitely win, Katie considered. Erin's face swam before her eyes as she remembered the first meeting in her office after the employee event at the hotel. That was the day life truly began to spin out of control, Katie reflected, or perhaps life had just caught up with her. Erin had almost died because of Alan's lackadaisical attitude toward Dale's actions, Katie considered. Then, she grimaced, of course he wouldn't care, his actions at the cabin were proof of the kind of man he was . . . no better than Dale. Both of them preyed on women. How many women had there been she wondered, and how many more would there be?

She looked up, and with no inflection in her voice, her face feeling as if it were made of stone, Katie said, "I left because Alan wanted to sleep with me. The night I left, he was drunk. He asked me to go to his room to get something for him, which," Katie held up her hand to quiet the attorney's protest, "which, was not out of the ordinary because I served as his assistant that weekend. It was no different from if I were a man, running to his room to retrieve files and various other items he needed for meetings and activities. The last night, he asked me to run to his room for him to get something for him. I was in his room, my back to the door. He entered the room. I didn't hear him, but there he was, and then he was all over me. He pulled me onto the bed, and it was quite obvious, if you get what I mean, that he wanted sex."

"And, did . . ." the attorney said.

"No!" Katie interrupted. "Are you nuts?" Losing her composure, she exploded—her flesh crawling at the memory. "I struggled to free myself from his grip, and when I managed to break free, I rushed to my room, packed and left. I drove straight home. The next work day I went to the office, packed my things, and left the key to my office on his desk, with a Post-It note," she reflected in satisfaction, "that said, I quit."

The attorney smiled, as she thought, this case has just gotten much easier.

"Katie," the attorney coaxed, "you were sexually harassed. It is your right as a woman to be treated with respect at work. *Clearly,* you have a case against Alan. You can sue."

"I know," Katie said. "I knew that the night I left Alan's cabin. I knew when I placed that Post-It note on his desk. I knew then and know now that I have a case and might win, but at what cost? Would the win be greater than the loss when Alan allowed—encouraged—his attorney to shred me in front of him and whoever else happened to be in the court room?"

"I'm not saying it will be easy," the attorney admitted. "But anything worthwhile rarely is."

"Oh, I know it wouldn't be easy, and that worthwhile things rarely are, but this is a man that I knew, trusted and respected," Katie said, frowning. "A man that . . . yes, did something horrible to me." And, Katie thought, he woke the slumbering giant of a nightmare—a nightmare I thought I had effectively put to rest long ago.

"To stand before him, watching him, and watch his attorney further destroy me, to save him from admitting to himself and everyone he knows that he hurt me, would be . . ." Katie thought for a moment, trying to find the words. "I knew Alan for years, and I respected him. He was good to my family and me. If I were to sue him, he would methodically set out to destroy me, by every means necessary. He would do what is done in these cases—try to tarnish my character by making me seem like some loose woman, and I'm *not.* It's the fact that he would *try* to make people think that of me, that would hurt even more than what he did to me in his bedroom at his cabin. He tried to invade my body that night, and that . . . it was . . . it hurt . . . was an indescribable pain, but what happens in court to victims is a methodical, intentional destroying of their spirit. I think that would be my end, to know, to have someone I once trusted set out to extinguish . . . to . . . to . . . to murder my spirit. I would win money," Katie acknowledged. "But I would lose myself, parts that I would never get back, and I don't have enough of me that I can sacrifice."

Katie knew that she'd lost pieces of herself the night she was gang-raped, pieces of her spirit that were never healed and regained, and knew that there just was not enough of her spirit to carry her through suing Alan, not sure what would be left of her after it was over. Her trust had taken a tremendous blow, trust for any one person, and she knew a certain amount of trust was needed in all relationships. To lose what was left in her small bag of trust would mean a life of fear, loneliness, and emptiness.

"I just—I can't," Katie said firmly.

"Katie," the attorney said as she reached over and touched her forearm. "There is a lot at stake here. You could help other women by coming forward and suing Alan, by being an example for them. This case will send a loud and clear message to other companies, that they will be held accountable for their actions, that this behavior will no longer be tolerated."

The attorney leaned back on her chair, and tapped the pen she held in her hand on the counter.

"You know as well as I do, this over-sexualized attitude is pervasive in the business world," the attorney said. "Men think women are there to amuse them, that women are simple sexual playthings. Men have a difficult time separating their personal lives from their professional world. Men that own companies are on a power trip." The attorney scowled, shrugged her shoulders, and waved her hand in the air. "When a man is in a power position, in a role where he makes decisions, where people report to him—a man at the top, a head of a company—he has no one to hold him accountable. And rarely, if ever, hears the word no, at home or on the job. If he *does* hear the word no—his powers of influence and salesmanship helped get him to the power position he enjoys—salesman that he is, a no is never a no. There needs to be checks and balances on this kind of over-inflated type of power. And this case," the attorney leaned forward, and clicked her pen on the counter, "you can do that—help create a check and balance for these men."

"You don't really think," Katie said skeptically, with a hint of smile playing on her lips, "that this case, any case for that matter, will make men stop wanting to have sex with women on the job, stop trying to use women at work as some sick form of foreplay . . . or . . . or for sex?"

Feeling as if a dump truck of anger had unloaded at her feet—years of the stinking garbage of what men, boys and society had done to her, with one goal in mind to protect the sick sexual lives of abusers—she let loose.

"It's what they do, and what we," Katie said, waving her hand erratically in the air, "allow them to do. Yes, everyone knows it happens, men at work—male bosses and male co-workers—grope and grind the help, and if you complain, well *hell*, it's like being a slave. No, not totally, these days we receive a paycheck from corporate America when men grab us, so . . . so . . . it's like we're a bunch of prostitutes! When a young woman enters the work world, there's what, a seventy percent chance that she'll become a company prostitute! Jesus! Or a stripper! Not that I have ever been to a strip joint, but we've all seen the shit in the movies. Men watching and grabbing. That's the statistics, right, seventy percent of women are harassed on the job?!"

"You sound angry," the attorney said, her voice rising, angry right along with Katie. "Do something about it, Katie. Now is your chance."

Katie ran her hand through her hair and looked across the kitchen, out the window at the garden. Nan's robins came to mind . . . they weren't singing today, she thought. No, her world had grown cold . . . as cold as the pre-winter air outside. She inhaled to calm the storm of anger that had been stirred within her, and exhaled a ragged breath.

"No," Katie said, resolutely. "Suing never changes anything. You and I both know companies have insurance for this type of thing. It doesn't impact their bottom line, not large companies like Alan's law firm. The insurance he pays into for just this sort of," Katie made the quote sign with her fingers, "'transgression' covers what he pays out to his victims." Grinning, Katie said, "Rich men have got it all figured out. And why shouldn't they, all the time they have together on the golf course discussing the logistics of sex on the job, cigars, and liquor, while a bunch of worker-bees run their companies. They don't work, not the big boys—companies, and firms like Alan's. They have nothing but time on their hands—idle minds and hands. They're just little boys, all grown up, looking for a toy to play with." Katie laughed bitterly. "It's our male leaders making the rules and the laws. Most judges are men, but of course, they can't deny *every* sexual harassment claim, so they had to come up with some fall back plan for their little on the job sex-capades. It's called insurance."

"Well—Yes—I mean," the attorney stammered. "Yes, they do have insurance to cover their asses, but their premiums go up. There *is* a cost to being sued. They have attorney fees, and then there is the beating they take in the community."

"No, they don't," Katie said, angrily. "They don't. Or maybe you're not reading the news I'm reading. Politicians that harass women—people actually stand behind them, defend them as if they're entitled to ruin a woman's life because being rich is somehow *stressful!* It's sickening! And *why* does this happen?" Katie said. "Not because people don't know it's happening. Regular folks hope that by standing by rich people, they'll be rewarded. It all comes down to money. We all need money, right?" Katie said.

Standing, the attorney said, "Change is never easy, Katie. But be a part of change anyway."

"Not like this," Katie said. "I won't be party to this circus . . . this rich man fun land. Even this will have no impact on them. Sexual harassment lawsuits are just like the women they harass, a notch, a company notch, nothing more than a locker room, or golf course joke to them, to be shared with their rich buddies. Nothing more."

Crossing her arms across her chest, an idea growing, Katie said, "I plan to be part of change, but not this way. It's going to have to be my way, on my terms."

The attorney raised her hand in the air, and then let it drop to her side. She shook her head.

"What can one person do, Katie, to end a problem as old as the first day a woman joined the workforce?" the attorney asked.

Katie picked up the attorney's discarded pen.

"The pen can be a mighty sword if wielded in just the right way," Katie said.

Puzzled, the attorney cocked her head. "I don't follow," she said.

"My next book," Katie said firmly.

Staring at Katie, the attorney recalled that she was an author. Maybe she's on to something, she thought. She placed her hand on her hip.

"Now that's a creative idea," the attorney said. "Do it, Katie. Write your story, just be careful how you write it so you don't end up on the wrong side of the courtroom. It's a shameful reality, but these bastards have rights to, as I am sure you are aware."

"Completely aware," Katie acknowledged. "More rights than the victims. The law and legal proceedings are set up by men to protect men in these cases."

The attorney raised her eyebrows. Sharp lady, she considered. Very sharp.

"Well then, I guess there is nothing more I can do here," the attorney said as she began placing her legal tools back into her bag.

Katie walked her guest outside, pulling her sweater tight against the bitter November wind.

The attorney extended her hand, and Katie took it in her own firm grasp.

"Good luck," the attorney said. "I'll be watching for your book. If you ever need anything, a legal perspective for your book, you have my number."

"Thanks," Katie said, "and good luck with the case."

Katie watched the car pull away from the house, and then rubbing her arms, walked back into the house.

"Hey, you," Katie said to the yellow lab as he looked up at her from where he had been laying on the floor of Nan's bedroom. "You can come out now, Hunter."

32

Later that evening, Nan sat on Katie's bed watching her apply her makeup. Nan had made a beeline for Katie's bedroom the minute she had arrived home from the coffee shop, knowing Katie was leaving soon for dinner with Jack. Curiosity was not going to wait until, who knew when the cat would drag Katie in, or if it would drag her in at all before morning.

"So, how'd it go this afternoon with the lawyer lady?" Nan asked.

"Fuh," Katie mumbled.

"Huh?" Nan said.

Katie turned toward her aunt, her mascara wand in her hand, and repeated, "Fine," then turned back to the mirror over her dresser, and continued applying charcoal colored mascara to her lashes.

"Uh-huh, fine. Do you think you could be a little more specific?" Nan asked.

"Um," Katie mumbled as she ran the mascara brush through her lower lashes. After she screwed the top back on the applicator, she turned toward Nan.

"Sit with me a moment," Nan said as she patted the space on the bed next to her.

Knowing she had plenty of time, Katie tugged on the belt of her robe and climbed up onto the bed, scooting next to her aunt who was propped with the many pillows at the head of the bed.

"Okay, sweets," Nan said, "so what'd the lady have to say? Was there still plenty of coffee? I made a special pot for your meeting?" She patted Katie on her robe-covered knee.

"Yes, Nan, there was plenty of coffee. I hadn't managed to drink the entire pot by the time she arrived at one o'clock. Thank you," Katie said as she clasped her aunt's hand, "for making your special coffee."

"I thought some special coffee might be nice," Nan commented.

"It was," Katie smiled.

"Now stop stalling," Nan insisted, with a squeeze of her hand.

Laughing, Katie said, "Nan, you are one feisty lady. Okay. Um. It was fine. I mean, at first, by the things she was saying, I thought she was planning to sue me along with Alan."

"The hell you say?" Nan said in surprise. "Someone wanting to sue my Katie. They're gonna have to get through me first," anger firing her up.

Katie lay her head on Nan's shoulder, smiled, and sighed.

"I can always count on you," Katie said comfortably.

"Yes, you can. I will always have your back, Katie," Nan assured her niece.

Lifting her head, Katie continued, "Well thankfully, the attorneys of the world are safe because no one is suing me. So . . . the attorney meeting today. She started by asking questions related to my role as the HR Manager at the firm. I think she was trying to corroborate what Erin had told her, that she had reported the assaults to me and that I had then reported it upward to my chain of command, to Alan. I was honest and told her that everything Erin told her was how it happened. That Erin had reported the incidences per procedure and I followed procedure as well. The break down occurred at Alan's end."

"That attorney had my heart pounding for a good fifteen minutes, wondering if I needed my own attorney," Katie admitted.

"Sounds like a cut-throat lawyer," Nan said.

"At one time I would have responded . . . is there any other kind," Katie, grinned. "Erin has a good attorney, that's for sure. Good thing because she's going to need an attorney that has the stomach for this kind of case. It's brutal having people you trusted—thought were your friends—attempt to rip you to shreds in a court of law, while an audience watches and listens."

"Think she'll win the case?" Nan asked.

"Oh, I have an inkling that she will, but even still, at a devastating emotional cost to the victims. I think Erin will fair okay because she has a very strong family of men to support her, but the other women involved in the case, I'm not so sure they'll walk away the same women. A lot of lives have been shaken up by what Alan has allowed to happen at his firm, and even by his actions, but they haven't seen anything yet. An earthquake is about to happen, turning their worlds upside down," Katie said thoughtfully.

Wrinkling her forehead, Nan commented, "By the way you're talking, I take it you declined to be part of the lawsuit."

"Yes, my dear, Nan, I did decline," Katie said, looking at her aunt to gauge her reaction.

"You're going to give up all that money," Nan said.

"Yup," Katie said, and nodded.

"Good girl. Who needs their filth money anyway," Nan said as she patted Katie's hand.

Katie grinned.

"Uh-oh," Nan commented with a laugh. "I see that gleam in your eyes. You're up to something."

Laughing, Katie scooted off the bed and asked coyly, "Now why ever would you say that?"

"Um . . . I know my niece," Nan said playfully. It was nice to see some fire sparking in Katie's eyes, something she had seen little of since high school.

Running a wide toothed comb through her hair, Katie glanced at her aunt through the mirror and saw that her aunt was watching her.

"What!?" Katie laughed. "I'm just going about my business, you know, life as a writer and all that."

Nan inhaled dramatically. "The dickens if you're not gonna write about what happened at the firm," Nan admired her niece's spunk.

"Lady, have you done lost your mind!" Katie said in a mock southern drawl, with a grin planted on her face. *"Puhlease.* I'm not getting sued."

Katie placed the comb on the dresser, and slowly turned toward her aunt.

"But I could write a work of fiction about the goings on in the business world. That," she said pointing her finger playfully at her aunt, "I *can* do."

"Well I'll be. Girls got spunk," Nan laughed.

"I got the idea from the attorney today, something she said. She said that change is never easy—be a part of change. And it clicked. I want to be part of change, to make the world better for all women. We have to work, need money just as much as men need money. We have just as many bills as they do, and are raising kids. But like me, there are thousands of women losing their jobs because they don't want to have to screw the boss to keep their job, or pretend to be okay with men pawing at them. It's a big secret, this . . . this *nastiness* that goes on at work, but not really," Katie said.

"Change . . ." Nan said thoughtfully. "So how will the book help? I mean, what kind of book is going to be?"

"Well, the workforce nasty is an unspoken part of the workday for women," Katie reflected. "Unspoken because they never know who they can trust, feeling that they're supposed to pretend it's all cool." Katie waved her hand in the air. "No one wants to stand out as the uptight, frigid lady at work, even when it means laughing off a man trying to rip her clothes off, and then drinking and taking sleeping pills at night to numb the disgusting memory of it all," Katie said angrily.

"Yeah . . ." Nan encouraged.

"So, why not a book with secret messages hidden within, letting women know they're not alone. Communicate to women that more women than they could possibly imagine, are feeling their pain. Let them know that there's a sisterhood in all this, that, and to encourage them never to give up. A book that gets women talking, sharing their stories with one another over coffee, tea, or a glass of wine. The sisterhood that'll grow in strength and numbers as women begin to take a stand for one another at work, speak out for one another. Millions strong..." Katie reflected. "You know," Katie said perkily, "that kind of book!"

"God love you," Nan said, with tears in her eyes as she pulled her niece into her arms.

"Thanks, Nan," Katie said as she hugged her aunt back. "For never giving up on me, and for always being here."

"I'll always be here for you, sweets," Nan said, her voice thick with tears.

As the women parted, Katie knew that her aunt always would be.

"Well you best finish getting ready for your date. Jack will be here in a few minutes. Can't go to dinner in that robe, even as pretty as it is," Nan smiled.

"I don't know," Katie grinned as she posed like a runway model. "Wrap a fancy belt around me and I think I could be setting the next fashion trend!"

Nan kissed her niece on her cheek, and smiling, walked out of the room.

Hours later, Katie sat across a table from Jack at an upscale Italian restaurant in Asheville.

"I'm stuffed," Katie announced.

"Me too," he said with a smile, as he leaned back on his chair. "Desert?" he asked.

"No, thank you!" Katie laughed. "I swear to you, if I even *try* to eat another bite, I'll vomit all over this nice white table cloth." With a grin, she asked, "How's that for a visual after all that pasta you just ate?"

"I have *the* most disgusting girlfriend," Jack grinned, trying out the word to see Katie's reaction.

Girlfriend, Katie considered. *Girlfriend.* It sounded right, she decided, and looked across the table, and smiled.

"Probably," she agreed, playfully.

"Think you have room for a cup of coffee?" he asked. "We could walk off a little of the pasta first. I know where we can grab a great cup of coffee and sip it in front of a crackling fire.

"After a walk outside, I think a hot cup of coffee would be perfect," Katie agreed.

Katie sat curled next to Jack as cozy as a cat, on a yellow and brown striped couch sipping a cup of lavender tea, and watched the flames flicker and crackle in the fireplace at the coffee house. The coffee house had been one of Jack's favorite hangouts when he lived in Asheville.

"How's the case going?" Katie asked, knowing he could provide few details about the human trafficking case he was working on, but wanting him to know she was interested and proud of the work he was doing.

He wrapped his arm around her, and pulled her closer.

"Rough," Jack shared. "What those girls went through—it's tough for me to imagine how they lived through what they did. That men could force little girls or women into what the victims were forced to do, and that men, knowing what was going on, paid to rape them. Katie, that's what it was. They paid to rape them. Men know how old girls are, that's the key word— girls—and they were buying a little girl's body. Even if the victim were a grown woman, for a man to have such lack of regard for her—that he would pay to savagely use her, rape her. That's what sex trafficking is," he said angrily. "I just don't understand how the human race has survived, as sick, twisted, and heartless as so many are. I'm sorry," Jack breathed. "I didn't mean for all that to come out."

Katie patted his leg, attempting to sooth and comfort away his thoughts about the case and the girls he was helping. Jack had turned out to be quite the surprise—so dedicated to helping women. Initially when he'd told her he changed from corporate law to specialize in women's rights issues, in this case, sex trafficking, she'd thought there must be some money angle. But he'd proven true to his word. Maybe it was his childhood that had made him care so much, maybe living with all the kids in the children's home seeing all he had as a little boy, or maybe, she reflected, he just had a uniquely beautiful nature. He had a genuine passion for helping victims. Not since her father, had Katie known such a champion for little girls and women. Her dad, she thought, would approve of Jack. She smiled, and rested her head against Jack's shoulder.

"It's a great thing you're doing for those girls," Katie said with emotion. "You're such an amazing man. *A great man.*"

Jack cupped her chin gently in his hand, and just as gently, lifted her face. Their eyes met. He leaned toward her and touched his lips to hers, lingering. Then, he pulled away.

"You're pretty amazing yourself, Ms. Katie," Jack said huskily. He tried to catch his breath. The last thing he wanted to do was scare her away by moving too fast, asking for more than he knew she was ready to give.

Flushed, Katie said, "You're so silly." She tried to catch her breath and emotions as they ran wild along with various other parts of her.

"It's early," Jack noted. "Would you like to cut out of here and go somewhere else?"

"Where'd you have in mind?" Katie asked curiously.

"Somewhere with a little more noise and a lot more action," he said mysteriously.

"Sure," she smiled, and wondered just where he was about to take her.

Twenty five minutes later, the buzz of voices and music from Nan's coffee shop met their ears. The wisps of sleepiness from the pasta they had eaten were gone. They'd walked into a surprise, a few changes to Nan's wine night.

The typical soft and elegant music had been replaced, Nan said, just for the night, by a little more lively music—country music. And she'd added beer to the wine list.

Katie grinned, when Nan shared, "Stu thought it might be a nice change to shake things up a bit."

Well, Katie noticed, it was working. On wine nights, most of the tables and chairs were moved to one of the storage rooms to give guests more space to mingle. Now, Katie noticed in pleasant surprise, there was space enough to be used for dancing. She found herself tapping her booted foot to the beat of an Amanda Lambert song.

"Nan," Katie laughed, raising her voice to be heard over the music, "you better watch it. Stu might just change you from a coffee shop owner to a tavern owner."

"Oh, Katie," Nan said in a loud voice. "There'll be no talk of a tavern. This is just for one night. Although," Nan said, "everyone does seem to be having a good time, don't they?"

"Yes, they do," Katie, said with a grin. "Maybe you can alternate your weekends, you know, elegant one weekend to satisfy the fancy crowd!" Katie laughed. "And then the other weekends have country night."

Katie looked around at the dance floor.

"It's kind of fun!" Katie said. "Where'd you get the music?"

"One of Stu's boys made me a file on his IPod," Nan shared.

"I see," Katie said with a smile. "It looks like Stu had this all figured out." Shaking her head, Katie said, "Now wait a minute, how did I not know you were having country night?"

Waving her hand casually in the air, Nan said, "Oh, with all your worrying about that attorney, I didn't want to bother you with some silly thing like country night."

"But I was just in here the other day!" Katie laughed, "And no one said a word."

"It was a surprise," Nan said. "I didn't know how it would go over, but it seems to be right nice."

Stu, a man a few years older than Nan, and a few inches taller, walked up to Katie's aunt and wrapped his arm around her waist.

"Hey there, Katie," Stu said with a twinkle in his brown eyes. "What do you think?"

Smiling, Katie said, "I think you did a good thing here, Stu." She watched as Jack walked toward them, and when he was close enough to hear, she asked, "Jack, what do you think of country night?"

Gently Jack grabbed Katie around her waist.

"I'm ready to get my country on!" Jack said, enthusiastically. "Yeehaw!" he shouted over the music.

Wrapping her arms around his waist, Katie swayed with Jack to a Jason Aldean song. It was the first time, Katie realized, that they had danced together, if this could be considered dancing.

"Go dance, kids," Stu insisted. "Be young before you're all rickety like me and Nan."

"Hey," Nan said, with a swat of her hand. Grinning, she joked, "Speak for yourself, old man."

"Oh my God, Nan," Katie laughed, as the words *country girl shake it for me* reached her ears.

"Don't look at *me!*" Nan said, in reference to the song that had people swaying their hips to the beat.

"Not me!" Stu said as he pretended to avoid the dig into his ribs from Nan. "It's not *my* IPod. I don't even have one of those things. I don't need no device to hear music. Every time I get around your aunt, we make our own music."

"Oh Lord," Katie groaned. "Okay, I'm coming," she said as Jack tugged at her hand.

They danced with the rest of the crowd to several songs, and as a slow song crooned into the room, Katie allowed Jack to take her into his arms, snuggling into his warmth, loving the way his body felt against hers.

33

As Jack held Katie in his arms, swaying to a country song at Nan's coffee shop—country bar for the evening—Alan was enjoying his own evening out. Clenching a cigar between his teeth, his hand on the steering wheel of his black Mercedes, he looked in the rearview mirror and asked the two men in the backseat, "You all ready for some fun?"

"I'm ready to rock it!" the older, more distinguished man shouted.

"Let's get this party on the road!" the other occupant of the backseat shouted.

Turning to the man riding shotgun, Alan said, "Let's rock," and peeled out of the driveway and sped, with a car following, down the long driveway at his cabin in the southeastern part of Kentucky.

Alan had invited several of the attorneys from the firm, and a few of his old business buddies from Northern Kentucky, to a weekend of fun at his cabin. Since being notified that he was being sued by women at his firm, and discussing the lawsuit with his attorney, Alan had felt the itch to get out of town and cut loose. He deserved to cut loose for a weekend, he justified, what with the headache of his life—the lawsuit. Women, he thought angrily, as he sped down the winding country road toward town—toward the best steak he could find, scotch, and some tits and ass. He planned to get wasted tonight, he thought with resolve, as he chomped down on his cigar and turned the steering wheel.

Alan brooded as he drove the ten minutes to town. Women were constantly playing games—smiling, swaying their hips when they walked, wiggling their asses, shaking their tits, bending over just right so a man could catch a peek of her tits, or bending over real low, ass up, so a man could just almost see the goods. They knew what they were doing, he stewed, and then they sued when a man acted interested in what they had stirred in the first place.

As countryside flew by, his thoughts turned to Katie; she hadn't been listed as a plaintiff in the sexual harassment suit against him. Katie was a tough one to figure out, he considered as he shifted his man goods. The weekend of the retreat she'd wanted him, wanted it, he was pretty sure. The way she'd smiled at him. The way she kept bending over when he was in a room with her, pretending to pick something up. Or was I wrong about her, he wondered. She's not part of the suit. That has to mean something. Damn women and their wiles, he thought, almost biting off the end of his cigar. He chunked the cigar into the beverage holder, spitting loose tobacco into his hand and wiping the remnants onto his navy colored dress pants.

"It's your first sexual harassment suit, the red haired burly man sitting in the passenger's seat said. "We got to celebrate you cutting your teeth as a business owner. Hell, I can't believe you've gone this long without getting sued!" The man laughed. "I remember my first," he said, comparing the first time he was sued by a female employee for groping her to losing his virginity. "God, she was hot!"

The car erupted in laughter, and soon Alan was pulling into the parking lot of the restaurant where they served the best steaks in town. As the two cars full of men walked into the restaurant, one of the men slapped Alan on the back and said, "Welcome to the club, old man. Sure took you long enough to catch up!"

Steak, potatoes, onions, four beers later, and Alan was ready for the next phase of his night—tits and ass. Banging his empty beer mug on the table, Alan bellowed, "Titties!"

"Titties!" the group of men shouted and burped.

The group of men threw over two hundred dollars in cash on the table for the waitress for her tip—their befuddle states of mind gave up trying to calculate the tip percentage.

Sipping on scotch, Alan watched with surprisingly little interest as the girl, looking to be not much older than his own daughter, gyrated above him, her nipples, attached to very obvious artificially enhanced breasts, almost touching his face. Typically, in this situation, Alan would make the most of the opportunity by lunging forward and getting in a lick, nibble, or a pinch. More of an ass man, he would be squeezing some stripper ass by now too. Bouncers always rushed at him, warning him to keep his hands off the goods, but they never kicked him out, not *the* great Alan Weaver, Alan thought. Many perks in the life of the rich and bored, he thought as he tucked a one hundred dollar bill in the girl's thread of a G-string as she climbed off him, and then hips swaying, walked away.

Bare skin flashed all around him—a blur—as he thought of the conversation he'd had with Nancy about the lawsuit. Of course, he'd had to tell his wife the law firm was being sued before she read about it in the newspaper or online. He'd told her his version of why he was being sued, his version of the truth that a few of the women who worked for him were uptight, frigid bitches looking for an easy money score. Nancy had wanted a few more details than what he initially provided so he had shared the Dale and Erin relationship gone bad situation. 'Lover's tiff,' Nancy had said. Nancy had suggested he have the new HR person write a no dating policy in the employee procedure manual, that way these things would never happen again. Alan had explained to her how tough it was for business leaders to date, not as if they could hit the bars without being scrutinized. The average man could hit a bar for a little fun, but a leader of the community had to find different ways, find other places for female companionship. Business was a large part of a business leader's life so that was where his pool of women was typically found. She had understood, understood how stressful it was for men in power and the complexity of their lives.

Looking across the smoke-filled room, taking in the girls shaking their tits in men's faces and grinding their stuff on stage, Alan watched his buddies as they sat next to a stage hooping, and hollering for the girls to strip it all off. They were paying to see pussy, not a G-string, they shouted. Alan downed his glass of scotch, his fuzzy mind wondering if this was really all there was, sitting in a titty bar with a bunch of middle-aged, horny men, watching girls young enough to be their daughters simulate sex in front of them. A cheap, sick, turn on that would have them beating off later at the memory of someone's daughter on a stage, or beat off in front of them while they shook what God gave them, all for just a few dollars. Had life always been this way, Alan wondered, as he ordered another scotch.

Closing his eyes tight, Alan ran his hand down his face. Sitting up taller, he allowed his hands to rest on his lap, and then shook his head to clear the crazy thoughts from his mind. Must be some bad alcohol, he mused as he tried to clear his conscious and get back to his night of celebration with his buddies.

"It's all just good fun," Jack said aloud to himself.

"Sright," the drunk stranger sitting next to him said, and slapped Alan on the back.

34

Katie, her face pressed against Jack's shoulder, peeked at her aunt Nan and Stu, now swaying together to not only their own internal music, but to another country song. Katie sighed.

"You okay?" Jack asked, pulling away and looking down at her, concerned that he was holding her to tight.

"Perfect," she said softly, and tucked back into him. And she was, she thought as she closed her eyes for a moment. She'd never known life could be this way—living—realizing up to now, since her senior year of high school, she'd only been existing because she'd been too fearful to let the world in. Life had quietly and slowly been passing her by, she mused. She hadn't realized that she'd just been existing, not fully living; she'd unconsciously chosen safety in everything. Had the reality of now, of fully living, not crept in, she never would have known the fullness of emotions . . . of life.

Jack's lips brushed her forehead as the song ended.

"Drink?" he asked as he pulled away. Taking both her hands in his, hands clasped, he pulled her back to him.

"I am a little thirsty," she said, with a glint in her eye that he noticed as he led her to the library room.

After Jack had finished his beer, and Katie her glass of wine, Jack asked, "Go to my place for a while?"

She rose from the couch in the library room, took his hand in her hand, and pulled him to his feet.

Once outside, they paused under the awning and watched the gentle rain. Katie and Jack looked at each other.

"You ready to run for it?" Jack asked, with a broad grin, the dimple in his cheek deepening.

"Ready!" Katie shouted, and they sprinted to his truck down the street.

"Damn!" Katie said. "Nothing colder than a November rain." She rubbed her shoulders and then swiped her wet hair off her face.

Jack, his hands on the steering wheel, mused at how beautiful she was, her hair in messy wet tendrils about her face, and droplets of water wetting her cheeks. He reached across the truck and brushed her rain kissed cheek. Then he scooted closer, and tangling his hand in her hair, leaned in and kissed her softly at first, then with heat, burning brighter. She returned his kiss, matching his fire.

They parted, the fire between them burning deep in their eyes. Jack started his truck, pulled away from the curb, and headed for his house in the country.

35

～

"**D**amn! Where's Art?" Alan slurred to his buddies at the strip club.

"He's getting his jizum on," one of the senior partners laughed.

"No point in ordering another drink," Alan observed. "As old as he is, it'll take all of thirty seconds. Oh! There he comes now!" Alan shouted, as his companions broke out in laughter.

"Thought we lost you, buddy," Alan said as he leaned against his red headed friend.

"I was helping some lovely with her college tuition," Art slurred.

"More likely her high school tuition!" the senior partners laughed.

"Let's head to another bar," Alan said. "All these titties in here are starting to look the same."

The rowdy, drunk group of men stumbled out of the bar, and barely registering that it had begun to rain, stumbled down the sidewalk to several other bars before deciding to call it a night.

"Now where's my car?" Alan slurred as he stood in the rain looking bleary-eyed around him at the headlights of passing vehicles, and then at his friends. "Anyone remember where we parked?" he burped.

"This way, the driver of the other car said," waving his hand for the men to follow him. "This way!"

Alan smacked his head on the side of the car before he fell back onto the driver's seat with a thud. He fumbled with his key as he attempted to insert it into the ignition, dropping it to the floor.

"Lemme do it," Art insisted. "Alan, my man. Let's switch places. You can't even find the damn key hole, so I know you won't be able to find your cabin."

"Good point," Alan agreed.

After both men stumbled and swerved drunkenly around the car, Art, the lesser drunk of the two, pulled the car out of the parking garage, flipped on the windshield wipers, and slipped into the stream of traffic.

"Where we turn?" Art asked as he ducked his head and squinted his eyes thinking that would help him remember the directions to Alan's cabin and make something seem familiar.

"Up there," Alan said, flinging his arm in the air. "Damn, red! You missed the turn!"

"Hang onto your nuts!" Art said, as tires slipping on the wet pavement, he did a U-turn.

"Shit, Art!" Alan laughed. "You're driving the wrong way. Get on the right side of the road," he slurred, as he grabbed the wheel and tried to veer the car into the correct direction of traffic.

"I got it!" Art laughed, and swerved across the lane of traffic, now driving in the correct direct.

"Shit!" Alan said as he heard sirens behind them. "Let me do the talking."

"License and registration, and proof of insurance," the stern officer insisted.

Alan leaned over, and smiled up at the officer who looked uncomfortable in the downpour.

"Hey, Tim, how's your daddy doing?" Alan asked.

The officer, looking young enough to have just graduated from the police academy, leaned down, placed his hand on the car, and grinned.

"Alan, is that you, man?" the young officer asked. "Dad didn't tell me you were in town. How the hell are you?"

Alan and Tim's dad were buddies from way back.

"I'm in town for the weekend on business," Alan slurred.

"Awe, well you guys better take your business on to your cabin," Tim said with a grin.

"Tell your daddy hi for me!" Alan said with a salute.

"Alan, my man," Art said. "You are a man of many talents and connections," and pulled back into the stream of traffic.

36

"Do you want anything to drink?" Jack asked, as Katie hung her coat in the hall closet and kicked off her boots.

Following him into the kitchen, she watched as he flipped on the sink faucet, filled a glass with water, and then took a gulp.

"That," Katie said, indicating a glass of water, "would be perfect."

Katie opened a cabinet nearby, selected a clear glass and filled it with cold water. Jack leaned with his backside against the counter and watched her intently as she drank, and then set her glass on the counter beside her. He held out his hands to her. Thunder boomed, and startled, she jumped.

She went to him, walked into his arms and wrapped her arms around his neck. They consumed one another in a hungry kiss. A moan escaped her when he pressed his lips against her neck. Their lips met again, and then they pulled back, their breath ragged, their eyes probing one another.

Katie shifted away from him, and took his hand in hers, giving it a gentle tug. He followed her from the kitchen.

Much later, curled into one another on Jack's bed—covered only by a sheet—they slept to the soft soothing rumble of the November thunderstorm.

37

"Who's drinking with me?" Alan shouted over the boom of thunder, from the kitchen on the second floor of his cabin. Reaching for a bottle of scotch, he filled a glass with amber colored liquid.

Most of the men mumbled thanks, but they were ready to call it a night, and headed to bed, barely able to stand from all the alcohol they had consumed, that and the fact that it was four in the morning.

"Bunch of pussies!" Alan called after them. "The party is just getting started!" He was alone in the kitchen with his friend, Art.

"Have a drink with me, Art," Alan insisted as he handed his friend a glass filled with scotch.

"It's the good stuff," Alan insisted. "Not the shit they sell at the bars."

"To you!" Art said, and raised his glass. "You have arrived at the doorstep of success, joining me in the world of seshual harasssssment," he slurred.

An hour later, and after another glass of scotch was downed, the house bathed in the November rain from the thunderstorm, Art helped Alan down the stairs to the theatre room. At the state beyond drunk, they decided to watch a movie.

"If you really wanna party," Art said, "I've got what you need."

"The hell you say," Alan said. "Art, you know I don't go that way."

Art fell onto the couch beside Alan, and slurred, "No, you dumb shit." Leaning up against Alan who was slumped against the arm of the couch, Art held up a small plastic bag with something inside. "This," he said.

"Whatsat?" Alan asked curiously. "Is that what I think it is?" He took the bag from his friend's fingers. "Well, shit! I've always wanted to try this."

"For special occasions," Art slurred, with a grin.

"Let's fire this shit up, and cook it, or whatever we do with it!" Alan insisted.

"Ahhh, no need for cooking. We're gonna do like coke, and snort it," Art said as he leaned forward and placed the bag on the table.

Fifteen minutes later, Art looked down at Alan, appearing to be in a deep sleep on the couch in the theatre room. "Welcome to the club, Alan," Art slurred. "Anyone can be in the mile high club, but few are allowed into the sued for sexual harassment club. Today, you are a true man!" He raised his fist in celebration. "I'm going to bed. Don't wake me in the morning!" He giggled as he walked toward the door, leaving his passed out friend in the room alone.

Hours later, Art heard a pounding on his bedroom door, and rolled over, pressing his pillow over his head. He felt someone pull at him, shake him and yell his name.

"Art!" shouted one of the senior attorney's from Alan's law firm. "Get up, man!"

"If you don't get the fuck out of my room . . ." Art shouted as he rolled over, and sat up.

"It's Alan!" the senior attorney, said.

"What about Alan. He's in the movie room, now get the fuck out and let me sleep," Art said as he flopped back against the bed.

"He's dead," the senior attorney said.

38

The next morning Katie woke to Jack's arm draped over her waist, and the sound of rain—a perfect pairing for a lazy morning. Not ready to leave the warmth of his body, she snuggled into him. She realized he was awake when she felt his fingers run the length of her arm.

She rolled toward him, looked into his sleepy eyes, and draped a leg over him.

"Morning," she murmured.

He kissed her forehead, and returned, "Morning," and pulled her closer.

They lay nestled in one another's arms in no hurry to leave the bed. Lazily they explored each other, finding parts undiscovered from the night before.

Later, after they had showered—Katie dressed in one of Jack's shirts long enough to skim her knees—they sat on the back porch that overlooked the small pond and forest of trees, and sipped mugs of hot coffee. The rain had stopped, leaving the world fresh and clean, Katie noticed as she sat snuggled next to Jack on the cushion covered wicker couch, her feet tucked beneath her.

"The world sure is beautiful after it rains," Jack commented.

Agreeing, Katie smiled contentedly as she looked up into Jack's face, rugged with morning stubble. "It certainly is," she agreed.

"I'd suggest a walk," Jack said, "but I'm afraid you'd ruin your pretty boots."

Katie laughed. He'd been surprised when she'd worn a pair of cowboy boots, a change from her city girl image from life at the law firm. She'd explained, that like him, she had two sides; she would always be a lady who loved to dress up in heels, but also loved to stomp around in a pair of worn out boots. She loved both worlds, the always knowing you would hear a hello and see a wave of a hand in a small town, and the not so good aspect of everyone knowing your business. In the city, waving at someone as you drove by might have the recipient of the wave thinking you were wanting drugs, and although just as many people knew your business, you could get lost in the million-large crowd. The city could be a heartless place to be, unless you found your little community within the larger community, such as in those areas nestled in the heart of the inner city, like Mainstrasse Village in Covington, Kentucky—a place where those of less snobbish origins, yet lovers of the city, converged.

Jack loved that Katie could be comfortable in a small country town, and yet also felt at home in the city. She was never boring, that was for sure. He was finding that, as she let her guard down, she was layer after layer of pleasant surprises.

Katie stood up and walked toward the window of the enclosed porch. She stretched as she looked out over the pond. A thick curtain of evergreen trees met her eyes, and beyond the trees was a mountain. She mused, it will be beautiful in the spring with the cattails blowing in the breeze around the pond, ducks swimming lazily, grass a rich green, and wild flowers beginning to bloom.

"What's going on in that brilliant and creative mind of yours?" Jack asked. "Thinking about your next book?" Katie had shared the idea for her next book with Jack. He'd loved the idea, and had even provided food for thought about character development.

She craned her neck toward him, and said, "No. Just daydreaming about spring, and how beautiful it will be back here." She turned back to the picturesque view, and continued, "With the flowers in bloom, and the pond . . ."

Standing next to her, Jack pointed toward the pond, toward the end closest to the path leading to the house.

"I plan to build a small dock at that end," he said. "There used to be one, years ago. Great place to spend the day fishing, or just being. Over there," Jack pointed to an area where trees would provide shade in the spring and summer, "would be a great place to curl up and dream of the books that need to be written, and even write them. There'll be an outside living area there, after I have a concrete floor poured, and with furniture, on Saturday mornings, I can fish and you can write . . ." Jack dreamed.

Leaning back against him, Katie looked where he pointed and envisioned a summer day, and sighed.

An hour later, Katie stood on the first step that lead to the porch of Jack's house. She looked down at the water that had invaded the front yard from the previous night's storm and contemplated her path choices to his truck. She considered what strategic plan she could devise to avoid wading through the miniature lake that was now his front yard. She sighed and thought, from the looks of his yard, he now lives in a boathouse. She looked down at her boots, then back at the water covered yard.

She shrieked in surprise when Jack grabbed her and gallantly waded through the puddle that swallowed his booted feet. Katie laughed and clung to his shoulders.

When he made it to dry land, he dropped her to her feet, and with a bow, said, "Me lady."

"Oh my Lord," she laughed. "Your gallantry needs some work! You almost dropped me in the water."

Jack leapt forward, picked her up, and spun her in a circle. She shrieked as he pretended he was going to drop her in the puddle, but instead he stopped and kissed her as she wrapped her arms around his neck. He allowed her to slide the length of him to the ground, her arms still wrapped around his neck. On her tiptoes, face to face, they kissed one last time before she turned and walked to the passenger side of the truck.

"Hey, Nan," Katie called out as she bent down and patted Hunter. She walked into the kitchen where she found Nan doing what she loved, cooking.

"Well, looky what the cat done dragged in, "Nan said with a smile. What a change, Nan considered as she looked up at her niece, watching as she pulled out a stool and sat down.

"Do you want some coffee?" Nan asked as she watched Katie turn on her cell phone.

Smiling, Katie said, "I could use a cup. Thanks." She opened a text from Erin. As she read, the smile slipped from her lips.

"Sweets, are you okay?" Nan asked as she saw the smile slip from Katie's face, and the color in her cheeks fade away.

Katie inhaled and reread the text to confirm that she'd read the message correctly. She had.

"It's—it's from Erin . . . the text," she said, and flipped her cell around so Nan could see the words lit up on the face of her phone.

"Is she alright?" Nan asked.

"She's fine," Katie said flatly. "But, Alan . . . he's dead."

Furrowing her brow in surprise, Nan said, "What? *The* Alan . . . your ex-boss, Alan . . . the untouchable man, Alan? What happened?"

"Drug overdose," Katie shared. "The man overdosed on heroin. My God, I didn't even know he used heroin." She closed her eyes, and shrugged. She blinked. She lifted her hands, palms up toward the sky, and continued, "I—not that I would have known . . . but maybe I should have known," she murmured. "That would explain his actions . . . I suppose." Her hands fell to her sides as she exclaimed, "What a selfish bastard!"

"Now, Katie," Nan chided. "You do *not* know what goes on in another person's mind, heart, or life."

"He had it *all*, Nan. A family, extended family, friends, and all the money a person could want. What possible struggle could the man have had? Hell, he took whatever he wanted, even things that didn't belong to him!" she insisted, angrily.

"Katie!" Nan said sharply. "The man is dead. Don't be walking on his grave with angry feet. Any person that does drugs—dies like that—was a tormented soul running from something. You just wish his spirit well. Pray God has him in a place where he finally feels peace."

"I'm sorry, Nan," Katie said, embarrassed by her anger and sorry for lashing out at a dead man. "You're right."

"Take a drink of your coffee," Nan insisted, and then asked, "What else did the text say?"

"Erin said Alan and some of the attorneys were on one of their boondoggles at his cabin, you know a weekend of drinking, and probably women—strip joints," waving her hand, "what they do—did. One of the guys found him on a couch in the movie room, stinking of vomit, at least according to Erin. I'm sure she has details that aren't in the news. Which, she said I could read a brief statement on the internet. There's a link in the text."

"Holy shit!" Katie said.

"Katie!" Nan said sharply. "Language."

Katie laughed, and said, "Seriously, Nan . . . now . . . language?"

"Well, I guess that will end the lawsuit," Nan said thoughtfully.

"Not necessarily," Katie said. "They can still sue the firm. The firm's still in existence. But I do wonder how it's all going to work out now that Alan's gone," she considered.

"I'm going to do a little writing," Katie said absently as she pushed back the stool she'd been sitting on. Grabbing her coffee mug, she walked out of the kitchen with Hunter trailing behind.

Katie left the door to the writing room open and walked across the room, stood in front of the large window, and looked out over the yard—across the road at the field. She wrapped her arms around her waist, closed her eyes, and inhaled deeply. Opening her eyes, she stared out of the window again, at the November day. She felt Hunter bump her leg, wanting her attention.

"What is it boy?" she asked. Walking over to her desk, Katie said, "Come here. Come see me."

Wagging his tail, Hunter followed her. He brushed her hand with his large head.

She sat down on her desk chair. Hunter bumped her knee, getting as close as possible for some earnest scratching. Leaning down toward him, looking into the dog's eyes, she said, "You are so lucky to be a dog, so the good life." With one more scratch of his head, she rolled her chair toward the desk, and then clicked her computer to life.

Katie stared at the computer screen, and the computer screen stared back.

"What?" she asked the screen. She sighed. Closing her eyes, she shook her head. She opened her eyes, her computer screen still staring at her.

"So much for getting an apology from the man," she said, and then laughed, the sound of her laugh brittle to her ears. "What is wrong with men?" Katie asked her computer, wishing the machine could provide all the answers to her many life questions.

"How many more? How many more miserable power pricks are going to end up like Alan?" Leaning forward, Katie clicked the mouse to access the internet, searching for an article about Alan's death.

Several hours later, Nan said, "Hey, sweets. Fresh cup of coffee?"

Leaning back on her chair, Katie said, "Thanks, Nan," and accepted the coffee mug from her aunt's hand.

"Sure is dark in here," Nan said as she switched on the small desk lamp.

Katie blinked as the room was bathed in a soft glow of light.

"How's the book going?" Nan asked.

Placing her hands behind her head, Katie stretched, and said, "Okay."

Nan examined Katie, knowing Alan was weighing heavily on her mind. It was who she was. Death bothered her—reminded her of her parents—triggered waves of emotional sadness memories.

"You know, Nan, something's bothering me," Katie said as she reached toward the ornate silver pencil holder and grabbed a pen, twirling it between her fingers.

"What's that?" Nan asked.

Katie paused and considered how to say what she wanted to say, sorting her thoughts and emotions.

She tapped the pen on the desk a few times, and then said, "That night, you know, at the cabin. When I was driving home—after what happened at the cabin—I prayed about Alan, *for* Alan."

"Well that's not so unusual," Nan said.

Katie looked up, and grimaced at her aunt. "It's *what* I prayed that might be considered unusual," Katie said.

Nan scooted the armchair toward the desk, getting settled in for what looked to be a long talk.

Tucking a foot beneath her on the chair, Katie folded her arms across her chest, and stared over the desk at her aunt.

"I prayed that Alan would lose everything—every penny he had hidden in accounts around the world—his job, law firm, wife, his children . . . but . . . but, not in death," Katie said quickly, with a wave of her hand. "And I prayed he'd lose *every* paid for friend he had. I prayed that *no one* would give him a penny, or *loan* him a penny even with a ridiculously high interest rate." She sighed, and with a sad smile continued. "My prayer was my gift to him because I wanted him to know what it meant, what it was like to be human, to feel like the rest of us. To know the pain of what life is really like—loneliness, loss, and things that matter. I prayed for him to lose his money because I knew that was such an important part of him. It was his identity. His money was why he could do all the evil shit he does, I mean, did, and got away with it. And . . . and, all that money he had squirreled away around the world prevented him from really living. When you have *nothing*, you have the chance to see and feel what is around you, and appreciate what *really* matters. You know, like the brilliant blue color of a morning glory flower, or feel the kiss of a November rain on your face," Katie said, as she reached up and touched her cheek.

Nan watched Katie, the depth in her eyes making her eyes a deeper color of green, her heart, and soul pouring into the room as she shared her prayer.

Katie lowered her hand to the armrest of her chair, and said, "I prayed he would struggle in life, on his own, so that life would give him the opportunity to grow into a person of substance that could actually contribute something to the world on a warm human level, something of value. God, I didn't mean for him to *die*, Nan . . . to kill him with my prayer. I—I just, you know, by struggling, by losing parts of us that are dear to us, we gain so much in life . . . a sense of self, purpose, empathy and a true sense of love for the world." With tears in her eyes, Katie said, "I didn't pray for him to die . . . to die."

Nan rose from her chair and walked around the desk to her niece. She bent down and hugged her.

"Oh, sweets," Nan said gently. "You didn't pray the man to death, if that's what's going on in that sweet head of yours."

Nan pulled away, grabbed a tissue from the box on the desk, and handed it to Katie.

Leaning against the desk, Nan said, "You can't pray someone to death; if you could, there'd be a lot less people in the world. Prayers just like the one you prayed are sent heavenward every day!"

Katie blew her nose, and then laughed at how silly she had sounded.

"Bad is just bad," Nan insisted. "Some people just can't be helped, and those with more money than conscious, well, a person can't survive like that . . . live a real life. I mean," Nan said, with a shake of her head, "people want money, do all kinds of things to get it, not realizing that if a person doesn't have a fully functioning, strong internal compass, it becomes a cancer. Money and power can eat a person up, like it did with Alan. Folks with more money than they need never know who their friends are, because really, money shines pretty bright in those kinds of friendships."

"We're blessed we don't have that problem," Katie said as she smiled and looked up at her aunt.

"Count yourself blessed that being filthy rich will never be on your list of troubles," Nan said with a wink. "You okay," Nan asked.

"Yeah," Katie said with a thoughtful smile.

"What do you have going on tonight? Date with *Jack?*" Nan asked with a flutter of her lashes.

Laughing, Katie said, "Stop! *Lady!* What do *you* have going on? Stu for dinner?" Katie teased.

"Shameful!" Nan said as she swatted playfully at her niece's leg.

"You started it!" Katie laughed as she followed her aunt out of her writing room.

Leaning against the counter in the kitchen, Katie said, "We're going to the wine tasting on the square tonight."

"Oh, yeah?" Nan said. "It's an event they have each year the week before Thanksgivinsg. You'll have fun. They'll have tents set up for three blocks, with warming stations placed along the way, outside of the tents. The music is always real nice."

On the drive to the town square, Katie and Jack discussed Alan's death.

"My mom and I lost my dad to his drug addiction, but even before it took his last breath, it had already taken him from us," Jack shared. "The demon of drugs—addiction—doesn't discriminate. It'll take a man or woman of any economic status, the only requirement's a feeling of emptiness that can't be filled . . . like with my dad, and even Alan."

Dressed warm in a coat cinched at the waist, fingertip-less gloves, jeans and her brown cowboy boots, Katie stood at one of the three warming stations rubbing her hands together. The wine she had sampled from several of the local wineries had helped warm the November chill from her.

"Hey," Jack said as he wrapped an arm around her and pulled her to him. "Are you warm enough?"

"Hmmm," Katie grinned. "With the wine I've consumed, this toasty fire thingy here, and the large snuggly man next to me, yes . . . yes, I'm warm enough."

She laced her fingers through his, turned toward him, and raised her other hand, resting it at the back of his neck, her eyes on his lips. She rose on her tiptoes.

"Katie," Jack said.

"Jack," she said playfully.

"I need to talk to you," he said, his voice serious.

"You are talking to me," she teased.

When he didn't smile in return, she said, "Oh." Her hand fell from his neck. She stepped back, putting space between them.

Bluntly, he said, "I was offered a job in D.C."

"D.C." she said, confused. "But you have a job. Your private practice in Asheville."

"I know," he said, shaking his head. "The job I was offered in D.C. is related to the work I do at my practice."

Katie wrinkled her forehead, and said, "Jack, you are making *absolutely* zero sense."

"There's a human trafficking task force that's been created in D.C., and they want me to take part in it, which means a move to D.C. They want me closer to the policy makers," he explained.

"You're talking about hobnobbing with politicians, which essentially is one step away from hell . . . even worse than . . . than people like Alan!" she exploded. "You sell out!"

The sight of the man she cared about, selling his soul to the devil, disgusted her. Angrily, she turned away from him, and walked away, away from his lies.

"Katie . . . *Katie,*" he shouted after her.

Seeing she wasn't going to stop, he followed her. Catching up to her, Jack grabbed her elbow and turned her toward him.

"Stop!" he insisted.

"Did you accept the offer?" she demanded.

"Katie . . ." he stammered.

"You did," she said, and jerked her arm away. Dismissing him, and with resolve in her step, she briskly walked away. For her, the evening was over.

He followed her, shouting, "Katie, let me explain!"

"How long have you known?" she demanded as she spun around.

He stopped short of colliding into her, and confessed, "Since Thursday."

She flung her arm in the air as angry tears burned her eyes. "I *trusted* you! I let you in. You, *asshole!* What . . . what . . . last night, and this morning? Knowing that you were leaving?" Flinging a hand on her hip she stared at him and angrily, asked, "Just what do you think I am? Use me and then toss me aside? Is that how it is?"

"Katie—Katie, I have to move if I want to make a real impact against this nightmare, human trafficking," he pleaded. "I thought . . . hoped, that you would come with me."

"Jack," Katie said, her voice thick with tears, "I think it's great what you're doing, representing women. But I can't—*won't*—be part of that world. A world of filth and corruption."

"Katie, I love you," Jack pleaded. "Please go with me. Be with me."

"I can't—I—I love you too, Jack, but I can't," Katie said. Bitter tears glistened on her cheeks. "It will change you . . . that place . . . those people. Some of those 'policy makers' are the same types of men that use, that *rape* girls and women, like the girls and women you defend. You know I'm right."

Katie felt as if the last part of her—the part that had survived after she'd been gang-raped, and then slowly begun to slip away when Alan had assaulted her, and she discovered Brad's infidelity—was dying.

"I gave you all of me, all of me I had to give . . . *all of me*. And now there's nothing . . . nothing," she said as hot tears slid over her lashes.

Katie stood on her toes and brushed her lips against his, then pulled away.

"I love you, Jack," she said. "But I won't watch you become Alan."

She walked away as he stared after her.

SEVEN MONTHS LATER

The two couples were enjoying a lazy June afternoon at Jack's house, sitting under the trees in the expansive backyard—in the outside living area on the concrete slab where slate tile had recently been laid. The living area was situated at one end—the end where they were celebrating—with a heavy wicker couch, love seat, and chair snugged around an oversized coffee table. There was a table and chairs positioned at the other end for dining purposes. It was the space where Jack and Katie whiled away evenings drinking tea, or glasses of wine as they watched the wild flowers and cattails sway in the early summer breeze, and the ducks swim on the pond.

"Cheers," Katie said as four champagne glasses clinked together. Careful not to spill any of the liquid in her glass, Katie hugged her aunt, and then Stu. "It's about time you proposed, Stu!"

"I'm glad I have your blessing," Stu said with sincerity warming his voice. "Your aunt stole my heart years ago, and I've been asking her for years to be my bride. You can't imagine how happy she made me when she finally said yes."

"Awe," Katie said, and hugged him again, moved by the sweetness of the man who would soon be her uncle.

"So, what made you finally cave, Nan?" Jack asked.

"Oh, a little something—someone—inspired me," Nan said as she looked at Katie, "not to be afraid to live. And I said . . . *yes!!*" She beamed, and raised her hand so Katie could see the engagement ring, again.

Jack had grown close to Nan over the past many months, and had offered his house and backyard for her wedding. The couple were going to say their *I Do's* on the newly built dock, with most of the town in attendance, Katie mused. Nan had chosen the end of July for her wedding, before school began in the fall, so that Stacey and Emily would be able to attend.

Since the wedding announcement, several weeks ago, there had been many excited conversations over the phone, and via Skype with both Emily and Stacey. Emily had grown a great deal since Katie had seen her the summer before—now so very grown up, Katie thought. Tears of pride and love had sprung to Katie's eyes when Emily shared, via Skype, her little world of friends and school. And she had excitedly shown her a letter she'd written that said 'I love you, Aunt Katie.' Stacey too, was adjusting well to her new life and her job as a civilian nurse.

A lot had happened since last summer, and since the wine tasting event last November, Katie reflected—many surprises.

Jack had accepted the job in D.C., but he'd presented a condition to working with the human trafficking task force, and that was that he would only do so if it was in an advisory capacity. That way, it wouldn't be necessary to live in D.C., or even attend meetings in person which satisfied Katie's no elbow rubbing with corrupt politicians. Jack knew he would be a positive force in creating laws that would protect victims of human trafficking—enforcing the maximum punishment for both pimps and Johns—and he could do so all from his office in Asheville, or his office at home in Marion.

Erin and the other ladies had won their lawsuit against Alan's law firm, which was not much of a surprise considering the statement Katie had submitted corroborating that Erin had followed proper procedure when she reported the assaults. But, Katie reflected, the statement she'd provided in support of Erin's case, as the HR representative at the time of the assaults at the Weaver law firm, had played just a small part in the ladies winning the class action suit.

Alan's death had been considered suspicious by the authorities, which had resulted in an autopsy of his body. The autopsy revealed there had been alcohol, cocaine, and heroin in his system at the time of his death. The questions his family and the authorities needed answered were, was Alan's death the result of foul play or an accidental overdose, and who was the supplier of the cocaine and heroin?

Those in Alan's personal and professional circles had been questioned, and his office, home and cabin had been searched for any evidence that might provide a clue. The supplier of the heroin had been found, and something more—something unexpected—had been found during the search at his cabin. It was what had spurred Katie to join the class action suit against the Weaver law firm.

Frowning, she remembered the morning she'd driven to Northern Kentucky, at the request of an FBI agent. During the investigation into Alan's death, discs had been found at his cabin—several were videos of Alan having sex with known prostitutes, many underage, and other unidentified women. And another disc had been found, one linking Alan to Katie, the disc an FBI agent wanted her to review with her in her office in Northern Kentucky. The disc the FBI wanted Katie to review was a video from the night she'd been sexually assaulted in Alan's bedroom. Not only had Alan sexually assaulted her, he'd had the nerve, or stupidity, to record the assault.

Katie had sat in the FBI agent's office, next to the agent, as she'd played the disc. The night of the assault, Katie had felt Alan's hands all over her, but as she'd sat in the FBI agent's office, she'd *watched* Alan's hands tug at her, touch her. She'd insisted the FBI agent stop the video mid-way into the assault, having seen enough, barely able to hold back the vomit burning the back of her throat.

Katie was informed that Alan had small cameras installed in the ceilings of the bedrooms at his cabin, barely detectable to the human eye. The small light that had caught her eye while lying in her bed at Alan's cabin, had been a camera recording her. He'd recorded her every move while she was in the bedroom, and quite probably watched the recording later. He'd even installed a camera in his own bedroom at the cabin, which was how he had filmed the assault.

After seeing the sexual assault with her own eyes, on a computer screen, filmed by Alan, Katie had been deeply and darkly humiliated, shamed, and angry. He'd not only sexually assaulted her, but recorded the attack so he could watch it over and over again, and possibly shared the videos with his buddies, she'd speculated. She still had difficulty wrapping her head around such an evil mind, and actions.

Katie had still feared becoming part of the lawsuit, knowing she could be met with ridicule and cruelty by those she knew, and those she did not know—similar to the rape trial when she'd been a teenager. She knew that the Weaver camp—supporters of Alan—would be ruthless in destroying her and the other victims. But Alan was gone, she had assured herself, and could not personally hurt her—now it would just be strangers that taunted her, and the media.

But finally, she knew she was strong enough, and angry enough, to take a stand. Bravely, she had contacted the attorney who had visited her at Nan's house, and agreed to become part of the class action suit. And with the new evidence, the disc of Alan sexually assaulting Katie, and the other discs found at the cabin, his estate had settled quickly. His family had wanted to keep as many details about Alan's indiscretions out of the media as possible. Fortunately, for all of the women who had been part of the sexual harassment suit, they had been spared a media nightmare.

Just a month ago, Katie had received a check as her part of the settlement. The money would be useful, she reflected, as she started her own life—for a house of her own—not wanting to be a third wheel when Stu and Nan were married. She needed her own home—a place where she could grow her own garden, and dreams. And the seedling of an idea to develop an organization that would help women and girls who had been victims of violent crimes, including crimes in the workplace, had grown into a beautiful garden of an idea. A place where they could seek help to build new lives.

Jack had loved her idea, and considered that human trafficking victims, homeless kids, and foster kids aging out of the system might also benefit from such an organization. They would finally have a resource, a fighting chance, to make it in the world. The organization had grown quickly from the dream to the development phase. With Jack's legal knowledge and connections, and Katie's expertise leading teams, her business knowledge, and perspective as a survivor, their dream had taken wings with a business plan created and a building found in Asheville.

"Congratulations to you, too, Katie," Stu said.

"What?" Katie said, caught daydreaming.

"On your book. Congratulations," Stu said.

Katie had self-published her second book to great success over a month ago. Her books had been well-received, and were selling well on the internet—readers throughout the world were getting lost in her books, learning about the difficulties of being a young girl in a broken world where sexual violence was the norm. And about the challenges women face in the business world and in their personal lives—born into a world that places a lesser value on a woman because of her gender. Her books shined a light on power and corruption, and the eventual fall of those evils as those in power are consumed by the darkness of their never-ending emptiness. The books were messages for the sisterhood of victims and survivors, of hope for a better future.

"Thank you, Stu," Katie smiled.

"That's my girl," Nan beamed, "the author."

Jack squeezed Katie's hand, and when she looked at him—sitting next to her, his arm draped behind her on the loveseat—she saw his love for her glowing in his eyes.

He was proud of her for not giving up on the world, for fighting back, knowing it had been difficult to join the sexual harassment lawsuit, to open the door to a potential societal and media attack. And he knew the bravery it had taken to trust enough to open her heart and write about her past, and then publish her life, all in an effort to help other girls and women.

"Walk with me?" Jack asked.

Rising to her feet, Katie tugged his hand in response.

"We're going for a little walk," Katie said to Nan and Stu.

Hunter had gotten to his feet when Katie stood up, and Nan said, "Hunter, come here."

The yellow lab walked over and nudged Nan's hand with his nose, his tail wagging.

"Why don't you stay here with Stu and me," Nan said as she scratched Hunter's neck.

"You kids go right ahead," Nan said, smiling.

Nan watched, as hand in hand, Katie and Jack walked toward the pond. Such a handsome pair, Nan thought as she watched the breeze catch at Katie's white sundress, and blew her hair into her face. She watched Jack tuck a stray strand of hair behind Katie's ear, and as Katie smiled up at him.

"What are you thinkin' about?" Stu asked as he watched the love of his life tear up.

"What a beautiful bride Katie's going to be," Nan responded with a sigh.

Jack and Katie walked to the end of the newly built dock. At the edge, they stood and looked out across the water toward the mountains in the distance. As they stood watching the cattails sway in the North Carolina summer breeze, Katie thought about what Nan had said to her in her garden the summer before. Nan had told her that God—or the universe—was holding a door open for her, just waiting for her to let go of her fear and walk across the threshold to her destiny.

Katie reached for Jack's hand, and twined her fingers through his.

Jack turned toward Katie, leaned down toward her, and pressed his lips to hers. Her lips parted to receive his kiss.

"I love you, Katie," Jack said, his voice breaking with the intensity of his love for her.

"I love you too, Jack," she said with trust shining in her eyes.

For long moments, they enjoyed the comfort of one another's arms.

Jack pulled back and smiled down into Katie's upturned, expectant face. Her eyes, he noticed, sparkled brilliantly in the sun. Overcome with emotion for the gentle, loving woman leaning into him, he brushed her cheek with the tips of his fingers.

"You never told me," he said in a voice bridled with emotion, "the wish you made the night at the fountain, did it ever come true?"

Squeezing tightly into him, she looked deep into his eyes.

"Yes," she said, a smile tilting the corners of her lips.

Jack furrowed his brow in curiosity, and asked, "What was your wish?"

Wrapping both her arms around his waist, she stood on the tips of her toes, and gently touched her lips to his. She resumed her relaxed stance—no longer perched on her toes—and admired his smiling, rugged features.

"Actually," she said softly, "I wished for two things that night. I wished that one day I would find a way to help girls and women who've been the victims of violent crimes."

"The two books you've published are helping thousands of victims and survivors. So that wish came true," Jack said with a grin.

"*And*...I wished that my heart would be able to trust again. That there would be someone worthy of my trust," Katie said as she gazed intently into Jack's eyes.

"Where's that wish standing?" Jack asked as he held her gently, swimming in the intensity of her gaze.

"Right in front of me," she said.

About The Author

With over twenty years experience in management, human resources, and project management, it was during the recession that Carol Knuth changed direction and began her pursuit of writing and publishing. Her first book *The Garbage Bag Girl* was the first in the series, her break out novel. The book details the heart-wrenching unique challenges at-risk children face, their strong will to survive, and as with her own life, spirits of endurance.

Carol Knuth currently resides in Kentucky with her family. She is the president of Dream Swept Publishing and she advises various organizations and boards that support the improvement of at-risk children and women's lives. Her interest in at-risk children stems from her own childhood spent in the foster care system.

Author photograph by Nikita Gross
www.carolknuth.com

ALSO BY CAROL KNUTH

The Garbage Bag Girl
Rhodes' Home

www.ingramcontent.com/pod-product-compliance
Lightning Source LLC
Chambersburg PA
CBHW021516240626
47154CB00002B/660